Devilish ink

A DUBLIN INK NOVEL

SIENNA BLAKE

DEVILISH INK

A DUBLIN INK NOVEL

SIENNA BLAKE

Devilish Ink: a novel / by Sienna Blake. – 1st Ed.
First Edition: May 2024
Published by SB Publishing

Editing services by Proof Positive: http://proofpositivepro.com.

For my dark romance girlies

Who love a hand necklace more than diamonds

AUTHOR'S NOTE:

This book is darker than the previous novels in my Dublin Ink series.
It deals with SA and violence (not between the two main characters).
And contains dubious consent and breath play.

Please consider your mental health before deciding to read this novel.

Dark romance is a safe space for adults to explore their fantasies. The dark scenarios in this book are pure fantasy. I do not condone any of the behaviour in real life.

Full TWs on my website:
https://siennablake.com/devilish-ink/

RY

I was being followed. In between the click of my boots on the rain-slick Dublin sidewalk were the same boot-steps for the last four blocks. The hairs on the back of my neck stood on end, my breath leaving my tight chest in gasps. I scanned the streets for a passing car, a friendly face, a *witness*. But we were alone. Me and my stalker.

Fuck.

I knew I shouldn't have left Rian's apartment. As soon as I saw the tall broad-shouldered stranger in a dark hoodie just standing there watching from across the road, I should have slammed the door, locked it. Called in sick. Booked the first flight out of Dublin. Fled like I did five years ago.

Instead, I told myself I was being paranoid. I told myself that Rian needed me. That he wouldn't have begged me to come back to Dublin if he hadn't.

Stupid.

After five long years of that constant gnaw of paranoia unsettling my guts, you'd think I'd have gotten used to it.

You'd think that I'd have learned to ignore it, given how

many times I've thought someone was following me and it turned out they weren't.

Better paranoid than dead.

I made a show of glancing at my watch and sped up my walk, trying to do that thing that girls do where they pretend to speed up because they're late. Not because they're trying to get away from someone.

To my horror, his footsteps sped up, too. I *was* being followed.

I should have stayed in Berlin. Or Barcelona, Amsterdam, Paris, Rome. Moving around all the time, never staying long enough to make friends, might sound like a lonely life. Better to be lonely than dead.

Which I would be if I didn't get to the safety of Dublin Ink before he caught me. Two blocks. Just two more blocks.

I fumbled around in the side pocket of my large handbag for my keys. Keys. Where are my fucking keys?

My fingers closed around the cold metal. Thank God. I shoved the keys pointing out between my fingers and made a fist. When he tried to take me, I wasn't going down without a fight.

His footsteps sounded like they were getting closer. Fuck. He knew that I knew he was following me. He'd have no choice but to make his move.

I broke into a run. My handbag filled with my gear clattered at my side as I strained to jam it against my torso. I didn't even stop to think how much damage I'd be doing to my tattoo gun or whether I'd smash my ink bottles all over my sketchbooks. I just *ran*.

One more block.

My heart thudded against my ribs as I screamed inside. Terror gripped my throat making it hard to breath. I couldn't hear the footsteps behind me over the sound of my blood rushing around in my ears but I swear he was chasing me.

My boots skidded on the wet pavement as I rounded the last corner.

I didn't dare look over my shoulder. But it meant I couldn't see how close he was. Prickles stabbed all the way down my spine as I anticipated his hand closing around my shirt, my arm, my hair...my throat.

The neon pink sign of Dublin Ink and the light coming from its windows shone ahead like a beacon of safety. Please, God. I sprinted even faster, pushing my thigh muscles until they screamed with effort. So close. So fucking close to safety.

I slammed against the Dublin Ink front door, grabbing for the handle, my shaking hand missing before I finally closed my hand around it. The door wouldn't budge. It was locked. Mason must have left already. Shit. Keys. *Keys!*

I fumbled with the keychain, looking for the right one.

But all these keys were new to me: there were several keys for Dublin Ink, front door, back door, storage room, supplies cupboard. Several keys for Rian's apartment: front door, garage, mailbox.

In my panic I couldn't remember which one was the one for Dublin Ink's front door.

I tried one.

No, wrong key. For fuck's sake.

It was at that moment that the clouds above broke apart, showering me with rain. My fingers slipped. The keys jangled to the ground.

Fuck!

No time to get this door open, I had to stand and fight my attacker.

I jammed my hand into my purse. The prick of my finger

against the tattoo gun gave me a rush of much needed adrenaline. I felt brittle. At the point of bursting. Of falling apart. But with my fingers wrapped around the leather conformed to my fingers, I felt a wild fury rise up in me. I was tired of running, tired of being the prey. If I was going to die, I would die fighting.

I whipped around to face my stalker, holding the tattoo gun out in front of me like a weapon. I squinted through the rain, against the lights behind me that cast everything in front of me into a glare. I was the criminal now and I was stealing my goddamn life back. But instead of a guttural war cry, a desperate whimper escaped my lips.

The sidewalk was empty.

There was no one behind me.

The man in the hoodie hadn't been stalking me.

But *he* was still out there.

I tumbled into the studio after finding the right key and slammed the door behind me, locking it up again. I leaned my damp forehead against the door, waiting for my heart rate to slow down.

A laugh bubbled out of me as adrenaline drained from my limbs.

Fuck, I was certifiable.

I pushed off the door and set about getting ready for my shift. The clock on the wall read five past. I was late. Mason would have left already to drop Rachel, his wife, off to work.

It was tempting to relax in such a place. The faint pink glow of the neon sign was soothing. The floral couches with lumps and bumps made me think of kind grandmothers whose kitchens always smelled of freshly baked cookies (something I knew nothing of firsthand).

Mason mentioned that this townhouse had been his nan's

before she'd passed. They'd turned the lower floor into Dublin Ink but Mason lived upstairs with Rachel. The boys' art covered the walls and cocooned me in what I loved best of all in the world.

I had only just hung up my coat when I heard the door handle rattling. If it was a customer they'd ring the doorbell. Someone was trying to get in.

Oh God. My stalker was *here*.

I spun around, scanning the room for a weapon. I grabbed a fringed lamp and clutched it in two hands like a bat just as the handle stopped turning.

Keys jangled outside.

My stalker had *keys*.

Wait…he wouldn't have keys?

The door opened and Mason barged in, halting at the sight of me.

A smirk stretched across his handsome face, raindrops rolling off his mohawk. "Is that a lamp in your hands or are you just happy to see me?"

A flush heated my cheeks as I lowered the lamp. He must think I'm a lunatic.

"I just wasn't expecting…anyone…" I said lamely, as I straightened out all the fringing of the lamp shade. "I thought you were dropping Rachel off?"

A softness came over his eyes at the mention of her name. Something in me twinged; I wish someone—*anyone*—would look like that when they thought of me.

"I am. She just forgot this." He grabbed two red sparkly nipple covers from the key bowl. Then winked before he disappeared.

I shook my head at myself as I unpacked my bag. On my workstation, I unpacked bottles of Panthera, my favourite

Italian tattoo ink, my large notepad, and a set of pencils. I had just dumped out my bag in the back staff room when I heard a bell jangle over the door as it opened again.

I stepped back into the living room calling, "Did you forget something else, Ma—?"

The man who stepped into the doorway was *not* Mason.

Outlined by the blurry streetlamp outside, he was tall with broad shoulders, filling the open door like poured concrete.

He stepped into the light and I caught sight of his face, his strong jaw and wide cheekbones. For a second I was just a woman appreciating an attractive man.

But then I realized where I'd seen him before.

He was the man outside Rian's apartment.

He *had* been stalking me.

RY

The door closed behind my stalker with a click like a gun being cocked.

I wanted to scream but my voice box jammed into my throat. I wanted to run but my feet were frozen in place. For a long moment we just stood there on opposite sides of the room, predator and prey.

I took him in, trying to assess whether I should run or fight back.

Gods, he was tall, at least six foot two. The collar of his heavy-duty workman's jacket was turned up against the wind. His boots were covered in mud. His hands, hanging by his sides, were thick and scarred. His shoulders filled out his jacket and his thighs filled out his jeans.

He was a man used to hard work. He was a man who wasn't afraid to get a little dirty. He was a man who other men called when something was too hard.

He was not a man I could fight off. Unless I had a gun. I'd never hated Ireland's *no-guns* law more than now.

Run!

Except I had nowhere to run to. Upstairs was a dead end. Unless I locked myself in one of the bedrooms and called for help.

But I'd never been up there, it being Mason and Rachel's private residences. I wasn't even sure if the rooms were lockable. Or if any of the rooms had phones in them.

My Irish burner phone was still somewhere in my bag out the back.

The back door. When Aurnia gave me the tour yesterday, she showed me the back door leading to the alleyway. To freedom.

But that door was undoubtedly locked. And my damn keys were also in my bag. If I could even figure out which key was the right key before he grabbed me.

He seemed oblivious to the droplets of rain rolling off his messy hair. Oblivious to the silent terror building up to the bursting point inside me.

I couldn't just stand here waiting for him to make his move. I had to risk something…

Before I could move he spoke: "What's a guy gotta do to get a tattoo around here?"

I was not expecting that.

This was obviously some sort of ploy to get me to relax before he pounced.

"You want a tattoo?" I said, my voice betraying my disbelief.

"I do," he said as he stepped in farther, glanced around the tattoo studio with obvious interest, as if he were a real customer and not here to snatch me up like a nightmare come to life. "This is a tattoo parlour, right?"

"Right…" I said. I glanced over to the door behind him. All

I had to do was get between him and the door and I could make my run for it. I just had to play along…for now.

"So?" he said expectantly, walking into my line of sight of the door. Dammit. He was good. He knew I was going to make a run for it and he was deliberately blocking the door.

"So what?" I asked, my voice coming out cutting as I edged aside, glancing again at the door past his broad shoulders. So close yet so far away.

"Will you give me a tattoo?"

My gaze snapped back to his face and I felt struck again at how kind his eyes looked. What was wrong with me? I shouldn't be feeling *any* empathy with the thug hired to kidnap me.

"You want a tattoo…from me?"

His eyes swept over me from head to toe, but for some reason it didn't come off as predatory. It felt…appreciative. "Yes, from you, Miss…"

I frowned. He was obviously fishing for my name. But if he'd been sent by Balor, he'd already know it.

Come to think about it, why bother with all this… pretence? Why pretend to be a customer? Why not just grab me?

"What kind of tattoo?" I said, suspicion lining my tone.

He grinned and for a split second I was blindsided. It was a glorious grin, wide and showing off his straight white teeth, crinkled his expressive green eyes.

"I thought maybe you could pick."

My mind short circuited. That never happened. A customer giving their artist free reign was the holy grail for any tattoo artist. Usually it was, *I want three roses in this pattern with this exact shade of pink, five leaves and a realistic-looking skull.*

Never *you pick.*

For a moment I wished he *was* an actual customer.

I shook my head. *Focus, Ry.*

"Really?" I said. "You want me to pick."

"Yes. Where would you put it?" he asked.

I crossed my arms. Ha-ha. Got him. Nobody wants a tattoo that someone else picks. "Isn't that a question I should be asking *you*?"

He shot me that bashful grin again and shrugged. "You're the expert."

I snatched up my tattoo gun, I held it in front of me, ready to stab at him if he lunged for me. It wasn't much of a weapon but it was all I had. I braced for him to lunge at me. But he just stood there, seemingly happy to keep smiling at me.

He waved his finger at my gun, pointed at him like a pistol. "Is this part of your…artistic process?" He sounded so fucking sincere, I almost dropped my tattoo gun.

"Your back is broad," I blurted out. "It'd look good on your back."

His grin turned into a smirk. "You noticed that, huh?"

To my utter surprise, I blushed. What the fuck was wrong with me? I was blushing at my own damn stalker and would-be kidnapper.

"Take off your shirt and get on your stomach then." I pointed with my tattoo gun to the tattoo chair farthest away from the door.

I eyed his movements. It was now or never. If he was going to grab me, it'd be now…

Instead he chuckled. "Normally, I'd expect dinner before I took off my clothes." Then he winked at me. My would-be kidnapper, *winked* at me.

Was he *flirting with me*?

He shrugged off his jacket and hung it up next to mine by the pegs up along the left wall, looking back to give me a quizzical look as he nodded at one of Rachel's pink feather boas that was draped on one of the hooks. "You moonlight as a burlesque dancer?"

Underneath his jacket he wore a casual plaid button-up shirt rolled up at the sleeves that clung to his shoulders. My mouth went dry as he unbuttoned his shirt and shrugged it off.

Holy shite, he was built as fuck. I gaped at the smooth plains of his firm chest, his bleedin' eight-pack and those thick V muscles that disappeared into the tops of his low-slung jeans. I heard a choking noise before I realised it was coming from me. Jesus, Mary and Joseph, did he carry bricks for a living?

No, my sarcastic inner voice said, *he kidnaps girls for a living.*

I backed up as he walked through the centre of the room, my eyes mesmerised by the way his back muscles rippled —*fucking rippled*—as he walked.

He went straight to the leather table I'd indicated.

I stood there holding the tattoo gun staring with my mouth open like an idiot. I snapped my jaw shut. *Ry, stop it.* I did not need to be confusing my kidnapper for a love interest.

He picked up something from the headrest that clanked and held it up.

It was a pair of silver handcuffs.

Shite. That was Mason's usual station. It must have been from when he and Rachel...

"Tell me this is part of the service," he said, his voice suggestive and teasing, his eyebrow raised.

I flushed as an image of him handcuffed to the table with

me on top of him flashed through my mind. I shook that image away, trying to ignore the flush of heat within my body.

"They're not mine," I blurted out before chastising myself. Why the hell did I feel the need to justify myself to my would-be kidnapper?

He smirked. "Sure thing."

He dropped the cuffs and they clanked as they swung from the headrest.

He lowered himself to the creaky tattoo table and rested his head on his arms, facing me. "I'm *all* yours."

I should be running for the door, this was my best chance.

But I was mad. Mad that such an attractive man could be a villain. Furious that I was curious about him, confused by him, turned the fuck on by him. Outraged that I'd spent this long letting the darkness terrorise me.

I stormed up to him, jammed the tattoo gun needle into his neck.

"You're going to tell me the fucking truth..."

LIAM

I knew eventually I'd get caught in my lies. But I didn't think she'd figure it out so soon.

My brother picked a smart girl. Stunning. Sexy…

What did they say about men who covet their brother's girl?

I blame her.

Her eyes had been my undoing.

Perhaps if she hadn't had locked gazes with me as I stood outside Rian's apartment, we wouldn't be here, with her tattoo gun in my neck.

I'd stood there outside my brother's apartment, working up the courage to knock on his door, to beg his forgiveness, ignoring the ice-cold raindrops biting at my skin.

The streetlamps had flickered on around me, devouring the faint awakening of stars. The rain dampened the world, but all I heard was Alan, his voice screaming as I drove away from our family farm.

"Don't you ever come back! You hear me? Don't you ever fucking step foot on this family's land ever again!"

I had no home. If I wanted one, I needed to speak with Rian, the brother who hated me. I needed to make things right.

He was home. He had to be.

I had nothing else. No one else.

Then his front door opened. And my hopes lifted.

Instead of the brother that should have been my salvation, it was *her*.

Her long dark hair falling over her shoulders. Her pale skin was etched with tattoo ink like a lace collar all up her neck, peeking out from her open black jacket over a white button-up shirt. A plaid miniskirt, torn tights and black combat boots completed her *Danger! Stay away!* look.

For some reason, it just made me want to get closer. To know what was underneath.

Like I said, her gaze locked with mine. Her dark eyes, shadowed and lined with black, were full of a loneliness I recognised deep in my soul.

It hit me like a punch to my guts.

It was the briefest of looks. But it sealed her fate.

Through her sad eyes, she promised me that she would understand me. She whispered that I didn't have to be alone. With that single look, she tied me to her.

I didn't even care that she wasn't meant for me.

I didn't care that she was my brother's girlfriend. She had to be, coming out of his apartment so late.

When she tore her eyes away, I felt the loss of it in my fucking chest. Like she'd ripped something important out of me, something I needed in order to breathe.

I stared at her, chest aching, as she marched down the sidewalk, petite hands white-knuckled over a purse strap, black tattoos stark against her pale fingers. Her steps were determined, hurried even.

I wasn't going to go after her. Although fuck, how I wanted to.

I glanced back to the door, the door I should be knocking on, the brother I should be reconnecting with. Going after her would be a betrayal. I was determined not to give him one.

I didn't stop to consider why he'd moved on from Eithne, the girl he'd brought home only a few weeks ago. I didn't stop to consider what had happened. I didn't stop at all.

I leapt up the stairs two at a time and knocked on Rian's door, trying to remember the speech I'd prepared.

The sudden heat in my chest made me tug at the collar of my jacket as I waited for Rian to answer. I felt like I'd been working on the farm all day. Muscles warm from hard labour. Body aching, skin searing in the brutal, heartless cold.

But the door remained unopened.

It seemed so inevitable that he'd be there. That he and I were two cars barreling down the highway toward one another, intent on a fiery crash, that the silence took me by surprise.

Rian wasn't home.

And the one link to him, the one frail string connected to him was getting away.

I glanced back up the street. *She* was still in sight. Small in the distance, nearly anonymous in her oversized black coat.

I warred with myself. Go after her. Wait here for Rian to come home.

But then in that very moment as she turned the corner, the siren glanced back over her shoulder. We locked eyes again. That was it. She was calling me to her. Before the wind swept her black hair across her face, hiding her eyes like a mask.

If I'd taken a moment to consider it, I would have realized that I'd wanted it all along: a reason to pursue her. If I wanted to reconcile with Rian the last thing I should do is to stalk after his new girl.

But I couldn't stop my feet as I hurried after her. I tried to tell myself I was following her because she might lead me to Rian. Perhaps if I became friends with his new girl, it would give me a way into his heart.

But deep down I knew they were lies.

I wanted *her*.

I followed her, staying well behind her as I racked my brain trying to figure out how to introduce myself to her. I watched as she realised I was behind her, watched her break into a run. Anger fueled me. Where the fuck was Rian? If his girl was this jumpy, why the hell was he letting her walk by herself at night?

I wanted to make sure she'd never be that scared again.

I wanted to protect her.

If my brother wouldn't take care of her right, I fucking would.

So I walked into Dublin Ink pretending to be a customer, asking for a tattoo just for a chance to talk to her.

To be close to her.

To get to know her.

And it had been working. Sort of. Even I could see how suspicious she was of me. How she kept her distance, moving aside depending on where I stood in the room, angling her body to face me the whole time to make sure her back was never turned.

Someone had hurt her, I realised.

That realisation made anger flare through me. I had to look away, staring at the art on the wall, my face turned away in order to hide my reaction from her. The last thing I wanted to do was spook her.

Although it seemed that I did that already.

Which is how I ended up face down on her tattoo table with her tattoo needle in my neck.

"Now you're going to tell me the fucking truth…" she said, her voice curling with anger.

Shit.

Now what? I couldn't exactly admit that I'd followed her. That I was the brother that her boyfriend hated. That I'd come in here to get a tattoo from her just to get to know her.

I'd ruin any chance before I'd even started.

I flashed back to my father, his breath sour with cheap whiskey, one hand fisted in my collar, the other one held high. "Tell me the fuckin' truth, boy!"

I learned then never to admit anything.

RY

I promised myself I'd never be a victim again. Despite my constant moving the only constant was my self-defense classes. Krav Maga. Brazilian jiu-jitsu. Muay Thai kick-boxing. Judo. Whatever I could sign up to, I did.

It made me feel stronger, made me feel like I had armour enough to chase the shadows away.

It also meant I knew exactly where this fucker's jugular was. If he moved an inch, I'd make him regret it.

"Answer me," I said through gritted teeth as I pressed the needle hard enough against his neck to draw a prick of blood.

I stood in a fighting stance, ready for him to lash out in response. For his face to turn ugly and cruel. For his true colours to show.

To my surprise, he smiled and showed me his palms as best as he could in his stomach-down position.

"Okay, you got me." A hint of humour in his voice. "I've never gotten a tat before and I'm low-key shitting myself."

I scowled and jabbed the needle at him, making him wince.

"Wise guy. Who are you?"

"My name is Li—Lee," he said slowly, as if to not startle me. "I just moved here from a farm in County Cork and it's a big deal for me cause I know…barely anyone in Dublin. I just thought I'd get a tattoo to mark the milestone."

There was a sincerity in his words that I didn't want to trust. But there was something else as well. He was hiding something.

"Bullshite," I said with a growl. I wasn't going to let him get away with it that easily.

"You were watching me. Following me. I *saw* you outside Rian's apartment."

He frowned. "Who?"

"Don't play dumb with me."

"I get it," he said softly. "You're a pretty girl working late and here alone. You don't know me from Adam. I wouldn't trust me either."

I flushed. I was *not* crazy. I saw him outside the apartment. I did. He was standing there in his hoodie…

Although, it was dark. His face was shadowed. The guy outside Rian's apartment had looked like him…but then again don't all monsters look the same in the dark?

Shit. Was I losing my mind? Had this guy been the exact guy standing outside Rian's apartment?

"Here," he said as he pointed at the dangling cuffs, "how about you cuff me while you tattoo me? Would that make you feel any better?"

I— *What?*

This was a bluff. He was trying to lure me into a false sense of security.

I frowned. Well, I'd call his bluff then.

I nodded at the cuffs. "Go on, put them on."

He reached out slowly as if to not frighten me, and grabbed the cuffs, locking them around his wrists with a click before holding them up to show me.

"Wanna make sure they're on properly?" he said, his voice low and suggestive.

What the hell? Why would a hired thug willingly cuff himself to my table?

I narrowed my eyes. With the cuffs around his wrists and him locked to the table, I felt enough space to study him. Really study him.

Normally hired thugs had gang or prison tats, a crooked nose from being broken, bullet or knife scars on their torso.

He had none of these.

I noticed the tan line on his upper arm and around the back of his neck. The dirt beneath his fingernails. The calluses on his open palms. Like a *real* farmer. Who'd just moved here from Cork.

Not a hired thug.

Oh my God. I was such a paranoid freak.

I sank onto the stool, exhausted, and lowered the tattoo gun to the table. My fingers started to shake, the adrenaline wearing off.

The man—Lee he said his name was—stayed very still. He was silent as I caught my breath, drawing my trembling fingers through my hair.

"I'm sorry," I said, shaking my head. "Jaysus fuck, I'm sorry. I just—"

"It's fine."

I looked up to see him watching me.

He wasn't afraid. Wasn't weirded out by my freakout. Wasn't heading toward the door like any normal guy with half a brain would be at this point.

"I can't imagine what it must be like to be a woman in this world," he said, his voice soft.

"You have no idea," I said.

Lee laid his cheek back against folded hands, the cuffs clanking as they resettled around his muscled forearms.

All the while, his eyes remained on me, like he was appreciating me, studying me, not the way a predator studies his prey, but the way a man would appreciate a beautiful painting.

My skin flushed with awareness at his gaze.

When I realised he was waiting for me, I frowned in confusion. "Wait...you still want me to tattoo you?"

He smiled and the corners of his green eyes crinkled. "It is what I came in here for."

"Even after all," I waved my hand vaguely between us, "*that*?"

He grinned. "*Especially* after all that."

"What exactly does that mean?" I picked up my tattoo gun from the table and fiddled with it, needing a distraction from my embarrassment.

When he didn't respond, I looked over at him.

His gaze was distant on the exposed brick wall.

Sighing, he said, "I don't know. I guess my skin right now is like the land where I grew up. That I've only just escap—"

My skin prickled. There was darkness in his past, too.

He cleared his throat. "What I mean is that it's empty. Just these vast, untouched miles. And, well, I left there for a reason. Because I wanted...I wanted to share something with someone. I wanted a connection. I wanted to not feel like I was so alone in the nothingness."

His gaze shifted slowly toward mine. His cheeks grew

slightly pink as if he'd shared more of himself than he meant to.

I found myself leaning toward him. Wanting more. More of his voice. More of his fresh masculine scent of cut grass and wood. More of *him*.

"You've got heart," he said. "You've got this wild, thudding, maybe a little bit crazy thing inside of you. And, well, I'd like you to share a tiny piece of it with me. *On* me."

I froze. "What?"

"Tattoo me with something that means something to you."

That was insane.

He didn't know me at all. And this stranger wanted me to tattoo something personal of *me* on him?

I barely showed myself to anyone.

Even Rian, my best friend, didn't know the worst thing that ever happened to me, the thing I'd been running from for years.

But God, the way he looked at me, with his expressive hopeful eyes.

How could I say no?

He'd shared a piece of himself with me.

Was I brave enough to share myself—even a piece of myself—with this stranger?

LIAM

Rian was right. I was the worst brother in the world.

One thing had led to another. I'd gone from stalking my brother's girlfriend to her place of work, to pretending to be a customer just to talk to her, and now I was on her table while she tattooed me...

And instead of wincing with pain, I was getting *hard*.

I was like one of those eejits who kept saying just a little more, just another sip, just one more hit...until it was too late. They were addicted.

I'd barely flinched as her needle pierced my skin. It was more irritating than painful. But the vibration soon turned to a numb heat.

Then there was her nearness, the way her presence warmed my back, her fingers of her free hand rested on me as she worked, the way her arm or—God fucking help me—the sides of her soft breasts brushed against my skin, lighting me on fire.

I could lie to myself and say it was her fault. She was just too fucking sexy, too mysterious, too...haunted.

Every time our eyes met for a moment, I felt a punch in my guts like I'd leapt off a cliff, before she glanced back to her work all innocent, totally unaware of how utterly hypnotic she was.

I just lay there staring at her, fucking mesmerized.

At the way her small nose appeared perfect from every angle or the way she pursed her lips and tilted her head as she worked or the way her dark hair kept falling over her eyes, getting caught in her long lashes, before she'd tuck it back behind her perfect shell ear, a small semi-colon in black ink behind it peeking through the strands.

I was fascinated by the Medusa tattooed on the top of her chest with snakes fanning out across her collarbones looking like they were moving as she breathed. The falling rose petals along the pulse of the left side of her neck.

They were all done in dark lines, the shading made up of dot work. Splashes of what looked like watercolour staining the pieces.

She spoke in that soft lilt of hers, her breath caressing the back of my neck, only offering crumbs of herself as an answer to one of my many, *many* questions about her.

Where did you grow up? Which of the cities in Europe was your favourite? What do you love to do outside of art? Where did you study? Who are your idols? Did you climb the Eiffel Tower when you were in Paris? Did you leave a lock behind on the cliff walk of Cinque Terra?

I wanted so much more of her than she was giving. Surely she had to know she was making me hungry for her, desperate for her.

I'd heard her laugh earlier and it'd been like the sound of fucking angels. This tinkling girlish melody, so different to the way she presented herself with her "fuck off" bad girl aesthetic. I wanted to hear it again. And again.

So I flirted. I teased. I made sexual innuendos trying to coax that laugh from her.

But all it seemed to do was make me harder and harder.

I only realised I'd let out a low groan when she shut off the gun and the vibration stopped, the silence of the studio loud in my ears. Interrupted by the occasional snap from the neon light, the rare passing of a car, headlights slashing through the crack in the drapes.

Ry—she'd introduced herself as Ryleigh, Ry to her friends, so she was already *Ry* to me even if we'd just met—rested a gentle hand at the small of my back, sending a rush of heat through my cock.

I repressed another groan.

"Is it getting to be too much?" she asked.

What was I supposed to say to that?

No, Ry, it's you. *You* are turning me on to the point of madness. *You* are too much. *You* are all too much and yet not enough.

"It can be a lot," she said, stretching her arms overhead, the hem of her shirt riding up so I could see a strip of inked skin across the top of her skirt.

Fuck. I wanted to slide my hands across that patch of skin. To drag my tongue across it to see how she tasted.

I tore my eyes away before she caught me staring.

"I'm fine," I lied, but it came out croaky, my throat tight.

She studied me, as if she was trying to peel back my lies.

Fuck. You can't look at me like that, Ry. You're going to make me crack and I'll do something I'll regret to my brother's girlfriend.

"No shame in taking breaks," she said.

I shook my head.

I grit my teeth and forced a smile.

"Really, I'm fine," I said. "Keep going."

A tendril of her long black hair slipped across my skin as she leaned over me. It felt like a feather's touch but it sent a jolt of electricity through me.

"You're tensing up though." She ran her fingertips over the muscles along my back as if to make a point.

They were strained to the point of trembling. Her touch made me ache, made my cock throb painfully. I had to dig my fingernails into the leather to stop from grinding against the table.

Fuck. She was making it worse. Making it so fucking hard to hold myself back. And she had no fucking idea.

No fucking idea what her nearness did to me, the madness it infected me with. The way her touch made me want to wrap my fingers around her wrists. To leave my own hand-shaped mark on her covered throat.

Thank God I was handcuffed to this table. I may have grabbed her if I hadn't been, pulled her down on top of me, forced my tongue into her mouth, ground my cock against her, sought out her nipple with my teeth.

I wasn't sure I could live with myself if I lost control.

If betrayed Rian.

I was here to fix my relationship with him, not destroy it further.

If he knew I was lying on her table imagining all the dirty things I wanted to do with his girlfriend, I'd have no chance of regaining his trust.

"To be honest," I said through gritted teeth, "I might need…a distraction. Music, maybe?"

If we kept talking, if she kept giving me small pieces of her, I'd fall for her and ruin everything.

Her chair wheels squeaked as she stood. "I think I have the cure for what ails ye."

I couldn't help but stare at the way her hips swayed as she walked across the room to a Bluetooth speaker, her bootsteps as light as a fairy. At the way her pleated skirt skipped up the back of her thighs with every step. At the peek of her red lace panties when she leaned on the counter.

I repressed a groan. I was going to hell.

The grainy strum of a guitar melody filled the room. I tore my eyes away as she returned to my side.

"I find music helps distract me," she said, smiling.

She sat back down on her stool with her legs apart, the only thing preventing me from seeing her panties was the thin plaid pleat falling right over the front.

Fuck me. Did she realise what she was doing? Her face was so innocent and honest that I knew she had no fucking idea.

I groaned internally. That made it worse. I rubbed my eyelids against my forearm, praying that I didn't do something stupid.

She swept her hair from her shoulders. Leaned forward toward me, her fingers brushing my skin as she inspected what she'd done.

Her breasts brushed my elbow again as she got too close.

Fuck. I could feel the way her nipples hardened against my skin through her thin shirt.

I couldn't help it: I let out a low groan.

"Hey," she whispered, "hey."

Her hand lay flat against the space between my shoulder blades.

I shuddered beneath her. My fingernails ached from digging into the leather. I was seconds away from sinking my teeth into my arm to keep from screaming. Or groaning. Or fucking this chair.

Or fucking Ryleigh herself.

I need to stop this whole thing. Demand she uncuff me and leave, tattoo unfinished. I hadn't actually betrayed Rian yet. It wasn't too late.

But before I could, she started singing along with the music.

"...I'd give up all the stars

Live in an endless night

Just to have you come home.

I don't need the sun

We'd be each other's light

And we'd never be alone."

I melted into the leather. If I could have fallen, I would have. Another sensation took over my body, the painful need in my cock overtaken by something aching in my chest.

How could someone who looked like the devil's temptress sing like an angel?

Her voice wound round my throat as surely as fingers. The soft waves of her breathy inhales rolling over me as strongly as the tides themselves; I was underwater and I couldn't breathe.

I cleared my throat as the first song ended.

"What band is this?" I asked.

I turned my head to catch Ry smiling.

"The Untouchables," she answered. "A local indie band. They're pretty much the only thing I took with me when I fled Dublin..."

It didn't escape me that she said *fled* instead of left.

Her eyes grew unfocused. There. Whatever she was remembering.

I needed to know what gave her that distant look, what she remembered that caused her voice to falter and her lungs to stutter.

I wanted it. Coveted it like a dark cursed jewel.

I wanted to know *her*.

But I had to tread lightly. I couldn't seem too keen, couldn't beg for her past. Couldn't scare her by wanting too much from her too soon.

"Right. How long ago did you…leave?" I asked, trying to sound casual as she leaned over me again and restarted the tattoo.

"Five years…" *Five long years* was what I heard in the hollowness of her voice.

Whatever happened five years ago haunted her. It stained her eyes with sadness.

I wanted to wipe it away, to lift her curse. I wanted to repaint her life with laughter and singing and…love.

With *me*.

"Where did you go?" I asked.

She shrugged. "Everywhere. Nowhere. Europe… I moved around a lot."

I took in her hard swallow, the way her shoulders curled in.

I wanted to reach out and hold her, to take her into my arms and promise to protect her.

"Why did you leave?" I asked softly.

Something dark flashed across her face. Her hand jerked.

The tattoo needle caught on my back and I bit back a hiss at the line of pain.

"Shite." She threw the gun onto the tray, snatched up her

cloth and dabbed at my back. "Rian's going to eat the head off me. I run off all his clients by threatening and then stabbing them."

My ears pricked up at my brother's name. At the same time, it landed like a punch to the guts.

I wanted to keep asking her about this thing that happened to her.

But this was my opportunity to get her to talk about Rian. That's what I was here for, wasn't it? My brother?

I ignored the guilt pooling in my stomach.

"Who's Rian?" I said, aiming for nonchalant. I winced internally as my voice cracked at saying his name out loud.

Thank fuck she didn't seem to notice.

"Oh, um...he's the artist who actually works here." She studied my wound as she bit her lip. "I'm just covering his chair while he's...away."

There was a hesitation in the way she said *away*.

"I think this should be okay." She chewed on her lip. "The cut is shallow."

"Like holiday leave?" I asked, not caring two shites about the scratch on my back.

"Yeah, you could say that."

"Without you?" I asked, incredulous.

If she were my girl. I'd never fucking leave without her.

She frowned as the steady, numbing pain of the needle resumed its way across my back. "I mean, I'm taking care of his apartment and his chair."

He could have gotten anyone to look after his shite.

But then again, maybe Rian was so particular about his chair and his place that he'd only trust his girlfriend.

Fuck, shows how much I don't know about my own fucking brother.

"You must be close," I said, trying not to let the jealousy shine through.

"Yeah." Genuine affection lifted the side of her lips into a smile.

Fuck, it was radiant. My brother made her smile like that and I fucking coveted it. I wanted her to smile like that for me.

"I'd do *anything* for him," she said, "and he'd do the same for me."

Shite. Don't say that.

I let my forehead fall back against the back of my hand, cocooning myself into a small cave of my hot breath and disappointment.

She *was* Rian's.

Maybe if she was unhappy with him, I could justify pursuing her.

But it was clear she cared for him.

I had no fucking business wanting her for my own.

Maybe Ryleigh was my punishment. Penance for all the reasons Rian hated me. A mirage I could never reach. A jewel I could never touch.

I let out a sigh and lifted my head to face outwards again.

"Must be nice," I said. "Where'd he go?"

She frowned and held her gun between us. "You know, you ask a lot of questions."

I lifted up my hands. "Sorry. Just making conversation."

She sighed and ran a hand through her hair. "Sorry. I don't know why I'm so jumpy lately…"

But the way she said it made me think that she did know. She just couldn't say it.

She returned to my tattoo. "So…where were we?"

"You were talking about Rian..." I nudged. "Where he'd gone to?"

"Oh, right, well, he's—"

The bell atop the front door jangled.

I cursed the interruption.

"Sorry I'm later than promised," someone announced gregariously as he swept in, bringing the cold in with him. "Caught the first act, if you know what I mean."

I ducked my face into my arms and watched from my shadowed place as Ryleigh rolled her eyes at the man who I recognised as one of Rian's friends. I couldn't remember his name though.

"Didn't wait for the tits to come out?" she teased him.

"How dare you!" the newcomer said. "That's my wife you're talking about...and I never have to wait for the tits."

She snorted as the guy made his way through the kitchen.

"Hey, man," he said to me.

It was convenient, being a man sometimes. My noncommittal grunt was fully accepted. I kept my face hidden as he rummaged through the kitchen.

"Mason will go upstairs in just a second," Ryleigh whispered to me. "Don't worry about him."

I wasn't sure that Mason could recognise me from the few times I'd visited Dublin before, but I wasn't sure that he couldn't either. His presence here was like a watchdog.

Mason walked past us with a bowl of something. But he halted when he saw me.

"What the fuck, Ry?" he said, frowning.

Shite. He'd recognised me.

I kept my face buried in my hands, brain racking over how the hell I was going to talk myself out of this.

"W-what?" Ry said, sounding just as guilty as I felt.

What did *she* have to feel guilty about?

Mason reached out and tugged at one of the handcuffs still around my wrist and let out a laugh. "Babe, if you wanted to borrow them, you shoulda just asked."

I almost burst out laughing with relief.

Ry went as red as a tomato and began spluttering. "Oh my God. It's not—it's not what it looks like."

"Uh huh," Mason said, an eyebrow lifting almost into his hairline as he glanced between her and me.

"I swear—"

"You kids have fun now…" he said before he strolled off.

"Mason, it's not like that," she called after him.

"Sure it ain't," he called back as he mounted the stairs.

"Mason!"

"Try not to be too loud, yeah?"

When we were alone again, Ry turned back to me.

"I'm so sorry," she said.

I couldn't help it. I burst out laughing.

She slapped my arm before a muffled laugh broke through her mortification.

"You have to admit, that was pretty funny," I said.

She rolled her eyes but she was smiling.

"Get back into position," she said waving her gun at me.

I grinned. "Yes, ma'am."

I laid my head back down on my forearm and she began work on my back again.

I wanted to try one more time to get information about my brother out of her.

"So…you were saying about Rian?"

"Hmm, what?" she said absentmindedly. "Oh, yeah, he'll be back…soon, I hope."

He'll be back soon...you hope?

Something was up with Rian.

She shifted back, bit her lip. "And I think we're done!"

"Great," I managed, fighting to not sound disappointed when she unlocked my cuffs and freed me. I climbed off the table.

Ryleigh hesitated. Then she shook her head and laughed nervously. "It's not like it makes any difference now whether you like it or not. So fuck it."

She pushed me in front of a full-length mirror.

I'd told her not to tell me what she was tattooing. I wanted it to be a surprise.

I had no expectations of what she might tattoo on me and yet the end result still startled me.

It wasn't its beauty, though it was undeniably beautiful. It wasn't its uniqueness, though I'd never seen anything like it before. And it wasn't its striking nature, even though I struggled to find air for my lungs as I studied it with increasingly hungry eyes.

It was, above all, its honesty. Its vulnerability. Its aching sadness.

A compass, detailed and impossibly intricate, seemed to float as if on crystal clear water above a map. At its heart, Ireland. A homeland.

And yet it was darkened by shadows from the compass, shading so lifelike I swore I could pluck the compass from my back. Place it into Ryleigh's cupped hands. Guide her where she needed to go.

"You miss Ireland," I said, reading the tattoo as much as the sadness in her eyes.

She seemed stunned that I'd seen too much.

She didn't reply, merely turning her face away, her cheeks pink.

I studied the tattoo again.

"You yearn for…home," I said.

"Hiraeth," she said. It sounded like *Here-ryth.*

I frowned. "What does that mean?"

She shrugged. "It's Welsh. It means homesick for a place that doesn't exist anymore."

"You know Welsh?"

"I spent a few months there."

When I looked from the mirror to Ryleigh I found her just as lost as I had been in the tattoo. Her eyes shimmering like a well to fall into and never escape.

"Ireland's not home. Not anymore. No matter…" she bit her lip, "how much I want it to be."

Ryleigh hadn't just given me a tattoo. She'd given me a wound.

I could feel its familiar throbbing, its never ceasing ache.

I had many such wounds.

And I'd been the reason for many more in others.

They were heavy to hold, to carry.

I wanted to carry it for her. I wanted to carry it *all* for her.

But I couldn't. Because she wasn't mine to protect.

She belonged to my brother.

RY

Lee was dangerous. He saw too much.

He was the worst kind of threat. Because I hadn't expected his attack to come in the form of gentle questions, of an encouraging smile that crinkled the corners of his wide eyes.

I'd let my guard down. He'd slipped past my armour.

Worse, I'd let him. I...wanted to.

I should have stopped his lines of questioning, but it'd been so long since I'd shared myself with someone.

Without realising it, my shields had fallen as easily as a dress from my shoulders. I was naked.

I could have just tattooed another roaring lion and made up some story about how it was my favourite animal at the Dublin Zoo when I went as a kid.

Or a skull behind a rose with the words, *memento mori, "remember we must die"*, and said that it was a mantra I kept to remind myself to live each day to the fullest or some other cliched shite like that.

Instead I'd just tattooed the longing of my heart onto him.

I could hear it beating there on his skin, *in* his skin, as he admired his fresh ink in the mirror. He had a piece of my soul on him. Forever.

He was going to walk away with it. Take it with him. Leave me with a hole in mine.

And there was nothing I could do about it.

"It's really important that we keep it clean as it heals," I said, resorting to the well-rehearsed speech I gave every client when I was finished with their tattoo.

I'd fucked up. I'd given in to the temptation of Lee's alluring green eyes. I'd opened myself up and I was bleeding out.

I needed to get him out of there. I needed to close the door on whatever this strange night was, whatever it meant.

It was easier once I covered the artwork with a large swath of plastic. I could convince myself I was adhering medical tape to just another random man's back.

He wasn't the first guy I'd tattooed with attractive muscles.

If I spoke like a robot going through the aftercare instructions, it was all the better.

I'd been too forward with him anyway. Sent too many signals I never should have sent. The way I leaned so close to him, accidentally brushing against him, the way I touched him… I'd wanted a reaction. I'd played a dangerous game.

And lost. Best not to make things worse.

"It'll be sore for a few days," I said, letting my voice form the words mechanically, "but the tenderness should fade quickly, especially if you don't aggravate it."

He watched my fingers as they absentmindedly trailed over him even after I'd secured the bandage.

I snatched my hands from him, my cheeks flaring hot.

I spun around to hide my shame. "I'm going to give you a little tube of ointment to take with you."

I walked over to the rack of drawers along the left wall to collect some things, fingers shaking as I put the aftercare items in a small plastic bag. I forced my breaths to slow.

Fine. I was fine. Soon he'd be gone and I'd be safe…

I turned and bumped right into him, his bare chest against mine, the sudden proximity robbing me of my breath.

I'd been this close to him for several hours now. But this was different.

The intensity of his eyes with no barrier between him and me: not the crook of his elbow, not the vibrating gun between us, not the reflection of a mirror. His heartbeat directly against mine.

His gaze dropped to my lips.

I parted them on an inhale.

The way he looked at me like he'd been holding himself back for too long and could take it no longer, his eyes burning, almost angry. The searing warmth of his naked skin against my suddenly all too thin shirt, like tissue paper against a flame. The way he inhaled like someone who just realised he'd slipped off a cliff and there was no possible way now to stop himself from falling.

He was going to kiss me.

My core ached. Fuck. I really wanted him to kiss me.

My heart seized in my chest as he reached for me… reached past me to grab his shirt. The brush of his flannel shirt against my forearm felt like steel wool.

Could he see my disappointment? Could he sense in the way I lowered my eyes a little too quickly that I'd expected something more? Feared it, yet wanted it? Prayed it didn't happen, but begged for it to be true?

"I'll probably be needing this," Lee said, holding the shirt between us like it was an apology.

I forced a smile. "Of course. It's cold out there."

He winced as he tried to shrug it on but his fresh tattoo was restricting his movements.

He gave me a sheepish look. "Do you mind?"

He handed me his shirt and turned around, presenting his entire back to me. Fuck, his body was beautiful. Thick muscles like the rolling Irish hills on a wide V shape, lats I could hang off, his jeans showcasing his round ass.

I fought the urge to lick the entire length of his spine and helped him shrug on his shirt then his jacket, heat rising up my arms as my fingers brushed his warm smooth skin.

I was still staring when he turned, his fingers working the buttons of his shirt from bottom to top.

He smirked. "Wanna help me button it up, too?"

I scowled and stomped over to the main counter, hiding my burning cheeks.

I'd hoped he would stay on his side of the counter, but it seemed Lee had no sense of personal space. He stood right next to me, so close I could feel the heat radiating off him. Even fully dressed he affected me.

"Are you sure you won't let me give you the tattoo for free?" I asked as I fiddled with the buttons of the old-fashioned cash register.

He shook his head. "Nope. You did good work."

I rolled my eyes. "I attacked you then cut you."

He chuckled. "You're certainly not someone I will forget any time soon."

The warmth and heaviness of his words twanged something deep in my chest.

"A discount then," I insisted. "A *steep* discount."

"I'll accept no such thing," he said, holding my gaze with a comfortableness that I envied.

I tore my eyes away. "You have to let me do something. I mean, you're literally bleeding because of me."

"Drinks then."

I sucked in a breath, grabbing for the edge of the counter so that my knees wouldn't give out.

Fuck. It'd be so easy to just...be normal with him.

To go for drinks with this handsome man. To laugh and spill my secrets and dreams like diamonds over pints of Guinness. To let him pay and walk me home...

But I was not normal. I could never be normal. I could never have a normal life, not anymore.

"I...can't," I forced out. "I'm sorry."

"Oh." Something like realisation crossed his face, then a flash of guilt. "Right. Of course."

Of course? Did he see the reason I couldn't date him?

He couldn't possibly.

He handed me cash for the full amount and his fingers brushed mine. That single touch was so charged, electricity ran up my arm and I couldn't fight the shudder that went through me.

I was so close to breaking, so close to giving in and just yelling *yes* to the drink, *yes* to the date, and *God, yes* to whatever came after.

But he didn't push. Damn him, he didn't push.

I didn't fail to notice how bitter the disappointment tasted on my tongue.

We walked together to the front door, both of us slow, so slow, as if we were trying to squeeze out every last second left. Our arms kept brushing, goosebumps running across my skin and my hair standing on end as if reaching for him.

My gaze kept drawing sideways. Every single time our eyes locked because he was already looking at me.

I tore my eyes away and swore I wouldn't look again but without fail, a second later I found his green eyes as the centre of my vision.

Finally we reached the door. For a moment he just stood there.

So did I.

Neither of us reaching for the handle.

My fingers itched to reach to straighten his collar, to brush that piece of lint off his shoulder, any fucking excuse to touch him, but I dug my nails into my palms and pressed them into my sides to stop myself.

"Well," I said.

"Well," he said.

"I hope you like it. The tat, I mean."

He nodded. Then cleared his throat. "You, er, you did an amazing job. Thank you."

"Thank you for trusting me. I've never been given free reign as an artist before so…that's a big deal."

He smirked. "I'm glad I was a big deal for you."

I flushed. It was like he knew how much I was drawn to him.

He placed his hand on the handle, but he did not move to pull it open. "When do you finish your shift?"

"Oh, eh…soon. I just have to clean up. Lock up."

"It's getting late. It's real dark out there."

I studied the foggy darkness outside and chewed my lip. The black night felt less terrifying with him so close to me.

"Can I walk you home?" he asked, softly, respectfully.

I opened my mouth to say—yes, no, I didn't know—but he interrupted.

"Just to make sure you get home safely," he clarified with his palms raised. "No funny business, I promise."

Whatever I was about to say died on my tongue. I snapped my mouth shut.

I can't remember the last time anyone offered to walk me home. The last time anyone cared enough about my safety.

I blinked back tears and glanced aside, hoping he wouldn't notice how much his kindness affected me. Fucking pathetic, Ry.

I shook my head, wishing I could just say *yes*. "Sorry, I—"

He nodded. "Yeah, right. Of course."

The brush of his lips on my cheek was as gentle as the breeze, as burning as the sun that was yet to rise. He thanked me once more for the tattoo and then he was gone.

The door closing behind him with a jangle of the bell and a soft click.

I ran to the window like a little kid. Through the slit in the drapes I spied him walking away.

My mind went with him. To his home. What was it like? To his bed. Was it warm? Would he sleep all sprawled out, his limbs taking up space? Would he think of me when he closed his eyes?

Only when he was out of sight did I let the drape fall closed. I turned around to find Mason behind me with an empty bowl of Lucky Charms in his hand. Grinning at me.

I yelped.

"You scared the shite out of me," I growled in frustration, pushing past him.

"I came down for more luck," he said. "But it seems you took it all."

I rolled my eyes as I began to clean up my workstation for the night.

"Ryleigh's gonna get some!" Mason teased.

I shot him an angry glare. "He was just a client."

"Right." Mason nodded solemnly. "That's what I told myself…and them, in the morning."

I pointed toward the window. "He went home."

Mason pointed his spoon at me. "He'll be back."

It was pitiful, the amount of hope his words raised inside my chest.

"Trust me." Mason winked at me. "I'm the—I mean, I *was*, the King of Sleeping with Clients. And game respects game, ye know? He'll be back."

I scowled at his retreating back.

It was stupid of me to want Lee to return. It's not like I gave him a reason to come back. Chances were I'd never see him again.

Besides, I was leaving Dublin as soon as I could.

LIAM

I should *not* go back for her.

No. She was Rian's girl. I had to stay away.

And she made it clear *twice—no* to drinks, *no* to walking her home—that she was not a cheater. She wasn't even someone who entertained other men.

Which made me want her more.

But even my tattoo—her tattoo—throbbed with every step I took away from her.

I had to stay away. But I just…couldn't.

Which is why I found myself turning around at the end of the street, like an invisible band was tied from her to me and slipping into the shadows.

As I waited outside Dublin Ink, I felt like I'd gone dead, like a buried bulb waiting for the spring sun.

There she was. Ryleigh stepped out of Dublin Ink and my heart bloomed in my chest. I took my first real breath in minutes. Even her silhouette captivated me as she bent over the lock, then she slipped her key into her giant purse.

She walked down the sidewalk, and I followed, drawn to

her like a magnet. I made sure I stayed farther back this time so as not to scare her like I did earlier.

I told myself I was just making sure she got home safely.

Staying in the dark as her protector. Just a good man looking out for his brother's girl.

I would just watch her long enough to make sure she entered Rian's apartment and locked up behind her. So she was safe.

Yeah, right. So why did I end up crouching on the roof's edge of the building opposite hers, staring down into her window?

Ry was doing nothing more than stirring a boiling pot of pasta in her kitchen, but she took my breath away. She had changed out of her grungy "uniform" of leather and plaid. She now wore an oversized sweater with a frayed hem that reached just past the swell of her ass and nothing else.

The allure of sitting at her feet on her linoleum floor and tracing the tattoos that covered her long, naked legs as she tested a strand of spaghetti nearly had me running to her door.

If I closed my eyes I got vertigo. If I kept them open I saw stars.

Ry perched one bare foot atop the other as she leaned over the stovetop, steam misting her makeup-free face.

She paused to pull the window up to let the steam out. For one long horrifying moment I thought she'd seen me, locked eyes with me.

But then she waved steam out toward the open window with a "that's better," and returned to the stove.

A tendril of dark hair fell from the messy bun atop her head and she tucked it back behind her ear. With all that war paint off her, she looked younger, more innocent. Just as stunning. She looked so at ease. Like she'd seen less. Hurt less.

A pang stabbed at my heart. I wanted to give her this world. One as simple and warm as that little kitchen. One where she felt safe and at peace. One where she could sing along to The Untouchables, as she was doing now.

I imagined her so caught up in the song, swaying her body in the kitchen, that she wouldn't hear me come in from work.

I'd lean against the doorframe, admiring her with a contented smile and chuckling a little. She was so damn adorable.

It wouldn't frighten her when I came up behind her and slid my hands over her hips; we'd done this more times than we could count.

She'd turn around in my arms and we'd begin to slow dance as she continued to sing.

When the song ended she'd ask, *"When did you get home?"*

"Just now," I'd tell her.

A little white lie neither of us minded.

Alan didn't believe it was possible to find something like that in the city.

But even in that bitter cold, I knew it was no farther than Ry's kitchen just across a small stretch of darkness. It was so close I could almost reach out and grab it.

Ry began tearing up as she chopped an onion beside a stainless-steel pan shimmering with olive oil. Despite the tattoos covering her neck and the piercings dotting her face, she looked like a little girl as she bundled up the extra-long sleeve of her sweatshirt to wipe her eyes. I could just make out her sniffling.

I wanted nothing more than to wrap her into my arms and hold her tight.

"It's just the onion," I imagined her saying, looking at me with red-rimmed eyes.

I didn't care. I wanted nothing to make her cry. Nothing at all in the world.

I'd take up the knife and cut it for her.

She'd laugh when it brought stinging tears to my own eyes and I sniffled.

I'd cherish that laughter more than she'd ever know.

When Ry struggled to pry open the lid of a jar of pasta, I thought how nice it would be to open it for her. To hear her little grunts and extend my hand toward her without a word.

"No, no, I've got it," she'd say, stubborn as ever, adorable as ever.

My palm was laced through with the deep cold of the rooftop, but I imagined it warm from the stove as I just held it there. Waiting.

There in the dark I smiled, imagining her giving up and finally slapping the jar into my hand. I could almost hear the satisfying pop as I twisted the lid.

In real life, Ry banged the edge of the jar against the kitchen corner.

I didn't want Ry to have to fight that hard. I wanted to take her burdens. And I knew from the look she sometimes got in her eye that they were far heavier than a jar of pasta sauce.

But it was a place to start. And that's all I wanted: to start.

To start with her.

After the lid finally relented, the onions cooked down, and the pasta softened to her liking, Ry plated a heaping serving and carried her meal to the little dining table. This coincided with the end of The Untouchable's album and the sudden silence was overwhelming.

The merry kitchen scene seemed like just another figment of my imagination. I almost couldn't remember the sound of the music or the water boiling or the sizzle of onions hitting the pan.

As Ry stared down at her plate, it seemed there was only ever silence. Horrible, invasive, all-consuming *silence*.

I recognised it all too well. I'd experienced the same for most of my adult life. After Rian left, I had Alan and then Anna, Alan's wife, and eventually their kids, but they were never really *mine*.

When I was alone in my room, that was the very sound I heard. A silence deeper than just a lack of sound. A silence inside of yourself.

It was the soundtrack of loneliness.

Ry sighed and twirled a bite of pasta around her fork, only for an overhead light to go out.

"Not again," I heard her say, frustration clouding her voice.

In the dark she made her way back toward the kitchen and switched on the light above the stove. She then returned to eat in the dim amber glow.

In my mind, she never had to get up.

"I've got this, babe," I'd tell her, patting her knee in the dark.

I'd twist the new bulb in and catch her with her fork buried in my pasta.

She'd say, *"It always tastes better stolen,"* and her sheepish look would turn into the doe-eyed smile I could never get angry with.

I'd kiss her on the forehead before taking my seat again.

I ached to sit with her, ask her about her day as our fingers intertwined, slipping so effortlessly into one another's, playing as we ate. Our knees touching under the table because we've both known what it was like to be alone, because neither of us ever wanted to feel that again now that we had each other.

Conversation flowing like water, laughter easily given and received, our eyes finding each other's and every once in a while pausing, lingering.

Ry finished her meal and tidied up before going into her bedroom. Her silhouette moved through the room and for a while she disappeared into the bathroom, leaving me waiting with an ache in my chest.

Her hair was down when she returned. It caught the light of the moon as it cascaded around her shoulders. She was little more than a shadow as she gripped the hem of her sweatshirt and pulled it over her head. I only saw an outline of her naked body before she slipped beneath the sheets.

As I shivered in the lonely cold, I imagined her shivering, too. I imagined her reaching out across the sheets for me.

"I'm here," I'd tell her, bringing her against the heat of my chest. *"I'll never leave you."*

Where the fuck was Rian to do all of this for her?

He left.

He went...*away.*

An anger rose up in me. How dare he leave her behind to suffer on her own, to fight stubborn jars alone, to walk home late at night *alone.*

I vowed that she wouldn't be alone. I'd look after her, watch her from the shadows, make sure she was safe.

And to do that, I had to break into her apartment.

LIAM

It worried me how easy it was to break into her apartment.

Alan was right about that, at least. "They build things fast and quick and cheap and wonder when they all fall apart," he grumbled at least a dozen times at the dinner table after we heard that Rian had moved to Dublin.

All I had to do was flip the teardrop latch on Ry's shitty casement window with nothing more than a credit card slipped through the crack, and I was in.

She was at work, of course.

I'd "walked" her there earlier myself, made sure she was safe inside with at least one of the other tattoo artists—Conor, the big gruff one—before I turned back.

It was dark inside her bedroom and for a moment I crouched on the old wooden floors without reaching for a light. I believed what they said about losing one sense. I could smell her so intensely.

I closed my eyes to block out even the faint haze of the city's lights through the heavy mist and breathed her in.

There was the musk of her perfume. But there was more.

I could smell her scent of wild cherries and Easter lilies from her lotions and oils in the bathroom. I imagined her hands trailing up her long tattooed legs, foot propped on the toilet.

There was a slight sweetness of sweat: had she carried it in after a long run through the fog? Had she tossed and turned all night, making the sheets damp?

Ry's life circled around me like a ghost and all I could do was grasp at it. I wanted something tangible in my hands.

I wanted *her* in my hands.

From the inner pocket of my jacket, I brought out a small torch and switched it on. Its beam fell on the doorway, lighting the path I was supposed to take down the little hallway toward the living room.

I told myself that I was just here to look for clues to my brother's whereabouts.

But I couldn't help but linger in her bedroom, my torch-light drawn toward her bed.

I covered every inch of it with light, studying the wrinkles in the unmade sheets like they were the contours of Ry's own body.

I thought I could make out where she'd slept, her dark hair fanned out around her pale face. Her fingers laid softly across her stomach, across her breast. Her knees bent slightly, her toes poking out from the bottom of the duvet. Her chin turned slightly toward me.

I lay on the bed despite everything inside of me telling me not to. I turned on my side toward where she would have been. I could almost see her pink lips parted just slightly, her exhales tickling my nose like a feather. Moonlight on her nipples as her chest rose and fell evenly.

I buried my nose in her pillow.

Had her hair been damp from the shower when she laid down to sleep? Wet from the rain? Sticky from sex with someone else? Or was there a more nefarious reason for the slight damp of her pillow?

How much I still didn't know about her. How much she kept from me.

There I was in her most intimate of spaces and she remained a mystery. It only increased my desire to know her.

I found her laundry basket and let the light from the torch scan over its contents. Crumpled band t-shirts, plaid pleated skirt with leather buckles, fishnet stockings.

It both aroused and infuriated me. There was so much of her to have and yet I shouldn't want any of it. It was enough to drive me mad.

Perhaps that was why I reached down and pulled a pair of silk panties from the basket.

I was insane. There was no other reason to press them against my nose and draw in a shuddering breath and release it on a groan.

It was pure masochism. No rational being would willingly torture himself like that.

She was there. Ry. All of her. Her scent. Her moisture. Her essence. And yet she'd never been more out of reach.

My instant erection ached as I breathed her in again. I dared to dart out my tongue and taste her. I licked the taste of her from her panties. I throbbed against the zipper of my pants as an urgency stole my breath and stopped my heart.

I pocketed Ry's panties. The thought of coming into them almost had me pulling my cock out right here. But not now.

I went out into the hallway, picking through the mail stacks.

All of them were addressed to Rian.

The latest one was postmarked almost two weeks ago. Rian had been gone for two weeks?

But…where to?

I found a small desk in the living room with papers in small piles. I paused at the sketch book lying on it, Ry's name in soft script across the front. I couldn't help myself. I opened it, eager to know more about her.

I was startled at what I saw on the page.

It was a monster, some kind of demon who peered out at me through torn paper.

No, it only looked torn. Ry had shaded it to look as if the edges were curling back.

I blinked and peered closer.

It wasn't a demon. There were no horns upon his forehead, no fangs in his snarl. It was just a man, a man whose features had been so corrupted by evil that he looked demonic.

Dread settled into my stomach. The details of this creature were so lifelike, it was as if he were cursing me from within the page…

He was real.

Obviously this drawing was pencil and paper. But whoever had inspired this dark piece of art was real.

My lips pressed thin.

In the way she'd shaded under his eyes to make them more sunken, the way his lip curled up with disdain, it was obvious that Ry was scared of him.

Whoever this demon was.

I vowed that if I ever met him…I'd end him.

I closed the sketchbook, banishing him back into the confines of the paper.

I kept searching across the desk, riffling through papers, drawers, trying to keep everything in the same order after I'd searched it, one ear open for the sound of keys in the lock.

I snatched up a letter. An admission letter dated just over two weeks ago addressed to Rian.

Mr Merrick,

We're pleased to offer you a place here at Cherrywood Estate...

What the hell was Cherrywood Estate?

I pulled out my phone and took a photo of the address in the top right corner before folding it back up and placing it among the papers on his desk.

There was one last thing I came here to do.

I dragged a chair from the little table where Ry had sat alone to her dinner and climbed up to pull off the light cover. I unscrewed the broken bulb and replaced it with the new one I'd bought earlier. I slipped the old one into my jacket pocket.

I returned the chair to its rightful place and nodded with satisfaction at the light.

There. My baby didn't have to eat in the dark anymore.

Before I left, I checked the key hooks by the front door. I was both angry and giddy to find what I had been looking for: a spare key.

Ry should have known better than to leave it out in the open like that, even if it was where Rian had kept it when he was living here.

Dublin was dangerous.

I took the spare, knowing that it would help me to make it a little less dangerous for her.

Walking out the front door felt so *right*. Like I already belonged here with her. Like this was *our* place.

I forced those thoughts into the recesses of my mind as I locked up behind me.

Ry was not mine. She never would be. She was Rian's.

If all I got were the glimpses of her I stole from the shadows, that'd have to do.

~

I stood in front of the very last mechanic in town: O'Sullivan's Garage.

Fine, I was probably exaggerating but it was pretty damned close to it.

Shop after shop in Dublin I watched managers scan over my scant work history, flip it over, and say, "That's it?"

The conversation inevitably went something like this:

"It was a family farm."

"References?"

"Family."

A wry smile here. A yellow-toothed chuckle. "Can't exactly trust them to be honest, now can I?"

I never told them that they really didn't have to worry: Alan had not a single kind word for me.

I always promised I did good work. That I knew my way around engines— motorbikes, cars, tractors—even though I'd never had any formal experience in a mechanic shop. I just needed a chance.

The doors slammed pretty fast. In my face. Time and time again.

In front of O'Sullivan's Garage, the wind rattled the last of my resumes printed on cheap paper from the hostel's internet café that I held loosely in my hand.

I considered for a moment not even trying. Giving up. Holding out my hands to the city and saying, "Fine, you win." Crawling back to Alan.

I suppose that was what made me move. One foot in front of the other. Up the driveway.

I couldn't let Alan be right. All the wrong he'd done… I wouldn't let Alan be right.

The big bay door of O'Sullivan's Garage was closed save a couple feet or two.

I leaned down and shouted in. "Hello in there!"

From beneath a beat-up old Bronco, a man rolled out flat on his back. If I hadn't known this was a mechanic's shop, I would have guessed he just finished a shift at the old coal mine. Grizzly beard. Weathered skin. Heavy duty gloves. Wary eyes.

"You're not selling dictionaries, are you?" he asked.

"Do people still sell dictionaries door to door?"

The man assessed me with narrowed eyes. I figured his shop wasn't exactly known for its warm welcome and friendly service.

"I don't know," he said. "You look like the type."

Did I really stick out as such a country boy in this city? Like some sort of Boy Scout on a field trip?

"I'm looking for a job," I said, waving the stack of resumes in my hand as evidence.

The man grunted and tugged himself back under the Bronco. "Sorry, don't need anyone else."

The sudden rumbling of the garage door startled me. I turned to see a woman pulling into the drive.

A redhead with a baby face and a big smile hopped out of a beautifully restored baby blue Cadillac, jangling a large set of keys.

"We're open, don't you worry," she said to me with a melodic Cork accent so much like home I felt a punch in my stomach. "The door's not supposed to be down. My husband should be around here some—"

"He's selling something," the man beneath the Bronco grumbled.

I held up my resumes. "I'm looking for work."

The woman frowned at whoever was hidden beneath the vehicle. "He's looking for work, Darren."

"He's selling himself."

The woman rolled her eyes and introduced herself as Kayleigh. She invited me into the back office, giving Darren's ankle a playful kick and a "stop being a grump."

I followed her into a tidy, warm space, quite at odds with the dark, cold expanse of the solely inhabited garage.

Kayleigh went through my resume, fingers drumming on the desk.

I glanced through the window at the equipment and tools.

The garage had top-of-the-line stuff. Basically a mechanic's wet dream.

"You specialise in motorbikes?" Kayleigh asked.

I drew my attention back to her and her splattering of friendly freckles. "That's right."

"But you don't have any specific work in that field?"

It was Groundhog Day all over again.

Except Kayleigh at least seemed like the type to let me down easily.

Out of the corner of my eye I noticed the man, Darren, now leaning against the hood of another gutted car. Wiping his hands on a rag and clearly listening, but clearly not intending to seem like he was.

"I've got more experience than anyone in this city," I said, focusing back on Kayleigh. "I never had any teacher. Or textbook. Or really any tools besides the basics. I got motors running because I'm a stubborn son of a bitch. Excuse the language."

"She's heard worse."

I was surprised to find Darren at the door, arms crossed, but there.

"I'm good, and you want me working here, because I always find a way," I continued, speaking mostly at Kayleigh, but also to Darren. "I don't stop. I won't stop. I'll do whatever it takes. *Always*."

Kayleigh drummed her fingers again on the desk, eyes scanning once more what little there was to scan on my resume.

"Any references?" she asked, sounding hopeful. Like she was trying to help me out. Like she really wanted to, if she could.

"Just my family and they won't exactly give glowing reviews of me."

Before Kayleigh could dismiss me with a kind frown and an apologetic apology, Darren asked, "Why's that?"

He'd just finished rubbing the rag over his grease-stained face. Cleaned, or mostly cleaned, he looked almost like a new man. Years younger. Less jaded. Less bitter. His eyes, though, remained the same: sharp, assessing, reserved.

I sighed and decided I had nothing to lose. "One brother disowned me because I didn't do what I should have done. The other brother disowned me because I came to do what I should have all along."

Kayleigh glanced over to Darren and gave him the slightest of nods but she remained silent.

Something unsaid had been communicated between them: this was now Darren's decision. Darren's alone.

I turned to him. Exhaustion had made me honest.

"Look," I said. "I've not been the brother I wished I could have been. But I'm here in Dublin to try and make things right. To fix what I pray is fixable. I need to explain. Or make him understand. Or, I don't know, just beg forgiveness. I'm not really sure. I'm not really sure of much these days actually. I just know I have to be here. Trying. Trying and trying. Just like with those motors. Not giving up. Never giving up. Doing whatever it takes. To the end. Whatever that may be."

Darren looked down at his dirty nails.

The new tattoo on my back ached. I felt Ryleigh as if she were there, pressing her hand against me.

"Please," I said, all pride gone.

For Rian. For Ryleigh. For me.

I hardly understood the grumble that came from Darren's mouth.

Before I could ask what the hell he said he was back in the garage, back beneath the undercarriage of the Bronco, clanging echoing in the hollowed space.

"I—uh, I—"

"Well, congratulations!" Kayleigh said, hopping up to give me a quick hug. "Welcome to the team!"

"He said 'yes'?" I asked, incredulous.

Kayleigh nodded her head from side-to-side. "Well, he said something like, 'We'll give you a shot. But only on a trial basis. You really have to prove yourself, mister.'"

I laughed.

"He said all that?" I asked, thumbing toward the garage. "With that one grumble?"

Kayleigh winked. "Sometimes he requires a bit of interpreting."

I grinned. "I'm glad you're the one doing the interpreting."

Kayleigh went back behind the desk. "When would you like to start?"

I rubbed my hands together. "How does right now work?"

~

In my palm, the copy of Ryleigh's spare key was still rough from the locksmith's saw. I squeezed it tight against the cold the next night.

The key worked without a problem.

I slipped inside her apartment and softly closed the door behind me.

First, I replaced the spare key on the hook.

Ry didn't notice its absence. I know because I watched her after she got home last night to make sure.

In her bedroom, I wedged the torch in my mouth once more and unpacked the tools I'd brought in a small black duffel bag along with the new latch.

I'd made sure to get her the most secure one I could find, though anything would have been better than what she'd had.

It made my skin crawl, remembering how easy it had been to gain entrance. Thinking of all the men who could have done the same…

I'd kill them.

I'd slit the throat of anyone who dared to even touch Ry.

For my brother's sake, of course, I lied to myself.

These thoughts didn't scare me, though they should have.

It should have been the moment I realised I'd gone too far. Fallen too hard for someone who could never be mine.

Instead all I wanted was to go farther, fall harder.

Perhaps it was the fact that I was in her bedroom and that her smell was all around me. By the time I finished replacing the latch, my need was so intense. I returned to the laundry basket and found another pair of Ry's panties.

I devoured her smell. It was becoming familiar to me, but that didn't make it lose any of its power.

Instead it only seemed to grow. I wanted her smell to mix with mine.

I lay again on Ry's bed and by the time I shakily unzipped my pants my cock was already leaking pre-cum. I rolled my fist over my head, whole body shuddering. My heels dug into her sheets as my back arched. If I had been in my right mind, I might consider the muddy marks I was leaving.

But I was nowhere near my right mind.

With one hand fisting recklessly around my cock, I suffocated myself with Ry's panties in the other. Pain filled my strained chest even as pleasure spread with a white heat from my lower stomach. She was in my nose, in my mouth, down my throat, and I wanted more still.

I stroked myself as I imagined her thighs pressed tight against my ears, blood rushing through them.

I imagined it was Ry's blood. It wasn't my racing pulse, but hers. Her inner thigh muscles twitching, her veins throbbing, her skin on fire as I drowned in her pussy.

I blinded myself with her panties, pretending it was her ass over my eyes. Her velvet skin softer than the silk I pressed against my eye sockets. Her hips would rock, ass undulating over me, as my tongue fucked her deeper and deeper.

My wrist was losing its steady rhythm on my cock. The

pace was growing more erratic and while I wanted to draw out the fantasy, I felt myself stroking my shaft faster and faster, desiring that release.

I licked my lips and I groaned as I imagined them wet from Ry's delicate folds. Her fingers would be running over her hard nipples, carding through her thick hair, slipping inside her hot, tight mouth and all the while I would be greedily lapping up everything she had to give me.

I was on the verge of coming, just about to give a strangled shout of her name into her panties, wet from being stuffed in my mouth, balls drawn in so tight they ached, sheets a mess beneath my writhing body.

I heard the key in the front door.

Shit. Ry was home early.

LIAM

Ryleigh was home early. And I was touching myself on her bed with her panties over my face.

Fuck. I had to hide. *Now.*

I rolled under the bed and dragged my duffel under with me just as Ry opened her bedroom door. My body pulsed with the buzz of adrenaline and the burn of unfulfilled need, my cock still hanging semi-hard from my zipper.

Ry threw her purse onto the floor with a frustrated sigh. I watched as she kicked off her heels, one coming dangerously close to where I lay.

She seemed agitated. Not bothering with the lights as she paced.

From beneath the bed I could see myself in the mirrored door of her armoire. I was in the shadows but still, I was there to be seen.

I should have moved deeper beneath the bed. Away from the mirror. It was safer. Where she couldn't see me.

Where I couldn't see *her.*

I remained motionless, not even breathing, as Ry

wrenched off her black lace top. She flung it down into the laundry basket with something like a growl. In a flimsy mesh bralette, she pressed balled-up fists against her eyes and shook her head.

I watched transfixed as Ry attempted to calm herself from whatever unspoken thoughts were causing her such anguish. Her measured breaths hypnotised me: curled in over herself, hand against her chest, her lips trembling slightly. When she straightened she seemed back in control.

She unzipped her miniskirt and laid it across the side of the basket instead of throwing it like the rest.

Her movements seemed glacially slow as she leaned over, her ass in black hose displayed for me. As Ry unrolled the stockings, her full breasts hung heavy in that barely there bra, and in the faint light I could make out the shape of her nipples.

My mouth watered beneath the bed and cum leaked from my dick. I was afraid I would come just like that, untouched, hand clasped over my panting mouth.

She opened the armoire to pull out an old oversized t-shirt and for a moment she disappeared from view. I saw the bralette fall onto the pile in the laundry basket, and when Ry closed the armoire door she stood completely naked, t-shirt hanging in a fist by her side.

She was perfect. Her alabaster skin was like the dark side of the moon, covered in all those tattoos: alluring and mysterious.

I wanted to map her, every fucking inch of her.

Ry looked at herself in the mirror for a moment and then turned hastily away. She threw the t-shirt over her head as she walked toward the bed and then the mattress compressed above me.

I thought she would fall asleep and then I'd slip out.

But instead of silence I heard her pound the pillow.

I tried to spy her in the mirror, but I couldn't make out much.

She rolled from one side to the other. And then back. She huffed impatiently.

Whatever had been under her skin earlier clearly wasn't gone.

I listened as Ry again tried breathing slowly and calmly. Again there was silence.

But not for long.

Ry *moaned.*

In the mirror I could just make out the crook of an elbow, the heavy rise of a chest in a too-thin old t-shirt.

I hardly dared to believe it.

But then she moaned again.

She was touching herself. Not even a foot from me, Ry was masturbating.

I had to grip the base of my cock with an iron grip to keep myself from coming uncontrollably right then and there. Even that, squeezing myself like a boa constrictor, was almost not enough.

To know that Ry's graceful little fingers were circling her clit, teasing her folds till they wet, slipping unencumbered into her tight pussy...

Surely she could hear my heart thudding out my chest.

Of course she couldn't because her own heart was probably racing. Her moans were rapidly growing louder and from the mirror I saw how quickly she was fingering herself, how strained the muscles along her forearm were.

Blood must have been thundering against her ears, skin

vibrating with electricity. Whatever had been agitating her had needed release and she was careening wildly toward it.

I began to stroke myself beneath the bed. Closing my eyes, I imagined my hand was her pussy. Her moans were in my ear, her hard nipples beneath her t-shirt brushing my chest. I'd never felt such pleasure masturbating before.

The bed was groaning, the springs of the mattress screeching and my hazy thoughts wondered what could have driven her to such need to make her writhe about, out of her mind with pleasure from only her own fingers inside of her. Her heels digging in like mine had, her back arching in the mirror, t-shirt damp against her heaving chest with sweat.

"Oh, God, *Lee,*" she moaned as she came.

My name.

Me.

She'd been thinking about *me* as she touched herself.

Not Rian. Not her boyfriend.

My fucking name.

I bit down on my bottom lip as I came beneath her. My cum came in searing hot spurts that covered the underside of her bed. My orgasm was almost more pain than pleasure because I had to force myself to stay absolutely silent.

I wanted to curl in on her, squeeze her tight to me, dig my fingers into her skin and my muscles screamed as I roped them in. I didn't even get the satisfaction of collapsing bonelessly as Ry did.

All I allowed myself was a single shudder that was more intense than anything I'd ever experienced with any other woman.

She had been haunting *me* this whole time.

But I was the one haunting her.

I wanted to hear my name on her mouth again. Closer. Louder. Even more desperately.

As Ry's pants softened, I used her panties to clean up the slats along the bottom of her bed.

I waited until Ry's breathing slowed and then steadied. I waited a little while longer to be sure, but it was soon clear: she was out.

How desperate had she been for that release? Had she been thinking about me at Dublin Ink? Waiting for me to return?

These thoughts consumed me as I snuck out from beneath her bed, carefully extracting the duffel bag, and made my way toward the door. I paused to glance back at her.

The sheets were pooled around her calves. Her t-shirt had ridden up over her hips and I could see the glisten of her come on her legs. I wanted to lick the small stain on the sheets so badly I felt myself already getting hard again.

I breathed in the smell of her sex, all that I dared, and it was intoxicating. I left her apartment feeling drunk. Wasted. Ruined.

Ry wanted me.

She could deny it all she wanted, she could refuse to date me, use her boyfriend as an excuse, but she and I both knew the truth.

I'd stayed away because I wanted to be respectful to Rian.

But this changed *everything*.

She had invoked *my* name when she came.

Me.

That was permission enough to pursue her.

Brother be damned. He wasn't looking after her well enough that his own girl was calling out another man's name.

She was *mine*.

RY

I used to watch couples in the park, fingers light, unobtrusive on a soft shoulder, tapping in time to a hummed love song. The brushing of a tendril of hair from a rosy cheek. Lips barely touching.

The longing hurt, but it was a bittersweet feeling.

So when I slipped into Dublin Ink earlier and caught Conor and Aurnia on the faded floral couch together, her knees draped over his lap, it hurt.

It hurt because I wanted it.

You said no *to Lee, eejit,* I reminded myself.

So it was a bad fucking sign that every night I waited till the last possible moment to close, hopeful eyes glancing one last time up and down the deserted street.

My head whipped up, hope bubbling in my chest, every time that damned bell above the door rang.

Every time it was *not* who I was hoping to see, and I forced a smile onto my face as another stranger walked up and asked for yet another rose or another lion or another skull.

I oscillated from annoyance (how dare he give up so easily), to regret (I should have said yes), to anger (whatever, he wasn't that special anyway).

It was becoming clearer and clearer, Lee was not going to return to the shop.

"You can head home early if you want," Mason said, spoon in his mouth as he climbed the stairs with a bowl of Lucky Charms and a bottle of wine tucked under his arm. Rachel wasn't working that night. "It's raining cats and dogs. If someone hasn't come yet, they're not coming."

"We can close up, Ry," Aurnia called from where she swept.

Conor let out a grunt of agreement from his spot in the corner where he was hunched over a desk and watching Aurnia the way he always did when she was in the room.

"I don't mind," I said, hunched over my drawing pad, trying to play it cool.

"*Ry…*" Mason leaned his head back at the top of the stairs so he could see me.

I lifted an eyebrow at him.

He grinned. "It's about to get noisy."

I frowned. "But you have Lucky Charms."

Mason winked. "Post-performance snack, if you know what I mean."

Everyone knew what Mason meant. All the time. He didn't exactly do subtle.

"Right," I said.

I was across the room grabbing my coat from the hooks when the little bell at the front door rang.

I forced myself not to turn around. It's not like it'd be *him* or anything.

"Conor is free right now," I heard Aurnia say. "He—"

"Actually, I came for Ryleigh."

My coat slipped from my fingers at his voice.

By the time I'd fumbled it back onto the hook, he was there. Within a foot of me. His shadow like a warm blanket I wanted to curl up in.

I failed, spectacularly, to keep the excitement from my face as I gazed up into Lee's eyes.

I saw the same light in his eyes. The same expectation. The same hope.

And it fed mine.

I was so fucking screwed.

"You came back," I said, and it came out all breathy.

I suddenly became hyper aware of Aurnia and Conor in the room. Aurnia with her chin atop her broom, girlish fantasies already weaving themselves in her little head. Conor sizing up Lee, assessing threat levels, judging douchebagerie.

I hardly knew Conor, but I was a friend of Rian's, so as far as he was considered, I was family. All he was missing was a shotgun laid across his lap.

Lee must have sensed we had an audience as well, because he cleared his throat awkwardly before continuing.

He kept his voice low. "Um, maybe I should have called to see if you were available first."

"You want another tattoo?" I asked, surprised.

Lee's eyes darted from under his baseball cap toward the corner where Conor sat scowling at him.

For a second he looked as if he were about to dash out of the tattoo parlour. To admit this was all a big fucking mistake and leave as fast as he came.

"Um, Conor," Aurnia said suddenly. "I forgot. We need to do inventory."

She earned a gruff, incomprehensible response in reply.

But whatever it was Conor said, Aurnia was having none

of it. It was rather funny, watching her tiny fingers tug at his tree limb of a forearm.

But he sighed and went easily after she gave him a prolonged look.

Oh, to have that power.

Lee ducked his head as they passed.

Aurnia gave me a wink and I smiled weakly.

Was I that fucking obvious? Had Lee made me that transparent?

Then they were gone.

Once more Lee and I had the space to ourselves.

He smelled of engine grease and soap. For some reason it was the most wonderful scent in the world, even better than fancy cologne or aftershave.

He slipped off his baseball cap and ruffled his hair, scattering raindrops. "I wanted to come sooner but— I'm sorry I didn't come sooner."

It seemed like he wanted to say more but I certainly wasn't going to ask for an explanation.

"W-what would you like me to tattoo this time?" I asked.

"Whatever the compass points to," Lee replied with a smile.

He shrugged out of his worn sherpa-lined jacket and our fingers brushed when I took it from him. That simple touch sent fire across my skin.

I hung it on one of the hooks, trying and failing to play it cool. He was standing way too close.

"It's your compass," I said.

His green eyes held mine. "It's your true north."

He stepped closer and took my hand.

My heart flipped over in my ribcage as he lifted my

fingers, brushed his thumb over the gothic letters twisting along the back of my hand: h o p e.

He lifted his eyes to mine.

"I want more," he said. Not softly this time. "I want you."

"You want...me?"

He nodded, his eyes fixed on mine.

I could have pulled my hand back. I'd be in the right. He was far too fucking forward. It wasn't appropriate. It was too much. I could have even told him to leave.

Pulled out my phone and booked a flight out of here. Been on a plane the day after tomorrow.

I could have saved myself.

"Whatever you want," he said, his words heavy with meaning, "wherever you want, as long as it means something to *you*."

I sucked in a breath.

Free reign again. Holy shit.

"You'll need to take your shirt off," I said.

He grinned. "Admit it. You like when I strip for you."

I swallowed hard, my throat too knotted to speak, as he unbuttoned his shirt one by one, then shrugged it off his shoulders, all the while he watched me, watching him, a smug knowing look on his face.

He hung his shirt on a hook and stepped in even closer. "Where do you want me?"

It was a dream. Lee's broad back there again beneath my hungry fingertips. His skin like a blank canvas.

I made him lie face down again on the table.

"No cuffs this time?" he asked.

I flushed, remembering how stupid I'd acted the night we met. How could I have thought this man was a stalker?

"Er, no cuffs needed."

"That's a shame..."

I did most of the prep in silence. Lee's steady breathing lulled me like waves against a small boat.

Night fell quickly outside the shop. The occasional beam of headlights flashed like a lighthouse. Otherwise we were alone without a shore in sight.

Lee gripped the edge of the leather chair when the tattoo gun made its first bite.

He laughed through slightly clenched teeth. "It doesn't get easier, huh?"

Most of my clients found the second tattoo the hardest. The thrill of the first had faded. The body provided slightly less adrenaline, slightly less natural painkillers. There was just the steady, unrelenting piercing of the skin.

"It must be a dream come true," Lee said, eyebrows pinched as I continued, "getting to travel around the world. Seeing everything life has to offer. I can't even imagine."

I dipped the tattoo gun into fresh ink. It gave me a chance to think over what I was going to say.

With most people I'd simply agree, give some bland triviality about how great travel was, and move on. With most people the easiest way was just telling them what they wanted to hear. This should have been exactly what I told Lee.

"To be honest, it's been hard," I said, wondering what it was about him that made me want to...share myself. To speak my truth. "It's like I've been carrying bricks around in my duffel bag. And each new city is another impossible distance to lug them."

Lee was silent for a moment.

"Bricks you brought with you from Dublin?" he guessed.

I sighed. Sitting back. Stretching.

I stared at the compass I'd tattooed first. Ireland beneath it.

My home. My hell.

"Sometimes it's like I can't even see what's in front of me," I said, leaning back over him. "I'll be in front of some of the most beautiful sights in Europe, places people flock from all over the world to see, and all I'll see is..."

Escape routes. Strangers. Long nights alone. Another day of surviving. Another plane to catch, a train to run after, bus to get lost on.

"It's all-consuming," Lee said in a voice hardly above a whisper, "when someone hurts us."

"When they won't stop," I added in a hollow voice.

I looked up to blink away the start of a tear.

I saw the man standing across the street.

Him.

I jolted with the familiar fear, tattoo gun tearing across Lee's skin. I stumbled back but didn't fall, Lee had caught my arm.

He pulled me back up to standing. "Ry, what is it?"

I glanced outside again.

The man who had been there was gone.

But like the impression the sun makes on the back of your eyelids, I saw him still.

A hazy figure in black. Facing the big windows.

Staring at me.

I felt a hand on my cheek, Lee's hand, and looked up to find his green eyes all-encompassing my vision.

"Hey," he said softly, "are you okay?"

His concern made my lungs shudder with a loosened breath.

"I just thought I saw..."

My nightmare.

I shook my head. "Nothing."

His eyebrows drew together but he didn't push me.

"Oh my God, I cut you again," I cried out when I saw the blood dripping down his back.

I cleaned up the blood with a wad of tissues, swearing between repeated apologies, fussing over Lee because I couldn't bear to look back through the window.

I only stopped when his fingers encircled my wrist. Nothing constricting. Nothing binding. Just steady, strong and calming.

"I'm fine," Lee said, smiling. "You're fine."

I finished Lee's tattoo quickly.

There was only so long I would be able to keep the tremble from my fingers. The panic was coming for me. I needed to get somewhere alone to fall apart. To shake as if with fear till morning.

I was grateful when Lee walked in front of the mirror himself.

The door I tattooed on him had a red slash across it. Biblical. Like he was marked. I couldn't remember if that meant he was spared. Or doomed.

"It's cracked," Lee said.

I winced. "Once that heals, I can fix it."

Lee shook his head.

"The shadowing along the edge," he clarified. "The door's cracked open."

I looked at it as if I hadn't been the one to tattoo it onto his skin.

It was the door of my childhood home. I hadn't meant for it to be open. Not open at all.

I didn't give Lee a response. I feared it like I feared the cracked door: once open, there was no closing it.

At the cash register I offered Lee a weary sigh.

He came to stand close once more. Too close. Torturously close.

"I really don't know what's gotten into me," I said, dragging my fingers through my hair.

Lee smiled through the wince as he dragged back on his coat.

"I think you just really want to buy me a drink," he said.

God, how I wanted to.

I shook my head.

"Then how about you let me buy you a drink instead?" he said, grinning devilishly.

"Wait, how does *that* work?"

He shrugged. "You could buy me the first drink if you really insist. But the rest would be on me. The gentleman in me couldn't let you pay for drinks."

"I'm sorry, I..." *I'm so fucked up that I can't. I'm not staying in Dublin so I can't.* "...shouldn't."

I wondered if he saw the sadness behind my eyes.

"You shouldn't..." he repeated.

"I shouldn't..." I said with a heavy heart.

"...'cause you're with Rian," he said slowly.

"Rian?" I said. "No, what? Rian? Ew, no."

"You're *not* with Rian?"

"Fuck no!" I laughed.

I was so amused by the idea of being with my best friend that I didn't even think to ask why he would so randomly assume that of two tattoo artists he'd never met before in his life.

"So there's not another man?" he asked.

Ice flooded my veins.

"So there *is* another man then."

"No," I said quickly. Too quickly. "No, I mean…"

There was a man…but not like that.

He haunted my every nightmare. He followed me around the streets. He was the reason I gave up Dublin, why I feared being here.

He placed his hand over mine. "Go out with me, Ry."

There was just warmth. Rough calluses, but soft touch. There was just a gentle squeeze.

I couldn't remember the last time I yearned for a man to not let go.

"Sorry, I don't date…" I said lamely, the closest to the truth as I'd let myself admit.

He raised an eyebrow. "Men?"

I'd experimented with women. When the loneliness got too much and I just needed the comfort of a warm body against mine.

But it felt like there was always something missing. I craved the roughness, the hardness of men. Even as I feared it.

"No, I date men—"

"Lucky me," he said with a grin, "*I* am a man."

"I mean…" I fidgeted with the edge of my skirt. "I don't date anyone."

"No one?"

"No."

"Ever?"

"I just… I don't date people I don't know. And I don't know you," I finished lamely.

He nodded and a determined look came over his eyes. "Yet."

"What?"

"You don't know me...*yet*."

"I don't want to give you false hope."

"I can be a very, *very* patient man. And..." he smirked, "there's a lot more of my body to tattoo."

I froze, my mind chewing over his words. Was he suggesting that he'd get the rest of his body tattooed in order to get to know me?

"You'll be waiting forever," I warned.

"I think you'd be worth it."

My stomach twisted at the seriousness of his words, the promise in his eyes.

Like last time, he held out the cash. His fingers brushed mine, causing a riot of heat to travel up my arm.

I pulled my hand back quicker this time.

We walked side by side to the door again, my eyes quicker to meet his, longer to pull away. He was already wearing me down.

"I've done hard labour my whole life, you know," Lee said, pausing at the front door.

I stared up at him, frozen as he leaned in.

"A couple bricks," he whispered in my ear. "They'd be nothing for me to carry."

Lee kissed my cheek and slipped out the door.

I sagged against it as it closed behind him.

Could it be that easy? Just unloading my burden? Sharing it with him?

My stomach tightened when I remembered the man across the street. The man who was hunting me.

No, as soon as Rian was out of rehab I was gone.

I couldn't stay in Dublin. Not ever.

Not even for Lee.

LIAM

She was not Rian's girlfriend.

She was his *best friend.*

Thank fuck.

Rian might still hate me for pursuing her. But it was too late. I was obsessed.

There was just some other reason, something I didn't know yet, that was keeping Ry from saying yes to me. I didn't buy her excuse of not knowing me.

She had shared herself with me, marked her biggest hope on my back.

I'd figure it out. Like I said. I was a patient man.

All I needed now was to find Rian.

I glanced through the glass doors of the Cherrywood Estate.

It was a drug and alcohol rehab centre.

Fuck. Had my brother fallen so far?

Guilt gnawed at my heart. I should have been there for him. I should have come to Dublin earlier, not waiting until our da had died to work up the courage.

This was my fault.

I forced my feet to step forward, to enter. To face whatever was waiting for me in here.

I smiled at the receptionist and asked to see Rian Merrick, my voice cracking on his name. I introduced myself as his brother.

The receptionist nudged her blue plastic frames back up her petite nose. "Your brother is a patient here, Mr Merrick—"

"Liam. Or...Lee."

That nickname was growing on me.

"I can inform him that you are here to see him but..." Her soft blue eyes softened even further when she looked from the computer screen to me. "...it's his choice."

I nodded.

She nestled the cardigan tighter around her shoulders and passed through glass sliding doors, disappearing quickly round the corner of a long hallway.

I paced in anticipation. Paced to keep warm. I feared the cold in my bones could only be relieved by my brother's forgiveness.

Even before the receptionist returned I knew it was probably still a long way off.

My shoulders sagged when I saw the receptionist's face: bad news. She reached across the counter to grip my hand, her fingers icy.

"It's often very difficult for our patients to see family members in particular," she offered kindly. "There's a lot of guilt. Shame. Drug use takes them to the very depths and the struggle back up can be ugly. I'm sure he just wants you to see him better, you know? Please don't take it personally, Mr Merrick."

I bit back a snort.

Rian's refusal to see me was as fucking personal as it got.

I don't think even our father raised from the grave would receive a bigger middle finger than me.

Rian expected cruelty from him. I was supposed to be better. Stronger. Braver.

"Can you pass along a message for me?" I asked.

"Absolutely!" She brightened.

"Can you tell Rian that I'm coming back every morning," I said. "Whether he sees me or not. Whether he spits at the sound of my name or screams his lungs out. Whether he curses me or wishes me dead and gone. I'm coming back. I'll be here. For him. I'm going to be there for him."

Even if he didn't want me to.

The receptionist gave my hand one last squeeze and promised to tell him.

"It's not your fault," she told me as I turned to leave, back out into the cold.

I smiled bitterly over my shoulder at her.

She was just trying to be nice.

But she was wrong.

"It is *all* my fault," I said as the cold of winter stabbed at my chest.

Kayleigh kept the garage warm under the excuse that she had poor circulation in her toes. In truth, I don't think she wanted Darren to get cold.

And he wasn't the type to ever admit something like that.

I appreciated the red glow of the portable radiator like a temporary stay of execution.

Kayleigh stood above me like a reproachful mother. "You wince every time you lie down on that shoulder."

I lay on an old leather creeper and stared back up at her.

Her feet wide, arms crossed tightly across her chest, a "don't give me any bullshite" set to her pretty pink lips. As stern as such a sweet face can look.

"I'm fine," I said and began to roll myself beneath a raised Harley Davidson.

Kayleigh's boot jammed behind one of the wheels stopped me short.

"*No*," she said. "You're clearly not."

Darren munched on a sandwich as he sat on top of a big red toolbox. "No workman's comp during the trial period."

Kayleigh hushed him.

I dragged a hand over my face and sat up with a sigh, drumming my wrench against my thigh.

"I'm not hurt," I explained. "It's a new tattoo."

"No workman's comp for tattoos," Darren grumbled.

I looked across the shop at him and he grinned over a mouthful of tuna sandwich.

"It's on your back then?" Kayleigh asked, fussing like a mother hen. "I don't want you lying on it till it's fully healed. You look like you're in pain!"

"They're on my upper back," I said.

"You got more than one?" she asked.

"I've got two and I plan to get more very soon. So it's not really possible to not lie on them."

"Oo, I know." Darren hopped off the toolbox. "How about…you *not* get another tattoo?"

He disappeared under the hood of an '80s muscle car that was more rust than paint.

"I don't really have a choice," I said.

Darren poked his head out and pointed a screwdriver at me. “There’s always a choice.”

“There’s a girl.”

Darren huffed, glanced at Kayleigh, and grumbled, “Right. You’ve got no choice.”

Kayleigh beamed toward Darren before smiling back down at me. “She’s a tattoo artist then?”

I nodded.

“Does she know how to tattoo anywhere other than your back?” she asked teasingly.

I blushed and prayed Kayleigh didn’t notice.

“I kind of let her tattoo what she wants…” I answered in a slightly sheepish voice, ”where she wants it.”

Darren slammed the hood of the car and planted his hands flat against it. He dropped his head between his shoulder blades and shook it. ”You’re doomed.”

Kayleigh frowned at her husband. “What do you mean ‘doomed’?”

Darren eyed Kayleigh.

“You know exactly what I mean.”

“I think it’s sweet,” Kayleigh said to me.

“I think it’s trouble,” Darren countered.

“There are worse ways to bond with someone,” Kayleigh said to Darren. “Certainly less painful ways.”

“It’s all painful,” Darren said. “Love ain’t nothing but it.”

Kayleigh dismissed Darren with a wave of her hand.

“Don’t listen to him,” she said to me.

“She’s going to permanently mark you,” Darren said. “Are you ready for something like that?”

The look Darren gave me meant that he was talking about much more than just tattoo ink.

She was going to mark my body. To mark my soul.

And I would let her.

"That's the plan," I said as I lay back down on the creeper.

Now that I knew she didn't belong to Rian, she was mine to pursue.

Now that I knew it was my name on her lips when she came, she was mine.

I wasn't going to let her get away.

I just hoped that Rian could forgive me when he found out.

RY

The ring of the bell above the door was like the call for our boxing match to resume, Lee stepping in through the door into the empty parlour like an opponent into the ring.

I was better prepared this time. I wouldn't be knocked out quite so easily.

"You should have called ahead," I said, my voice purposely as cold as a first punch.

I'd planned my attack, my first move decided in advance.

Last time I'd let my heart speak first: *"you came back."*

Stupid, pitiful eejit. Not this time.

Lee stepped back like I had, in fact, struck him. The hurt on his face stung worse than I'd expected.

"Ry, what's wrong?"

The initial shock on his face had quickly worn off, now there was only concern. He moved toward me as if he were ready to scoop me into his arms, to comfort me, to soothe me.

That was not how I thought this would go. He was supposed to argue back, get defensive. To stab me back.

Not…this concern. This compassion.

No, I couldn't let him get near me. I couldn't let him touch me. I'd falter. I'd utterly fail in my attempt to push him away.

I stepped back. "Only my friends call me Ry."

"I don't want to be your friend."

I stumbled. Guess I wasn't as prepared as I thought. I forgot to keep my hands up.

"What? Then what—?"

"Let me be clear," he said, his voice hard, his focus narrowed on me as he advanced like a determined opponent. "This will only ever be *more* than friends—"

"How presump—"

"Let me finish," he said, his tone more biting than before.

I slammed into the back wall. I was trapped. I had nowhere left to go.

He stopped only when he was toe-to-toe with me, close enough to me to make my throat seize.

He invaded my senses, his masculine scent filling my lungs, his heat crowding me, even though he kept an inch between us, not touching me.

Every inch of my skin screamed for him to touch me.

"I understand you have trust issues. That's okay," he continued, his voice softening. "I don't need you to get over them. But I'll be here every week until you learn to trust *me*."

His response caught me on the chin. Warmed me like blood on my tongue.

I found my chest rising and falling a little too rapidly. The cool demeanour slipping off me like a dress, pooling on the floor. Why is it that he could strip me of my defences so damn easily?

"So, no." He spoke low, his tone managing to sound both

dangerous and inviting. "I'm not here to be your *friend*. I'm here for *you*. All of you; the best and worst of you."

My heart squeezed.

No. What he was offering wasn't real. It couldn't be real. Broken dolls like me don't get their fairytale ending.

I should have demanded that he leave. Told him I was getting on the first train out of the city. Pushed past him without a word even, leaving him with my cold shoulder as his last memory.

But inside there was a part of me that still believed in fairytales. That hoped, dreamed, that one day a prince would come and save me.

It was a stupid part of me that was going to get me hurt.

"Y-you barely know me," I said.

"I bet I know you better than most already." He shrugged his shoulder, the one where I'd laid myself bare on him in ink. Twice.

I laughed, nervously. He was so close to the truth it hurt.

"What you're feeling…it's not special," I said, trying to brush off the tension, trying to regain some sort of control over this sparring match. "I see it all the time, in fact."

He lifted an eyebrow. "Is that so?"

"It is," I said with an indignant sniff. "It's easy to get addicted to the ink."

My gaze trailing over the tattoos that covered my fingers, my hands, that twisted up my arms.

"To crave the pain," I continued. "To miss that flood of numbness when your body responds to the pain, endorphins soaring, adrenaline making every one of your cells come to life. It's like *coming*."

The word caught in my throat like a forbidden curse.

Lee placed his palms on the wall on either side of my head

and leaned in closer, as close as he could possibly get without touching me.

His heat hovering just above my skin like an aura. His gaze tracing my cheeks down to my lips then back to my eyes. He looked like he was holding himself back through sheer willpower alone from crashing into me. Consuming me.

Heat pooled between my thighs. My eyes fluttered closed.

I hadn't had a man's touch in so long. I did my best on my own. But there was only so much strength in my hand. It was never enough. Never what I longed for. Never took me where I wanted to go.

A shiver ran down my spine because I knew that Lee, with those callused hands, with the rippling muscles along his tanned forearms, he, *he* could give it to me. He would be strong enough to totally dominate me.

"You should try a different tattoo style," I said, grasping for straws, the wild shots of a desperate opponent, one who already knew she had lost.

"Conor or Mason," I continued, pretending that I didn't understand that the only reason he even cared about tattoos was to be close to *me*, "they can give you what you're looking for."

"I've already found what I want," he said, his lips brushing my ear, his husky voice sending shivers down my spine. "I want…you."

~

Lee kept his word. Week after week, he came back to Dublin Ink.

Maybe if I hadn't been so eager to see him again, I'd have noticed he only ever showed up when I was alone.

He'd stand way too close to me as he unbuttoned his shirt, as my fingers flinched toward him.

But to my utter frustration, he didn't make a move on me physically. No crowding me against walls, no demanding I let him into my heart.

He just lay down on his stomach on the tattoo table and turned his face toward me, his head on his forearms.

"What do you want tattooed on you today?" I'd ask, even though his answer was always the same.

"Something meaningful to you."

I'd ignore the tightness in my chest and take my time, readying my inks, as if I didn't already know which piece of my soul I was going to mark him with.

I added ivy to the door on his back and the brick walls of my childhood home. I added the oak tree with its tire swing out the back that I used to swing in. A sunset view between the mountains of Glendalough where we'd vacation when both my parents had been alive.

Sunflowers because they were my ma's favourite, nestled around a bowl of black pudding that she'd always make Sunday mornings. I added two angels, my ma and my da, with outstretched hands as they rose up to the sky, robes billowing.

Once all the pieces of my childhood covered his back, I had no choice but to move to the back of his thighs.

I gave him the art piece that landed me a full ride scholarship to the Limerick Art School. I added the real paw prints of my childhood dog, Marley, a mirror of the ones I had on my inner ankle.

Each piece of me, he bore without protest, asking gentle questions, coaxing their stories from me.

And I shared them with him. Every piece I handed him felt

like a piece I couldn't get back, but…I didn't want them back anymore.

I didn't want to carry them alone.

I only realised partway through my latest addition to the back of his right thigh that I was tattooing a shadowy face, shattered like glass. Unrecognisable save one uncracked eye. That one eye was drawn with such real-life detail that I expected it to blink. To search my face out in the mirror. To lock onto my gaze and never let go.

I hadn't meant to give him this part of me.

But once I'd started I had to finish it.

"Who is he?" Lee asked as he stared into the eye of my nightmare in the mirror when I'd finished, his voice low but firm.

"It's just an art piece."

I tried to keep my voice casual, but even I could hear the pinch of fear in my voice. I tried to busy myself with cleanup so I wouldn't have to look at him.

He saw through me anyway.

Lee grabbed my trembling hands. His fingers brushed over my knuckles. He reached out and tilted my chin up so I was forced to look at him.

"It's okay if you don't want to tell me about him…yet."

I sucked in a breath, needing to look away, but I just couldn't. Everything about him drew me in like a vortex I couldn't escape.

"I know whoever he is, he hurt you. Really hurt you."

I blinked as the backs of my eyes stung, as my pain threatened to tumble out into his hands. I clamped my jaw tight against the ache, as hot fat tears rolled down my cheeks.

Lee leaned in and kissed away each tear.

Between each kiss, he whispered, "When I find the man who hurt you, he is fucking *dead*."

His words should have terrified me. Instead I leaned in and for a moment I let him rest his forehead against mine.

I sucked in a breath and straightened, pulling away from him. I walked to the register, my back to him, wiping my eyes as discreetly as possible.

"So," I said, clearing my throat, "are you sure you won't let me give you a discount?"

As always, he stood too close to me as he shrugged on his jacket. "How about you let me buy you a drink?"

I smiled sadly at him as was our routine.

It never deterred him. He merely smiled and held out the cash. As our fingers brushed and electricity shot up my arm, he said, "Maybe next time, then?"

As I watched him walk away I'd always kick myself.

One day that man will get tired of waiting for you.

~

"It's time we move on," I said.

Lee was shrugging out of his coat when he stopped halfway, his eyes flying to mine. If I'd had my hand against his chest, I was certain that I would have felt his chest seize up and his skin go cold and clammy.

"To your front," I said, repressing a laugh, his panic adorable.

I wondered if one day I wouldn't hold myself back. I wondered if one day I'd just laugh as long as I wanted. Till Lee came over and put his finger to my lips with a wicked grin. Till he threatened to give me something to laugh about, his fingertips at my ticklish sides.

This was the problem with Lee: he made everything seem possible.

"Your back is fully tatted. We need to move on…to your front," I clarified, tapping the leather chair. "For your next tattoo, I mean."

"Jaysus, woman," Lee muttered, swiping off his shirt and tossing it across the back of a chair. "For a second I thought you meant…us."

I bit my lip.

"What if that was what I meant? That I wanted this…" I waved a finger between us, to whatever the hell *this* was, "to be over."

"I'd convince you otherwise," he said simply.

"Really?" I lifted an eyebrow at him as he strode to the table.

He grinned. "I'm very convincing."

I hid my snort.

He lowered his body to the table and stretched out like a cat before placing his hands under his head. With that cocky country boy smirk, and in that gravelly musical lilt, said, "I'm all *yours…*"

My brain short-circuited at the sight of him laid out on the table, adjusted today like a deck chair rather than a table. His firm pecs, wide torso and the ridges of his six-pack, and that mouthwatering V sliding sinfully into his jeans. His hands tucked like that made his biceps bulge around his handsome face.

And those damned green eyes, utterly unapologetic in the way they followed me around the room as I prepped for his tattoo.

I found myself fumbling with ink bottles and tripping over my own feet thanks to the heaviness of his stare.

But when I leaned over him, our faces inches away, our breaths fanning each other's faces, his smirk slid off his face.

I don't think either of us was ready for the intimacy of facing each other during the tattooing.

At least, *I* was not prepared for this.

I'd tattooed hundreds of guys' chests, glorious, muscled chests or good-looking men, and it was never like *this*.

As I placed my left hand down on his firm pec to steady my right hand, heat coursed through my body. Goosebumps broke out over him. God help me I couldn't help but brush my thumb across his smooth skin. Electricity sparked between us.

His eyes were like magnets, drawing my gaze to them. Under the lamplight, the green of Lee's eyes was so vivid it was distracting.

Jaysus, Ryleigh Elizabeth Carroll, focus.

I bent over Lee's chest even farther, trying to hide my eyes from him. But this brought my breast into contact with his arm. The friction against my nipple caused them to harden painfully.

I bit back a moan.

I cursed myself for attempting such an ambitious tattoo: an anonymous couple in a heart-wrenching embrace down the left side of his chest and along his ribs.

It was large and difficult. It required a lot from me.

Worst of all, it would need time.

The small of my back was already damp with sweat and I'd only just sketched in the rough outline of the love-stricken pair.

I shifted on my stool, trying to quell the ache, pressing my thighs together. He shifted just as much on the table. Our breaths grew heavier, sweat breaking out on both of us, his fingers at some point shifting from behind his head to gripping the leather at his sides as if to stop from grabbing at me.

Soon it wasn't his gaze I had to fight to avoid but the thick hard outline of his cock against his thigh, straining against the heavy material of his jeans. I swallowed as my mouth watered. As I imagined the pressure of it, the pain, even, of it splitting me apart. The way his muscles would move as he thrust into me.

I shoved back from him so abruptly, it drew a look of concern from him.

"Do you, er, do you need a break?" I said, just sitting there. I was soaked through my panties. That if I stood from this chair, I'd leave a wet mark of my desire.

"You noticed I was hard, huh?" he said, sounding unfazed.

"It's fine. It's just the human body," I said, my throat parched. I switched off the gun and practically threw it onto my rolling workstation. "It's just…a usual reaction."

Was I trying to reassure Lee? Or was I trying to convince myself?

"It doesn't mean anything," I added in a weak voice. "It's, you know, not personal."

Lee's gaze on me was steady. I hated how unembarrassed he seemed because I was dying of shame at my reaction and he couldn't even *see* how wet I was.

"Ry…believe me when I say, my reaction to you is *not* usual. And it is entirely *personal*."

"Oh."

My eyes flickered toward his crotch under his unflinching gaze, my cheeks heated even further.

Oh.

"Do *you* need a break?" he asked me, sitting up and nudging his chin at my nipples pointing out of my shirt.

I scowled and shifted my arms in front of me. "I'm fine."

"Really?"

He sat up and grabbed the section of stool between my thighs and tugged me to him, moving so quickly all I could do was yelp. Our faces were inches apart.

He smirked. "Are you sure? Cause I can *smell* the way I affect you."

I gulped, cheeks burning. I pushed at his hand still holding onto the stool, preventing me from closing my legs fully.

He caught both my wrists in his other giant one and stilled me.

"Don't ever hide yourself from me. I fucking love the way you smell."

My breath hitched.

Fuck me. I was going to come on this fucking stool, with his hand half an inch from my soaking pussy.

A languid smile graced his pouty lips. "Maybe you do need a break."

Before I could reply, his thumb brushed the front of my panties and a wave of pleasure exploded through me.

A moan tore from the depths of my lungs before I could stop it.

He pushed aside my panties and his fingers slid through my wetness.

"Soaked," he hissed. "That's *my* girl."

"Wait..." I mumbled even as I jerked my hips forward begging for more, not even sure anymore why I wasn't supposed to let him do this.

He paused his fingers and I let out a whimper.

For one long moment I just sat there with his fingers at my entrance, our breaths heaving around our cheeks and his gaze boring into me.

"W-why'd you stop?" I cried out, unable to stand it anymore. I needed him to move, to say something, to *do* something.

"You said 'wait'."

And I realised he was obeying me. Even though he was strong enough to do whatever he wanted to me, to take me, dominate me, one word and he would stop.

That last precious kernel of trust fell into place.

I bucked my hips forward impaling myself onto his fingers, causing a wave of pleasure so hard it knocked my head back and my eyes rolled into my head. I let out a long groan.

His hand, still wrapped around my wrists, trembled.

"Eyes on me."

I obeyed, the spring green of his eyes taking up my whole vision.

I rocked again, loving the way his thick fingers stretched me, the way he curled them into the depths of me, hitting that sensitive back wall. I was so turned on and he felt so damn good that I knew I wasn't going to last.

"You look so damn beautiful fucking yourself onto my fingers."

I moaned and bucked and he remained still, his pupils blown wide, as he watched me fall off the edge.

The orgasm hit me like a battering ram, electricity crackling across every inch of my skin in waves. I swallowed a scream, my head falling against his neck as my body trembled, the last of the waves fading out of me.

Only then did he let go of my wrists and brush the hair away from my damp forehead. He pulled his fingers from me and rearranged my panties before pulling them away.

I felt the loss of them instantly.

"Perfect," he whispered before putting both of his fingers into his mouth and sucking off my juices.

Oh my God, what the fuck was he doing?

Shame coated my cheeks.

But his eyelashes fluttered with pleasure and he let out a low appreciative rumble. "One taste isn't going to be enough."

He yanked my stool forward and I let out a yelp.

His lips were at my ear when he growled, "You're never getting rid of me now."

I shivered, the ache already building up in my core. How could I want him again so soon after coming?

This...never happened.

He pulled back, shifting to readjust his thick bulge. "I finished you...now finish me."

Right. This is when he expected me to suck him off or jerk him—

He grabbed the tattoo gun from my tray station and placed it into my hands before settling back into the chair.

For a second my mind short-circuited. "You mean, finish your...tattoo?"

The side of his lips twitched up. "Yeah. What did you think I meant?"

No, no man ever *gave* me pleasure without demanding the same in return.

Surely, he was just pretending to be a generous lover.

But he just lay there, his erection just as hard and present.

"But..." I waved at his bulge with my gun. "But you're...."

"Hard?" he offered.

"Yes," I blurted. "Don't you want to..."

"Come?" he said, his voice tinged with amusement.

My cheeks burned. "Yeah."

He must be dying to come.

To my utter surprise he shook his head. "Not until you trust me."

It wasn't my intention to tattoo the couple naked. I'd worked on a sketch earlier that day and the man and woman had been swathed in clothes, a plaid skirt for her, a red flannel shirt for him.

Had I lost myself so completely in my work that I'd accidentally tattooed them naked? Was my desire that overwhelming?

The idea frightened me even as it thrilled me.

The only fucking problem?

Lee could see it, too. Clear as day. It was, after all, right there on his chest.

I cleared my throat, suddenly embarrassed as Lee studied his latest tattoo in the mirror.

"Something else from your past?" he asked, tracing his finger along the chains that bound the naked couple together.

When I didn't answer, words stuck in my constricted throat, he looked up at me. My cheeks were already warm, but they burned when his eyes darkened.

"Something from *our* future, perhaps?"

"It's just art," I said, doing my best to keep the unsteady waver from my voice.

"Art imitates life."

"Isn't it the other way around?" I asked.

"Fuck, I hope so."

The enigma of him shocked me. His quiet air betrayed his boldness. He wasn't just please and thank yous, he had a dirty mouth.

There was kindness mixed with a roughness; he would offer to walk me home and in the next breath promise to kill for me.

The confusing combination sent a wave of heat through my body.

I licked my lips, finding them dry.

His attention was still on the tattoo.

I took this opportunity to drink him in with my eyes, to memorise how his serious brows looked alongside the crinkle of humour in the corners of his eyes, how his soft, pouty lips looked against his wide, sharp jaw, how such a ferocious, brutal-looking body, now covered in tattoos, protected a kind, thoughtful heart.

I'd tuck all these things away for later for my time alone with my charcoal pencils.

For my time alone with my fingers.

"They're in chains," I said. "Why would anyone want that for their future?"

Lee's grin was sly, his eyes flashing as he focused on me. "I suppose it depends on who you're chained to."

An image of myself chained to Lee—chained down by him, for him—rushed through my head.

All the things I wanted him to do to me. Things I hadn't allowed myself to desire in so long. I had to squeeze my thighs together to stop from moaning out loud.

I could never tell him that I'd tattooed my fucking fantasy onto his chest. That I'd cursed him to see what I saw in the mirror every lonely night: need unfulfilled.

The hair at the nape of my neck stuck, sticky with sweat. I pulled it up, rolling it into a messy bun to get relief. But it didn't help.

Not even the metal of the cash register had any coolness

left in it. I pressed my inner wrist against its sides like it was a tap of cold water, but it was as warm as freshly brewed tea. There was no escape.

Lee joined me and once again he stood too close.

He hadn't put on his shirt though.

I vaguely made it out still draped over the back of the couch; it seemed to waver like a mirage at the edge of my periphery. He normally put it on at this point, not standing there like an adonis half-naked still.

Was it the heat that made him forget it? Or did he know that there was no point in him putting it back on?

"Let me offer you a discount," I said, trying to cling onto the safety of our little routine.

"No," he said, his voice so blunt it stunned me. "We are *done* with this dance."

His hard torso seared into me as he pulled me against him. His lips crashed into mine.

I had no fight left. He'd taken me by siege and he had won.

The need for him was all-consuming, the orgasm that had temporarily sated me earlier, feeling so distant. I could barely string two coherent thoughts together as to why this was a bad fucking idea, why I shouldn't be getting involved with a man I was just going to leave.

I gave in. My fingers grabbing at his hair, his fingers digging into my back. My body burned as he pulled me tighter, as he explored my tongue with his, as we groaned into each other's mouths.

I moaned as Lee's kisses trailed down to my neck. I bucked against him, an ache in my chest, need between my legs.

He lifted up my thighs like I weighed nothing and sat me

onto the counter, holding my core flush to his very hard and very big erection.

We poured our twin groans into each other's mouths. I was seconds away from begging him to fuck me when a creak of floorboards made us both freeze.

Shite. Was someone creeping around inside the studio?

Lee had one hand inside my shirt, one hand at the small of my back, holding me close. My arms were wrapped around the back of his neck, fingernails digging into his scalp.

Neither of us moved and we were an almost perfect reflection of the tattoo raw and red on Lee's naked chest.

We waited. Breathing heavily against one another.

I heard the sound again.

A loud, long moan.

It wasn't an intruder.

Lee and I locked eyes and laughed at the same time. Covered our mouths to hide our laughter at the same time.

We parted only to avoid the plaster that snowed down from the ceiling above us as the bed upstairs thumped on the floorboards chorused with high-pitched moans.

"This might go on for a while," I whispered, a giggle on my lips which were still wet from his tongue.

"What time is it?" he asked.

I searched for my phone to check, but Lee interrupted my search. Hand in mine.

"Never mind what time it is," he said as Rachel started screaming. "Your shift is over."

"I'm not sure—"

"Your shift is over." He snatched his shirt and jacket off the couch. "And I'm taking you for a pint."

RY

"I thought 'pints' was code for 'back to my gaff'," I said with a grumble.

Lee smiled and held the door to The Jar open for me like a fucking gentleman, letting the merry strains of a live trad band out into the cold night. Asshole.

"Why, Ryleigh," he said, a teasing note to his voice, "are you objectifying me?"

I let out a *humpft* and stormed through the ancient wooden doorway, made harder because his giant build took up most of the doorframe, and I couldn't so much as stomp past as slide past.

The bastard grabbed me around the waist and kissed me long and hard.

I groaned and clutched at his shirt, fumbling for his buttons, need burning inside me so I was a single roaring thought: to get him naked and to ride him senseless.

He made me lose my feckin' mind. I forgot we were out in public, literally standing in a doorway, letting in the cold, until clapping, whistling and calls of "look at him eatin' the face off her," broke through my senses.

A group of pimply college-aged guys stood waiting to get into the warmth, all grinning ear to ear.

"Jaysus," one of them said, "I should come to dis bar more often."

I hid my face in Lee's warm jacket as he took a feckin' bow.

I tried to detach from him as he led me through the wood-panelled bar to a booth near the back.

But he held me close to his side.

His possessiveness should annoy me, but my inner feminist obviously lost her mind, too, cheering away like all the other parts of me for *Team Lee.*

There wasn't a single soul in this damn bar that didn't know I was with him.

As the other women in this bar shot him appreciative glances and me jealous ones, I found myself leaning against him, a smugness settling over me.

He was *mine.*

Jaysus, Ry, where the hell did that come from?

Okay, then, he was mine for as long as I stayed in this cursed town.

A hard knot sat like a weight in my stomach.

He ushered me into a booth and bought us two drinks: him a pint of Beamish, me, a "jammie and ginger".

He returned quickly and slid into the booth, trapping me into the wood-panelled wall, sitting way too close to me.

God, he smelled good. Like wood and spice and the hint of engine grease.

I scowled as I gulped down my drink, hoping the cold

Jameson whiskey mixed with sweet and spicy ginger ale would cool me off.

He was trying to torture me. Kiss me like that back at the studio then take me to a bar, then sit way too fucking close to me?

Two could play that game.

Under the table I rubbed my hand over his cock in his jeans.

He hardened instantly in my hand.

It was thick and hard and lord help me, it might hurt a little when he thrust into me but Jaysus, Mary and Joseph did I want that so badly.

Fuck going back to my gaff, there was a public toilet here somewhere. I'd never been a public toilet kinda gal. But then again, I'd never met someone so…sexy and frustrating as Lee.

"Ryleigh!" he hissed, grabbing my wrist to prevent me from stroking him any further. "What are you doing?"

I glared at him. "What are *you* doing?"

He groaned as I reached down with my other hand and rubbed the head of his cock. Fuck, he was growing even thicker.

"I'm trying to have our first date." He scrambled to grab my other hand.

"*What?*"

"Pints. Drinks. Our first *date*," he said between grunts.

I froze.

Our first date?

Here I was groping him like a hormonal teenager boy.

I snatched my hands off him and fisted them into my lap. I pressed my thighs together.

"Fine," I grumbled.

"Don't sound so disappointed." He chuckled and clinked his glass against mine. "*Sliante*."

I downed the rest of it, ice clinking in the glass. Then I stood, needing to get some room from him, needing to get some space, some air.

"I'm going to the bathroom," I muttered.

I didn't wait for him to get out of the booth, I went to slide past him instead.

Of course, that was a daft idea.

There was barely any room and I ended up practically sitting in his lap.

He grabbed my hips, not letting me get any farther, his chest against my back, our thighs pressed together like we were one animal.

I felt every single inch of his cock against my ass. Every. Single. Thick. Hard. Inch.

He let out a low groan. "You hussy."

Still pissed at him, I tried to push his hands off me and get the fuck out the booth. But all I managed to do was wriggle around on his lap.

He wrapped one arm securely around my hips. The other arm went around my chest, settling between my breasts and his hand wrapped around the front of my throat, firmly but not painfully.

Instantly, I stilled. Then melted against him, my body responding instinctively.

He let out a curse, then his lips brushed my ear.

"Date's over."

~

The door banged open and Lee and I tumbled into his apartment with a crash.

His neighbours would hear everything, but he didn't seem to care. He shoved the door closed with his foot.

I scanned the dark apartment. "Where's the bedr—"

His lips crashed with mine. He shoved me against the wall, holding tightly to the globes of my ass as he kissed me, stealing my breath. There would be bruises in the shape of his fingerprints left on my skin and, dear God, I wanted to be marked.

My pleated skirt parted easily as I wrapped my legs around his body, aching to get closer to him.

His kisses felt hot against my skin as his lips travelled down my neck, making me moan for more. The scruff on his face added a slight hint of pain to the pleasure of his kisses, making me shudder.

This wouldn't go past one wild night… It couldn't. But I planned to enjoy every moment of it.

"Do you know what you do to me?" he growled into my ear.

I shook my head.

He shoved my coat off my shoulders. It pooled onto the floor and he kicked it away, kissing down my neck as I moaned.

He had been so careful and controlled back in the tattoo studio when he'd made me fall apart on his fingers. I could hardly believe that this was the same man, a wildness taking over his eyes, a reckless hunger in the way he moved.

He grabbed me by the back of the neck, forcing me to look at him, as if he *needed* me to understand how serious his next words were.

"You make me fucking crazy."

The growl of his voice, the intensity of his stare, the feel of his hard body against mine, all of it, made my head spin, made every single cell of my body *ache*.

The fucking tension built up over the last few months of us pretending to just be artist and client, all that time with him stretched out and half naked, all that time with his warm body under my hands, under my control, it left my core twisted and needy to the point of insanity.

"Off," I hissed, pushing at his jacket, the soft wool tickling the palms of my hands before he flung it aside.

He grinned and it was beautiful and devilish.

The next few moments were a fury of movement. My shirt was torn off my head, my bra undone and flung aside, my black hose torn in two, stretched out in tatters, before it fell away from me like a shed skin.

Finally he snapped my thong off me, muttering, "I'll buy you fifty more."

The cold air hit my soaking pussy and I shivered.

He unzipped his cock and pulled it from his jeans. I reached for him. I just needed to fuck it out. Then I could move on from the butterflies he gave me whenever he looked at me with his hooded eyes.

But he stopped me.

My eyes widened in surprise when he growled and wrapped his hand around my throat like the perfect necklace, making me gasp.

It felt like such a natural reaction. Something inside me just *responded* to the utter dominance in which he held me.

For the first time in a long time, I felt secure. Safe.

I felt *protected*.

"I am going to take my time with you," he said, his voice low and firm. "I'm going to fuck the sass from this pretty little mouth. I'm going to devour your pussy until you're all that I taste. I am going to kiss every single one of your tattoos until you are *begging* me to fuck you."

I shivered with impatience. It didn't matter that this was a terrible idea, that letting myself be claimed by him would make it all the harder to leave when the time came.

But *all* I wanted was to feel him inside of me.

"Then what are you waiting for," I countered right back.

He squeezed my throat and I let out a whimper, stilling.

"Not right now," he said. "Right now, I just need to fuck you."

No more teasing. No more waiting.

He found my soaking entrance with his cock and thrust inside, filling me, making my head knock back against the wall as pleasure racked my body.

He let out a curse. "Fuck, you're so wet and tight. I'm going to fuck you so hard you'll be feeling me for days."

He squeezed my throat firmly, the lack of air made my lips part soundlessly as he devoured me.

His hips thrusted and pivoted until the base of his cock ground against my clit. My eyes rolled in pleasure at how his cock was perfectly hitting my g-spot. All I could do was writhe against the wall.

The sounds of how wet I was filled the room, but I couldn't bring myself to feel embarrassed with how intently he stared at me.

Sparks flew before my eyes as I hurtled toward my release.

"Your pussy feels like heaven," he growled. "It was made for me. *Mine*. No one else's. Ever."

This was supposed to be a fling. I was going to flee Ireland again soon and I'd likely never see him again.

But my heart rang with his words as Lee fucked me against the wall.

Stupid heart.

My fingers dug into his tattooed back. He barely winced even though I must be hurting his unhealed tattoos.

But he didn't stop me.

No, in fact he fucked me faster.

"So fucking pretty bouncing on my cock."

My pussy clenched around him, made him curse as he fucked me.

I was so close. I wanted to come more than I needed my next breath.

His hand closed even tighter around my neck. "I want my dick drenched in your cum, pretty girl. Give me what's *mine*."

Shattering, I screamed as I came, hard, my vision going white, my body shuddering against the wall as he fucked me through my orgasm.

My pussy fluttered around him as he slowed, his grip on my neck softening, his thumb brushing tenderly against my pulse point.

Nothing else existed except his touch and those damned green eyes.

As he—finally—carried me into the bedroom, he grinned like the devil.

"I'm not done with you."

RY

Lee threw me onto the bed like a rag doll. His strength should be frightening, but I found myself squirming, need growing in me again as I stared up at him, towering over me as he stood at the bed's edge.

My heels dug into the mattress, pooled the sheets at the base as he unbuttoned his shirt and let it fall to the old wooden floorboards of his bedroom.

God, he was glorious. His wide shoulders covered in ink, his back tattoos curling around his thick lats and the naked couple so fresh and raw under its plastic wrap, over his firm chest.

Then his jeans were down and kicked off his ankles, his cock springing back as he straightened.

He was thick and long and perfect.

My pussy ached, remembering how good it felt to have his cock inside me.

I let out a whimper. I needed more.

"Fuck, you're beautiful," he whispered.

I watched his eyes trail up and down by body. His gaze

twisted round me so possessively that I swore I could feel it, like a snake itself around me, squeezing tighter and tighter.

He grabbed my ankles and tugged me toward him.

Our eyes met as he lowered his face into my pussy, his hands running along my inner thighs.

I let out a moan. “Please…”

He brushed the tip of his nose against my clit and let out a groan. “Fuck, you smell better than I remember.”

Something about what he said seemed…off.

But he licked me long and flat with his tongue and my mind short-circuited as glorious tingles spread through my body.

“Yes. Please,” I begged hoarsely.

I bucked my hips against him as he pressed me down with his weight.

He held me down as he punished me with his tongue. Over and over, until I was writhing uncontrollably and speaking in tongues.

Then he was on top of me, his weight pressing my legs open. He thrust into me with a brutality that made me scream. With one hand firmly around my neck, Lee lowered his lips to mine to swallow my cries.

Any breath I tried to take was his. Any gasp I tried to steal, he stole back. All I could do was cling to him as he fucked me like he hated me.

“Fuck,” he muttered. “You make me crazy.”

He rolled us so that I was now on top of him and in control.

I grabbed his chest, like a cat testing her claws, using him for leverage as I rocked my hips.

He hissed in pain.

I was pressing my fingers into his fresh tattoo. I gasped and snatched my hand away.

He caught my hand and pressed it back onto his chest.

"I need it, too," he said through gritted teeth.

Our eyes met.

He didn't need to spell it out for me. I knew. Just as he had.

He wanted pain, craved pain.

Just like me.

Something in him didn't believe he deserved pleasure without it.

As I ground on him, I dug my fingers into him.

He cried out, but I felt his cock twitch inside of me. Fingers digging in my hips, he held me down onto his cock, kept himself buried all the way.

"Fucking perfect," he whispered, hand twisting in the hair at the nape of my neck.

He wrenched my hair back and the flare of pain across my scalp turned into heat, into soaked need. He wrapped his free hand around my exposed throat.

My groans joined his. Every time I pressed against his tattoo, he twisted my hair further, closed his hand around my neck even more.

We hurt each other as we fucked harder, the moans of pain and pleasure were indecipherable from one another.

We locked eyes as I struggled to breathe.

This was my favourite part. This was the reason it was such a turn-on. This connection. This intense trust.

I was on the verge of passing out. Of going under. I was in his hands. I delivered myself to him fully and he did what I asked without ever having to: he tightened his grip even further.

My head spun, spots darting in front of my vision as I gave in.

I came, harder than I'd ever before.

Mouth open, I screamed silently as waves of white hot pleasure crashed over me again and again.

I sagged like a doll as Lee pulled out, flipped me over and came on my stomach.

I felt the loss of him instantly.

He fell to my side and curled me up against him, his big arms enfolding me as I drifted back down to earth. His hands traced soothing circles at the small of my sweat-slick back.

I inhaled what felt like my first ever breath, a rare storm of emotion threatening to overcome me. I worried I might cry as I exhaled so I held it in till I was steadier.

I clung to him. Hands everywhere. Looking for purchase.

His fingers intertwined with mine.

I squeezed back and felt a strange twinge in my chest.

"Easy," he whispered, pressing a kiss to the top of my head. "I've got you, babe."

The world stopped spinning beneath me. I wasn't steady yet, but Lee was. He was steady for both of us.

"I've got you. And I'm *never* letting you go."

If only I could believe him.

RY

If I didn't leave soon, I'd be sending the wrong message.

Lee held me like I'd been shaped just for him. Melting into him was as easy as melting candle wax. I liked the sweet nothings he whispered to me before fading gently into silence; and I liked the soft flutter of his carefree breathing even more after that.

But I couldn't fool myself. I couldn't tease myself.

If I let myself fall asleep, even for just a little while, I'd be telling myself—telling him—that this could be something. If I relaxed into the warmth of his arms around me, I'd be allowing myself to hope that there could be some kind of future in Dublin. If I didn't retreat from the steady beating of his heart, I might foolishly match mine to his.

Then I'd have to shatter my own heart when I inevitably had to run from this godforsaken city. Could it ever learn to beat on its own ever again? Would it even want to?

It was torture, pulling myself away.

"What are you doing?" Lee mumbled as I slipped my fingers from his.

He was already reaching back for me.

"I can't stay," I whispered, suddenly conscious of neighbours through the walls even though that had been the absolute last thing on my mind just a few minutes ago.

Lee surprised me by laughing. He didn't bother opening his eyes as he patted around for my hand and guided it back on top of his chest, steadily rising and falling.

"What's so funny?" I asked, still keeping my voice low.

Sneaking out of a guy's apartment usually didn't involve so much discussion.

Lee peeked an eye open, the haze of sleepiness over his features.

Had he really let himself get tugged under? Had he really not been faking it, secretly urging me to leave? Wasn't that how one-night stands went?

"Oh, you're serious?" he said, propping himself up on an elbow.

He rubbed his eyes like a little kid. His hair was ruffled from sex, but it made him look so young in the dim light. Like the weight he seemed to carry had somehow fallen from his shoulders.

I hesitated. "Well, yeah… I mean, I can't *sleep* here."

Lee nodded, pausing only to give a big yawn. "Yeah. Yeah, okay."

He flopped back down onto the mattress.

I should have sighed in relief that he wasn't going to argue. Instead the backs of my eyes stung and I was grateful that the darkness hide my rejection.

This was how it was supposed to be, I told myself. This was how I was supposed to protect myself.

I couldn't help but wonder why I wasn't soothed at all.

I rummaged around for my clothes (not my torn hose,

those were clearly beyond repair). I noticed Lee doing the same, his big arm fishing over the side of the mattress, pawing around like a St Bernard.

"I can get my clothes all by myself," I whispered, watching as he struggled against sleep.

"I'm sure you can." He rolled over to grin at me, eyes just slits. "And I can get mine all by myself."

I stopped, halfway into my top, arms craned overhead. Hair in my eyes. Miniskirt askew.

I tugged my top down. "Why do you need your clothes?"

"I'm not letting you walk home." He tugged on his jeans. "I'll drive."

He disappeared from the bedroom in his low-slung jeans and no shirt.

"I don't need you to drive me," I called after him.

There was no answer from outside the darkened bedroom.

"Lee?" I shouted. "What are you doing?"

Only silence greeted me.

With a grumble, I finished getting dressed.

I found Lee by the door, key swinging on his finger. He opened the door and held it open for me but taking up most of the doorway yet again.

I crossed my arms over my chest. "You don't have to drive me."

This was a fling, right? A one-night stand. Tomorrow didn't exist for the two of us. He simply *couldn't* drive me home. It would ruin everything.

"I want to."

"Lee," I let out a noise of exasperation, "I don't need you to, okay?"

Our stares warred, in silence. Who would give in first?

"Well then," I finally blurted out.

I pushed past him, my body brushing against his bare torso, sending a shiver of need through me. I almost stopped, almost turned into him and pressed into him.

God, how I wanted to beg that he take me back inside. I stumbled out into the cold, trying to outrun these thoughts.

I heard the door close behind me. Heard the lock turn. The sound stole the air from my lungs faster than the icy air. For a second I thought he'd just locked the door behind me.

But then I heard his footsteps behind me. I glanced over my shoulder to find Lee following me, his shearling-lined jacket open over a bare chest and raw tattoo.

The laces of his untied boots flicked against the frozen concrete. Lines from the sheets still etched across his cheek like a map I wasn't supposed to still have in my possession.

"What are you doing?" I whispered, hurrying my step.

Lee stuffed his hands casually into his pockets. The night backdropped him like he was on a photoshoot for some Nordic perfume. Lumberjack Noir. Goddamn him.

"I'm driving you home," he said. "Car's this way."

I halted on the icy curb.

"Lee," I hissed. "This isn't how it's supposed to go."

"No, it isn't." He thumbed over his shoulder. "The car is *this* way."

"I am *not* going to your car."

"You are," Lee said, grinning lazily. "On those pretty legs of yours *or* over my shoulder. You choose."

I clenched my jaw.

Lee clicked his keys. Red lights blinked on a car half a block away.

"I don't need you to—"

He stepped swiftly up to me as if to hoist me over his shoulder.

"Alright! Alright," I snapped, holding out my hands.

He chuckled and held out his arm as if to say *after you.*

I scowled as I stomped toward his damn car, trying so hard to ignore the heat between my thighs at his brutish stubbornness.

Damn him. I *wanted* him to drive me home, I *liked* that he wouldn't take no for an answer, I *craved* him putting me in my place when I was being a pain in the ass.

Our hands touched again as we both went for the passenger door. Heat shot up my arm and I snatched my fingers back.

"*I* get your doors," Lee said firmly.

He was supposed to be a brute—I liked brutes, but he wasn't *also* supposed to be this fucking sweet.

He held the door open for me. I avoided his gaze as I was forced—yet again—to brush up close to him to get in. I muttered a thanks as I dropped into the seat. But he did not get out of the way so I could close the door.

He leaned his bulk in and his nearness made me gasp. He smirked at me, his lips close to mine as he drew the belt across my chest, deliberately brushing my nipples with his arm, and taking a moment to inhale against my neck before he clicked the belt in.

I squeezed my inner thighs together. Driving me home was not supposed to be this fucking sexy.

He closed the door, muffling the late-night city noise outside so that the rushing blood in my ears sounded like drums. Only then could I breathe properly again.

He climbed into the driver's seat and my body tightened up again, the aching need growing between my legs.

As he pulled away from the curb I found myself wanting to reach out and place my hand on his thigh or on the back of his seat. All things that I should *not* want with a one-night stand.

I scooted over as far away from him as I could and pressed my hot cheek up against the cold window of the passenger door.

As he drove the nearly silent streets of Dublin, I tried not to look at him. But I found my gaze drawing to him. I found myself becoming mesmerised by the steadiness of his hands on the wheel, the flicker of his eye to the rearview mirror, the ease with which he shifted.

He could be driving me anywhere. Into a windowless basement. Over the edge of a cliff. And I wouldn't even know it.

Finally, the car came to a crunching stop outside my—Rian's—apartment. For a long moment the silence in the car rang in my ears and his steady gaze sent sparks rattling down my spine.

I clawed at the door, desperate to get out before I did something stupid like kiss him or invite him in.

But it would not unlock.

Panic clawed at my throat, as memories of being tricked slammed into my mind. Oh God. He'd trapped me inside.

He was a monster just like—

I let out a scream as Lee's fingers twisted into my hair and he tugged me back against him.

"I said, *I* get your doors," he growled, amusement fringing his tone.

What?

He nipped at my ear as his fingers loosened in my hair.

And then he was gone, out of the car and walking around to my side.

I was stunned into stillness as he opened the car door and leaned his frame in again.

"You're going to fight me all the way, aren't you?" he chuckled into my ear as his arm brushed across my body to unclick my seatbelt.

He straightened and held out a hand.

I moved automatically, grabbing his hand to let him help me out, as my brain tried to untangle how twisted up my insides felt.

I cleared my throat. "Well, then. Thanks again. Have a good one. Bye."

I walked fast, heels clicking on the sidewalk, face turned away from the wind as I fumbled in my purse for the apartment keys.

Footsteps behind me and his presence at my back caused me to drop my keys, heart beating too fast, fingers too slick with sweat despite the cold.

Lee retrieved them for me and brushed past me.

"What are you doing?" I asked, hurrying after him.

"*I* get your doors."

He unlocked my apartment door and stood in my doorway, his back holding the door open.

His face was in shadow, but his eyes were bright. The sleepiness gone. No little boy in sight.

Lee nudged me inside and locked it behind us.

I glared at him as he hung my key on the hook next to the spare. "What the hell are you—?"

"Bed," he commanded.

I frowned. "Are you tucking me in as well?"

He smirked at me. "Bed. Now."

I rolled my eyes. "You are *not* tucking me—"

He stepped in real close, so close I could feel the heat rolling off his bare skin in waves.

"Bed. On your own legs *or* over my shoulder."

Fuck. I scowled but I did what I was told. Having him pick me up was not going to be good for my current tenuous levels of self-control.

In my bedroom I felt the air heat up around us, making it hard to breathe again. Even as I had my back to him, I could feel his eyes on me as I stripped out of my clothes and tugged on a sleep shirt.

The sheets of my bed were blissfully cold as I slipped under them and curled to my side, my back to him. I heard Lee slide off his boots. Drop his coat on the dresser.

The edge of the mattress compressed beneath his weight and I gasped as his chest pressed against my back and his arm slid around my waist, his breath against the nape of my neck.

"Lee, what are you doing?"

His voice mumbled against the tangle of my hair. "Trying to sleep."

He held me tighter, kept me in place when I tried to turn around to face him.

He continued, "You said you couldn't sleep at my place so we came here."

I tried to protest, "Yeah, but—"

"Sleep," he said softly. "Rest. You're safe."

His words stabbed my heart. It was what I couldn't have.

It was *all* that I wanted.

LIAM

I moved quietly through Ry's apartment so as not to wake her.

In her kitchen, I turned around with an armful of eggs, tomatoes and a couple sleeves of black pudding to find the wall opposite me littered with pictures of Rian.

My brother's life illuminated in the cold white glare of the refrigerator.

I'd almost forgotten that this wasn't *her* apartment. That it was *his.* That she was just staying here temporarily.

I let the refrigerator door close. I dumped my armful on the counter and stood there with my back to the pictures.

Rian with friends.

Rian happy.

Rian successful.

Rian without *me* in his life.

I searched the cabinets and found a frying pan. I cracked the eggs into a bowl with a single hand. I knew my way around a good Irish breakfast, having lived all my life on the farm.

I pushed around the drawers for a whisk, my fingers grazing over the forks Rian touched, the chopsticks he waved around, laughing with friends over takeout, the saved champagne cork he might have been keeping for New Year's.

It was all guesses, of course. I created a life for my brother in my head. The truth was I had no idea if he was happy. If he was successful. Whether his friends were real.

I sliced the blood pudding thick, cut the tomatoes into juicy slices, lit the stove, heated the pan before laying down the blood pudding. It crackled and popped and I had nothing left to do but let it cook.

I couldn't avoid the pictures forever.

I slowly turned toward the wall and stepped over to it.

It was more painful than I thought, seeing the life he had without me. My chest tightened more and more with each one.

Pictures of the opening of Dublin Ink, Rian not looking at the camera, but standing proud.

Of him on a stage getting some sort of art award. More award ceremonies.

Pictures of parties where Rian sat brooding in a corner in a cloud of smoke.

A rare smile on his face as he wound his arms around the necks of Conor and Mason in the booth of a pub.

Here was my brother's life filled with friends.

No, not friends. *Family*.

My stomach twisted. I wanted what he had. Was that why I coveted Ryleigh so much? Because I wanted to *be* my brother?

I shook my head. My interest in Ryleigh might have started because of Rian, but whatever was growing between her and me was real. It was bigger than us. Bigger than this.

And…if his life was so perfect, how the fuck did he end up in a rehab centre?

My gaze settled on a Polaroid selfie of Ry and Rian, cheeks mashed together as they made faces at the camera. I leaned in closer for a better look.

She had fewer tattoos then, but that wasn't the most noticeable difference. It was something in the eyes. A brightness. I saw flashes of it sometimes, especially when Ry was tattooing. There was a joy in her that had been nearly extinguished.

Now I mostly saw a darkness, the suspicious guardedness of a wounded animal.

I found my hands curling into fists.

So many times I wanted to grab her and yell, "Who did this to you?"

But I didn't. I couldn't push.

She would tell me when she was ready. I just had to be patient. To give her time to trust me. To open up. I just had to keep refusing to let her push me away.

I checked on the blood pudding before walking into the living room, a soft dawn glow coming in through the window.

I kept an ear open for signs of Ryleigh waking as I carded through Rian's records, a collection of indie punk and indie folk, from Radiohead to Mick Flannery to Declan O'Rourke, all music that Alan would call, *"shite to cut your feckin' wrists to"*.

I took pictures of band names I'd never heard of to listen to later.

Then I scanned the titles on his bookshelf, mostly art and tattoo books and magazines.

I studied the art that he'd picked to decorate his walls.

A large colourful painting on canvas labelled "Dublin Rooftops", but I didn't see any rooftops in it. It was too wild, too organic in the way the curved shapes moved around the piece.

There were a series of line drawings of an orchid and... was that a pussy?

Some of them had creases in them as if they'd been crumpled and smoothed out.

How strange.

Did Rian do these? It didn't seem like his style.

Returning to the stove to flip the blood pudding was like coming up for air after too long under water. My lungs ached. A weariness settled in my bones as if I'd had to fight my way toward the surface.

It was strange, learning about your own brother through his things. But I was desperate.

Rian was still ignoring me when I visited his rehab centre every morning. I'd earned nothing but sad smiles from the receptionist and blasts of icy cold air to the face as I left.

But I'd do it again. And again.

Just like I returned to Ry again and again for a needle in my skin, I'd return to the rehab centre for a knife in the heart. As many as Rian wanted to stab me with his refusal to see me. I could handle the pain.

Rian might be stubborn. But I would be immovable. I'd prove I was serious with my persistence. Just like I'd proven it to Ry.

"I thought I smelled something tasty."

I turned to find her leaning against the wall outside the bedroom, one bare foot atop the other, fingers pushing back messy bedhead, her bottom lip held between her teeth.

Nothing on but my shearling-lined coat hanging open.

I smiled because she was the girl from the Polaroid. Playful. Eager. Eyes flashing with mischief. She wasn't hiding anything from me except a little bit of her hips and tits.

I never wanted Ry to have to go back to being the scared, haunted woman I met at Dublin Ink.

"No," I said.

Ry arched a jet-black eyebrow.

"No?" she asked, voice still a little thick from sleep, but seductive, nonetheless.

I shook my head. "You didn't smell anything, I'm afraid."

She narrowed her eyes. "I didn't?"

I crossed toward the stove and switched off the burner. Shame, I thought distractedly, the blood pudding was cooked to absolute perfection.

But I had something better to eat.

When I turned around, Ry had her palms flat on the island behind me. My coat opened just enough that I could make out the curve of her breasts. Naked as a newborn beneath it.

"You really should get that nose of yours checked out," I said, unable to tear my eyes away from her beautiful body, my cock pressed painfully against my jeans.

"Guess I'll book an appointment then."

I blocked her path, pushed her back against the counter, boxed her in with my arms.

"There's no one else for *you* out there," I whispered.

I pressed my hard cock against her lower stomach and she let out a low moan. I leaned over her to nip at her earlobe.

"There's no one for *me* out there," I said softly into her ear, relishing the scent of her lavender shampoo.

Ry's fingertips played at the waistband on my boxers, brushed along the coarse hair of above my groin, teasing me, moving so fucking close. Yet never close enough.

She stretched up onto tiptoes and blazed a trail along the pulse in my neck with her tongue.

"Where did they go?" she whispered.

"They never existed," I said, twisting her hair tightly in one hand, twisting it once more as she hissed and bit my jaw. "You've always been mine. Even before I found you."

I pulled Ry's hair till her throat was exposed to me. With my tongue I traced her tattoos. I pressed my lips to the faint bruising from my hands. I scraped my teeth along her throbbing vein.

"Now that I've found you," I whispered to her collarbone, "there will be *no one* else. Nothing between us."

"There's still this fucking coat," she said, lips curling wickedly as she arched her back.

I had Ry up on the counter before she could even gasp in surprise. My fingers tore at the coat. Like it wasn't the only one I owned and it wasn't the dead of winter. Like I had no need for it all as long as I had the woman beneath it.

I flung my coat somewhere behind me. It might as well have been over the edge of the cliff.

I had Ry now. Her warm, soft tits, her belly already fluttering, her fingernails scraping along my forearms as I pushed her back on the kitchen island.

Whatever was on the counter before us was now on the floor. If something shattered, we didn't hear it. If something spilled, we didn't care.

Parting her legs was easy. Ry's heels dug painfully into my shoulders as her head tilted back over the edge of the island. It was pure debauchery, us writhing on the cheap laminate.

I sucked at her clit. Lapped and licked.

When Ry bucked from the intensity of it, I flung an arm across her hips like a seatbelt to keep her in place.

I slipped a finger inside of her and her cries mounted, the calm of morning broken beyond repair.

Drawers and their contents rattled beneath us as Ry's fists grabbed at the counter beside her and rocked her pussy into my face.

"Oh God, I'm so close…"

"Say you're mine," I demanded between licks, needing to hear it. Needing her to admit it.

"Yours," she mumbled.

The laminate went slick beneath our sweating bodies. Saliva from my tongue mixed with the wet of her pussy and my chin became bathed in it. Her cries became piercing and I wanted to drown in the sound of her pleasure.

"Tell me you're mine *forever*," I demanded.

"Yours. Oh God. Forever. Please…"

It was not enough. She did not mean it, she was lost in the sex haze. She'd say anything at this point, anything to get me to let her come.

She would not.

Not yet.

Not until she was *mine*.

I pulled my face away from her pussy.

She let out a pained cry. "Lee, please—"

I dragged her toward me. Her ass on the edge of the counter, I thrust into her with a boorish grunt. Ry clutched at my back and moaned.

"You feel like home," I groaned as I watched my cock disappearing in and out of her tight pussy, enjoyed as her tits bounced with every thrust, nipples straining for friction.

"One day you'll realise my cock belongs buried in your tight cunt at all times. I'll keep reminding you of it until you believe it."

I fucked her hard and fast as I choked her with her hair.

Ry woke a beast inside of me. Stalking her. Breaking into her place. Choking her. Hurting her. She made me crazy.

And I fucking liked it. I'd worry later if I liked it perhaps a little too much.

For now I just wanted to leave my marks on her. I wanted her to stretch her tight little pussy so it ached and she was forced to think of me for the rest of the day.

I wanted to fuck the thoughts out of her so she'd stop thinking about ways to say goodbye.

Our connection was real.

Ry needed to believe in it the way I did.

I let go of her hair around her throat and she gasped in a breath.

"You'll breathe when I give you permission," I growled. "You'll come when I tell you, and you'll fucking love it."

I groaned at how tight her pussy clenched down around me when I closed my palm around her throat instead.

My balls tightened as I felt her pulse wildly jumping at her throat, her eyes streamed with tears as she got closer to coming.

"Come," I groaned. "Come all over my cock."

I released her throat as she screamed, her pussy constricting around me like a python.

If I stood any chance of lasting any longer, that went out the fucking window. My vision went white, my body spasming in blissful fits, and I came deep inside of her.

I'd been careful last night, pulling out of her. But now, I wanted to see her pussy filled with my cum.

I wanted to see her belly rounded with my child.

Then she'd never get away from me. She'd be tied to me forever.

If I had to explain it to anyone else, I'd sound like a sick fuck. But I knew that Ryleigh was mine. Mine to protect. To worship. To love.

And I was hers.

The only thing stopping Ryleigh from admitting it was herself. Her damn thoughts were way too loud in her mind. I could see the way she kept trying to push me away last night. Refusing to stay over, refusing to let me drive her home.

She could refuse me all she wanted.

I. Would. Not. Let. Her. Leave. Me.

Ever.

RY

I would *not* see Lee again. I would definitely *not* go on a second date.

I would not call him back or reply to the string of cute texts he'd sent me over the day.

He must have added his number to my phone while I was asleep because it read *Hubby* against his name.

Hubby: Glad you got to work safely, baby.

Hubby: Hope you have the best day.

Hubby: Miss you already.

Hubby: The guys at work think you're pretty. I took a pic of you while you were asleep ;)

Hubby: I'm listening to The Untouchables while I work and ur right, they're great!

Hubby: I can still taste u on my fingers.

Hubby: Fuck, I'm hard just thinking about eating u for breakfast again...

. . .

Lee was just a one-night stand. A fling. A perfectly brutish gentleman fling who made me do stupid things like let him take me on a date and let him stay over and consider *not* leaving Dublin.

I was already losing control over my damn heart. Already saying things like *yours* and *forever.*

Already liking the look of *Hubby* flashing across my phone when he rang. Again.

I should not see Lee again.

But then there he was. Smiling at me as the little bell rang above the door like we shared a secret. Like he'd come to make another secret between us. Like he wanted all the secrets I had to give him.

His eyes darkened as he looked me up and down from across the tattoo parlour. It made me shudder despite myself.

This was not a man who played games. He had no desire for the usual holding out: the delayed texting, the prolonged, aloof silence, the self-imposed restrictions on calling. He had none of the normal fear of appearing too eager, of not playing "cool".

There in the doorway he dripped with an easy confidence. Lee was a man who knew what he wanted and wasn't afraid of going after it.

What he wanted was *me.*

He hadn't said a word since stepping inside. The longer he silently devoured me with his eyes, that charming grin unwavering, the louder my heartbeat in my aching chest.

The sound of the heavy lock turning in the door made my inner thighs clench.

He turned to switch the sign from Open to Closed.

The intensity of it all frightened me. His boldness, his

swiftness. It was terrifying to have everything you'd wanted all at once.

With a voice I hoped didn't quiver, I said, "W-what do you want?"

"You," came his husky reply.

"I'm still on the clock. I only have time for customers right now."

"Then I'm a customer," he said, completely unaffected as he stalked slowly toward me.

I was struck again by how tall and imposing his figure was as he drew dangerously closer. Of course a man like that wouldn't need to play games. He was in a league of his own. Games were for lesser men.

Gods took what they wanted. Whenever they wanted.

"I have to work," I said weakly.

"You will be *working*," Lee said in a low tone. "I'm here for a private session."

Painfully arousing images of being "worked" around the tattoo parlour flooded my mind: my ass rolling hypnotically on his cock on top of the leather table, my lips swollen from sucking him off till he came in my mouth, supporting myself with shaking arms against the storage rack in the back as I tried to keep my ankles from coming unlocked behind his sweating back.

He chuckled, "A private *tattoo* session, Ry."

My cheeks warmed. Maybe Lee didn't mind a little game or two, after all.

I turned around and began to prepare my tools.

As professionally as I could manage, I asked, "Where were you thinking?"

"Whatever you want," he replied. "On my thigh."

I had to squeeze my eyes shut. He'd spoken so coolly, but he knew damn well the heat his words would send between my legs.

"Is that alright?" he asked from right behind me.

"Sure," I croaked.

I swore I heard a soft chuckle behind me. But my body was already buzzing with such anticipation that I couldn't be sure.

I'd insisted so long that I wasn't interested, that I didn't want him. This was my punishment. Lee was intent on showing me just how wrong I'd been.

I heard the rustle of clothes behind me and I tried to keep my fingers from shaking over the small metal work tray. As each item of clothing hit the floor, crumpled jeans, a plaid sleeve and belt falling into view at my feet, I lost more control of myself.

My nipples were poking through my white shirt. I was so wet under my black pleated miniskirt that I worried I might drip right down my leg to my patent leather knee-high boots.

When I turned around to face him, Lee was stretched out on my tattoo table in nothing more than grey Calvin Klein briefs. He had his hands behind his head, elbows wide, biceps bulging as he gave me a mischievous smirk.

Fuck. My pussy ached as I imagined straddling him and sinking down onto his hard cock. I tried to pretend I was unaffected as I rolled my stool toward him.

But I could feel how hot my cheeks were, how dry my throat was, how soaked my panties were.

My throat was constricted as I asked, "Can you show me where?"

Lee made a *hmm* sound as he circled his finger between

his thighs as if he was still deciding. He wanted me to notice how hard his cock already was, as if I hadn't already. I mean, how could I not? He was big even when he was soft. And he certainly wasn't anywhere near soft just then.

"This one," Lee said at last, tapping his left thigh.

The one I would have to lean over him to reach. The one with his erection like a fucking mountain range between me and it. The one I knew the bastard would pick even as he made a show of not knowing.

"And what do you want?" I asked. "Tattooed, I mean," I added when he shot me a wicked grin.

His eyes were so filled with lust that I had to tear my gaze away from them, too.

He had me cornered. There was nowhere to run. And for the first time in years, I *liked* that terrifying sensation.

"Something from your more recent history this time," Lee answered. "Say, something you had for *breakfast* this morning, perhaps?"

Brazen. He had no shame.

As I outlined the tattoo on his upper thigh, I had a hard time not brushing my forearm against his more than obvious erection. It was all I could see. All I could think about. That thick ridge stretching toward the waistband of his boxer briefs.

I wanted to lick him through the soft cotton till it was wet, till the fabric clung to his long shaft, his pulsing veins, his tightened balls. Then I wanted to slowly peel his underwear down his length. I wanted to see the way the muscles of his lower stomach twitched as I blew cold air from my lips against his moist cockhead. To see how long he could resist grabbing me as I caught him in the searing heat of my mouth.

He made no such pretences at covering up his reactions.

He groaned and moaned and hissed with abandon as I brushed against him as I worked. First accidentally. Just a brush.

Then I did it on purpose, dragging my nipples against his thigh hairs, letting my breath billow hot over him.

I was making him crazy. I could see how his forearm muscles strained as he clutched the leather.

But he was driving me equally as mad. His debauched sounds over the steady hum of my machine, my thighs pressed together to try to soothe the ache until I couldn't stand it much longer.

He broke first.

All of a sudden, he grabbed me by the hips and pulled me up to sit over his face. As his fingers urged aside my panties, I went for the waistband of his boxer briefs.

His fingers circled my wrist, holding me back.

"You're still on the clock, sweetheart," he said.

I let out a whimper.

"You said you *had* to work," Lee said, and I could feel his breath against my wet folds. "That I couldn't be here unless I was *just* a customer."

His cock was right there. I wanted it.

"Keep working."

"But—" I protested.

"Keep. Working."

I leaned over with the tattoo gun once more. Lee started to lick me. His tongue lapped at me and I could feel just how much of a wet mess I was down there for him.

I stopped tattooing and let out a moan.

"Keeping working," he murmured against me.

"I can't," I panted. "I'm going to ruin your tattoo."

"So ruin me."

How was I supposed to focus when he was giving me that kind of pleasure? How was I supposed to command my shaking hands or my hazy vision when his goal was to drive me out of control? It was impossible.

"Keep working," Lee repeated before nipping at the sensitive skin of my inner thigh, making me hiss with pain and pleasure.

I started tattooing again, but I hardly knew which direction was up and which was down when he thrust his tongue deep inside my pussy. I lifted the gun off his skin and pushed my hips down toward his face, yearning for even more.

But the absence of his tongue made me moan, forehead falling to Lee's knee.

"You stop working," he said. "*I* stop working."

Damn him.

I began working on the tattoo on his upper thigh just to bring his mouth back to my pussy. But it never got easier.

His tongue felt so good licking the length of my entrance and circling my clit that not even thirty seconds would go by before I was forgetting about the tattoo and rocking uncontrollably against him.

Each time he stopped my protests grew louder. Each time my palm was sweatier as I was forced to continue, my heart rate faster.

I was a wreck on top of him. Damp hair from my ponytail stuck to the back of my neck, sweat beaded down my undulating spine, and my inner thighs burned from squeezing so tightly for so long. My breath came in desperate pants and I had to squint to see Lee's tattoo as the needle continued piercing him.

I wanted so fucking badly to come, but it seemed impossible. Every time I felt that white-hot wave cresting in my lower belly, I forgot where I was, who I was. I stopped working, lost entirely in blinding, toe-curling bliss.

And this was always the very moment when I needed one last dart of Lee's tongue against my clit or one last violent suck over my pussy.

He never gave it.

I'd nearly come more times than I could count and all I could manage now were desperate, high-pitched whimpers.

"Keep working," was all he said, his own voice strained as the fabric over his cockhead grew wetter with his precum.

I hardly even heard myself murmuring, "I can't, I can't, I can't."

"Keep working."

I was close again. Lee's tongue was driving into me with an inhuman strength and his fingers were digging deep into the flesh of my ass, pulling me even farther down onto his face. Everything inside of me wanted to stop working, to squeeze my eyes shut and come all over his face.

I screamed as I held the tattoo gun tighter, forcing myself not to let go.

The needle went deep, deeper than it ever should have gone into Lee's skin, as I came.

After being denied it for so long, the release was so intense that I stopped breathing. My back arched like I'd been electrocuted and I held the throbbing needle in place because I was still coming and I didn't want Lee to stop. I orgasmed for longer than I ever had in my entire life.

When I finished, I looked down to see between lingering white flashes that the tattoo was complete.

I collapsed against Lee's torso and the tattoo gun fell to

the floor. I heard it vibrating against the floor, but I was incapable of moving. I'd never felt more spent.

I wasn't even capable of keeping my head up as Lee drew me into his arms.

He cupped the back of my head as he laid me down where he had just been. He brushed my hair away from my face as he gazed down at me. He leaned over to kiss me, tasting like me.

My fingertips tingled with pins and needles or I would have reached up to grip him around the back of the neck and keep him there.

"Don't move," he said.

"I can't," I would have said if I'd been able to speak.

Lee returned with a damp cloth. I lay there, still shuddering a little, as he cleaned me up. I'd been so wet for him. He had to wipe nearly to my knees. I could see the evidence of it all over Lee's mouth, chin, and neck.

When I finally had the strength to reach for the cloth to clean him up in return, he shook his head, eyes flashing dangerously.

"Don't you dare," he said, sounding more threatening than I'd ever heard him. "I crave the scent and taste of you."

His face softened as he ran his thumb over my cheekbone.

His tone was different as he added, "Don't take it away from me."

I saw a vulnerability in his gaze that hadn't been there before. I could hear the words behind his words: Don't take *you* away from me.

He didn't know it, but this frightened me infinitely more than any threatening growl.

There was a bond between us. A piece of each of us that we'd given the other. He was afraid to lose me.

I'd suspected he'd make it difficult for me to go. But now, I realised he would never let me leave. Even if staying would get me killed.

LIAM

For the next few months, Ry and I lived in our own world made for two. Every spare second outside of work I spent by her side, under her tattoo gun, in her kitchen, feet touching under the dining table, in her bed, in *her*.

Slowly I saw the hesitation leave her eyes. She talked about leaving Dublin less. About leaving me. Stopped trying to talk about us as if we were just a fling.

I learned her full name: Ryleigh Elizabeth Carroll and I learned how to write it out in Gaelic script.

I memorised her movements across Europe after she'd exiled herself and learned how to cook her favourite foods: osso buco, a slow-cooked veal in a white wine tomato sauce, a dish she'd grown to love when she'd stayed in Milan; paella (she pronounced it as pah-ye-yah) Valenciana, a fragrant saffron rice dish cooked traditionally with chicken and rabbit that reminded her of her time in Spain; and boeuf bourguignon, a beef stew simmered in a rich red wine sauce that she tasted in Paris.

I memorised the lyrics to all her favourite songs so I could sing them to her, badly, when she was having trouble sleeping.

And when she'd twitch in her sleep sometimes, a mumbled *no* escaping her lips, I'd tuck her close, and whatever nightmare was stealing over her fled at my fierce touch.

She took me to all her favourite places in Dublin, every piece making this city more and more my home.

She showed me Marsh's Library, the oldest public library in Ireland. Tourists all went to the famous Trinity library, she said with a giggle in her voice, but they always missed this one, a quiet eighteenth century brick building in the shadows of St Patrick's Cathedral, hidden by a lush garden.

I walked with her hand in mine through the rows of three-hundred-year-old ornate oak bookcases, vintage seating and weathered book spines, fingering the bullet holes in the shelves still left over from the Easter Rising.

I softly threatened to lock her away in one of the vintage reading cages where they used to lock up patrons while they perused books so they couldn't steal them. She laughed and skipped out of my grasp, the smile she cast me as she glanced back over her shoulder taking my breath away.

She pointed to a spot next to a window in the central reading room they call "Swift's Corner", where the author Jonathan Swift used to sit and look out onto the cathedral.

I asked her who Jonathan Swift was and she slapped my arm, called me a heathen then told me he'd written Gulliver's Travels.

She squealed when I pulled her into my lap in that spot for a long kiss as a response.

She took me to The Library Bar, her favourite secret bar tucked upstairs in a hotel on Exchequer Street that looked like a Victorian mansion's living room with plush velvet armchairs, deep green walls lined with towering wood bookcases and lit with ornate chandeliers. We sat curled up together in front of one of their roaring fireplaces and sipped hot coffee laced with Jameson whiskey.

We walked arm in arm along the willow-shaded footpath of the Grand Canal fringed with reeds, passing in single file over the wooden lock near Baggot Street, and throwing bread at the swans.

We stopped at her favourite tea shop called Wall & Keogh, the smell of sweet floral teas thick in the air as we made our way to the small shaded garden seating out the back and debated over steaming cups of Irish Mist, green tea brightened with Galway fruits, whether Dublin or Kerry were the better GAA team and whether Mayo would ever win another Sam Maguire cup.

That night after work, I drove to Dublin Ink and parked several blocks away as usual.

Dublin Ink had become like a second home to me.

It was where I'd come to know the woman I love. Where she'd left her mark on me forever.

Where I went when I closed my eyes and thought of her: the cold of the leather, the warmth of her fingertips. The grey of her eyes, the pink of the neon glow.

The abandoned street outside, the drapes cocooning us like there was only her and me and no one else.

The wind whipped especially cold that evening as I walked closer to the warm square of light spilling out from the Dublin Ink window into the damp street. Even with my collar turned up against it, icy tendrils managed to slither around my throat.

I paused at the door as voices filtered out to me.

I'd gotten used to Conor and Mason and Aurnia over the last few weeks. They didn't recognise me as Rian's brother, and I supposed why would they. He looked like our ma and I looked like our da.

I doubted that Rian had any photos of me anyway; even if he did, they were from when I was a teenager, not the man I was now.

Their voices shouldn't have made me pause. But there was a voice that caught my attention, the particular lilt of a male voice, the musical strains of the Cork accent worn out from living in Dublin for so long.

I crept to the window, staying pressed close to the wall, and peered inside.

It looked warm inside the cosy tattoo parlour, bright with the neon glow and all the fringed lamps, enough to fill a flea market, turned on.

There were open bottles of whiskey and plates of boxty, Irish potato pancakes, and corned beef and cabbage sliders.

Ryleigh and Conor, Mason, Rachel and Aurnia all stood smiling, laughing, arms slung round shoulders, hearts drawn close, around an all too familiar newcomer.

Like a family.

A family I didn't belong to.

My little world shattered.

My heart seized in my chest and I clutched at it. I stumbled back from the light and lurched back into the shadows where I belonged.

She'd weaved such a spell over me that I'd almost forgotten that her apartment wasn't ours, that her life wasn't only mine.

Ryleigh wasn't mine anymore.

Rian was back.

I'd gotten so used to being called Lee that I wasn't sure I'd respond to Liam anymore.

Liam, who had the brother who hated him, seemed so far away, like he was another man entirely. As Lee, a man with Ryleigh's love, I was reborn, remade.

I'd forgotten all the lies I'd told her. But as they say about lies... They never stay buried for long.

RY

A tightness lined my stomach with bitterness.

Lee didn't show up the other night, cancelling on me last minute. He'd never cancelled on me before, let alone *by text*. When I messaged back to ask what was wrong he replied: *Something came up. Sorry. Promise I'll make it up to you.*

Something was wrong.

Even though he texted me to say good night and good morning.

And now it had been almost twenty-four hours, the longest we'd gone without seeing each other. Why did it feel like I was missing a limb? Why did my chest ache?

Hubby: Missed ur face when I woke up this morning

Hubby: Didn't miss ur morning breath tho ;)

Hubby: Jks. u smell like roses

. . .

I still hadn't changed his name in my phone. It still gave me a thrill every time I saw a message from "hubby". From him.

It felt like nothing had changed except…

Me: Hey, missed u last nite

Hubby: I know. missed u too

Me: So how about lunch here today? There's someone I want u to meet

Hubby: Sorry, can't. I'm busy

I waited for him to propose a new time to come see me like he always did.

But minutes went by without another message and my guts twisted even further.

Was he getting cold feet? Growing disinterested?

Calm down, Ry. He's busy. Just because you and he have spent every single free waking moment together in the last few weeks, doesn't mean that it could have lasted. Life happens. People get busy. People need space.

Besides, him needing space couldn't have come at a better time now that Rian was back. I'd have more time to spend with my best friend. Right?

Lee had been practically living with me in Rian's spare room, and it's not like we could keep doing that now that Rian was back.

I hadn't told Rian about my new boyfri— wait, was that what he was? Lee and I never actually discussed that's what we were, but…

Shite, was he seeing someone else? We never actually *said* that we were exclusive.

Although I couldn't see how he would have time to meet anyone else let alone date anyone else.

Maybe I should stop by his work. I looked up O'Sullivan's Garage, the name of the mechanics he worked at. It was only a twenty-minute bus ride from here.

God, Ry, stop being so paranoid.

Besides, isn't that what you wanted? A way out? Him to lose interest so it'd make it easier when you inevitably left Dublin?

I threw my phone into my backpack. Fuck. I needed a distraction. Something to get my mind off Lee.

I didn't realise what I was drawing at first.

It happened sometimes. A pencil or pen would just appear in my hand, silence would drape over me like a blanket, I'd blink and there the start of something would be on the page.

I'd blink again and it would start taking shape.

I'd blink again and it would be there: the answer. All along. As if my soul was keeping a secret from me. As if it knew what it would draw and knew to not tell me.

So I wouldn't stop it.

It was a new butterfly breaking out of a tiny cocoon. A delicate thing. The size of my thumb. A tattoo for an inner wrist. Or the small patch of skin behind an ear. A tattoo to be tucked away somewhere private, somewhere safe.

There it was from my soul: a beginning, a miracle, a new life.

I'd been so fixated on it, my finger running over the delicate pencil lines, that I hadn't heard the door of the tattoo parlour open. The cocoon's warmth had become my warmth so I didn't feel any gust of misty wind from outside.

When the hand came to my shoulder I yelped.

"Ry, it's me. It's just me."

I sagged with relief, exhaling shakily: it was Rian. It was my best friend.

"You know how consuming work can be," I said, forcing a smile.

"Ry," Rian said.

His hand came to squeeze my shoulder. He'd gained back weight in rehab. Healthy muscle. His fingers no longer felt skeletal through my shirt.

"Rian," I said back.

He gave me a fixed look.

I rolled my eyes. "You just startled me."

"That was something more than just startled, Ry."

"I'm not used to anyone else being here when I'm working the late shift," I told him. "And since Rachel and Mason broke the bed upstairs it's been pretty quiet up there, too."

I closed my drawing pad and busied myself with cleaning up my workstation, an easy excuse to not meet his still worried gaze.

"Ry," Rian tried once more with a hand at my elbow, easily brushed away by my reaching for the trash bin.

"Are you alright?" he asked.

"Alright?" I dropped my pencils into a mug with a picture of the needle end of a tattoo gun with the words "just the tip" on it. "How could I not be alright? You're back. You're *better*."

Partial truth was always a safe retreat for the liar.

The happiness I felt looking at my best friend was true. His skin had a healthy glow back. His eyes were clear and sharp. I didn't notice any fidgeting of his fingers, any chewing at the inside of his mouth. He didn't stop mid-sentence to stare off into the distance.

I didn't think I'd ever seen Rian this...normal. This calm.

He was clean. He could see with clear eyes. So I was

alright because he was alright. And he hadn't been alright in a very long time.

I drew Rian into a hug and squeezed him hard, my face nestled against his chest.

"I was so scared for you, Rian," I said. "When I heard you were...sick. I—I can't lose you."

Rian squeezed me before he pulled away, holding me at arm's length. His eyes bounced between mine. He might as well have taken out a flashlight to shine at me, into one eye and then the other.

"You know I feel the same way about you," he said, his voice soft and earnest. "If I lost you..."

I thought about how I'd disappeared into Lee. How I'd barely spent time with anyone else. Guilt threaded through me when I realised I'd even stopped dropping by the rehab centre to visit Rian. He must have noticed.

Perhaps that's why I hadn't told him about Lee. Because I hadn't figured out how to make time for both of them. Not yet.

It doesn't matter anyway, a voice inside me said. *Rian's back. It's time to leave. You had a break from your life.*

But that's all Lee was: a reprieve.

Our life here, no matter how sweet, couldn't last. What he and I had here couldn't be real.

But the face from my nightmares was...

"You're not going to lose me," I said, forcing a smile, but even I could hear the lies in the hollowness of my voice.

Rian hesitated one last time. Did he remember when I fled Dublin? Or had it been hidden behind a haze of cocaine?

Was his gaze clear enough now to see through my half-truths? Was he seeing the haunted darkness in my eyes?

Rian's fingers tightened on my arms. I could hear him clearly: *I'm here for you. If I wasn't at some point, I am now.*

"Would you tell me?" he asked, still searching my face, still prodding for the truth. "Would you tell me if you weren't alright?"

I didn't trust my own voice. Rian would have to believe a nod. Another forced smile.

He let me go, reluctantly, it seemed. But I made it through. I'd slipped through the cracks one more time. Was it relief I felt? Or disappointment?

"Ready to go?" he asked, nodding toward the door.

It was only then that I saw the coat draped over his arm and the umbrella resting against his leg.

"Is it already time?" I asked, checking the clock.

Closing time was over an hour ago. I bit my lip. Lee still hadn't come.

I considered waiting a little longer. Sending Rian home ahead of me. Of giving Lee another chance. He wasn't going to go *another* night without seeing me, was he?

"Come on," Rian said, tugging at my arm. "It's cold. We'll keep each other warm."

We locked up together. I left Dublin Ink bathed in darkness, the neon light switched off. A steady rain fell on the slick sidewalks. It'd been falling since that morning.

For the first time in a long time, I checked the streets.

I realised I'd stopped doing that because Lee always walked me home. I frowned peering into the shadows across the street. The hairs on the back of my neck stood up as if…as if I was being watched.

I shook it off. I was being paranoid.

Besides, Rian was here.

Even if Lee wasn't by my side, I wasn't alone.

"Do you think you'll stay in Dublin for much longer?" Rian asked over the pitter patter on our shared umbrella.

I pulled him closer, glancing over my shoulder at the shadows before giving him a look. "Is this because I left my oatmeal bowl in the sink this morning?"

Rian laughed and I relished the clear, full sound. For so long his senses had been dulled that he'd stopped laughing as much.

"You know you're welcome to stay for..."

I lifted an eyebrow at him. "Really? You want a permanent roommate?"

He shrugged. "If we didn't kill each other living together after art school, surely we won't kill each other now that we're older and...?"

"Wiser...?" I added. I stepped over a puddle. "Um, didn't our attempt at being roommates end with you tossing your half-finished canvas out on the curb with the trash?"

"Your toyboy of the week threw his leather jacket over my still drying canvas." Rian pulled me aside out of the way of the muddy spray of a passing car. "He ruined it."

"I still agree with him," I teased. "The smears made it better. Postmodern, you know? Abstract."

Under his breath, Rian mumbled, "If I wanted to smear a masterpiece, I would have smeared a masterpiece myself." He shook his head. "I hope your taste in men has improved."

I know he was only teasing.

But for some reason, his words stabbed into my gut.

Would Rian like Lee? Would Lee like Rian?

They seemed so different.

My best friend was every bit a moody dark artist, secrets and darkness tucked away in every crack.

And Lee was a simple kind-hearted country boy turned

mechanic. I couldn't ever imagine him keeping secrets or hiding a dark side.

"I mean," Rian continued, "eventually, I'd like the place back, you know, when Eithne forgives me. When she's ready to..."

"She loves you," I said, squeezing his arm. "She'll come around."

"I hope so," he said as we rounded the corner onto his street. "She just...we just...need more time."

I patted my friend's hand over the umbrella. He looked distant for a moment, but then shook it off.

"Really," he said, the tightness falling away from his voice, "why not stay in Dublin? The parlour could use your talent. Even with me back."

I was quiet. Rian didn't know how complicated the answer to that simple question really was. How much I wished it were different.

"I mean, I know you said it was just to cover my chair, keep it warm," he continued, oblivious to the sting in my jaw, "and I know there's that big old world out there to explore, but..."

Don't say it. Please, don't say it.

"...but Ireland is your home, Ry," he said.

Home.

I swallowed thickly.

"Dublin Ink could be your home," he said. "Me and the boys. Aurnia. Rachel. Eithne. Home, Ry. *Home.* Don't you want a home?"

I remained silent as we ascended the steps to his apartment.

"What are you chasing out there all alone?" he asked.

It was the wrong question.

The right question was what was I running away from?

Under the small canopy in front of the door, he closed the umbrella as I pawed through my bag for keys, avoiding his eyes.

Rian grabbed my upper arm and turned me round to face him. His eyes still held the clarity of sobriety, but now they were laced with something far too close to a drug: love.

"Ry," he said, fingers squeezing my shoulder, "when Mason and Conor dragged me out of that hellhole, I didn't think it was possible. To find home again. I thought... I thought I would always be lost. Always be on the outside looking in..."

He dropped his eyes for a moment and I grabbed his hand.

"I thought there'd been too much damage done," he admitted. "I thought the best that could happen was a few sober weeks and then a relapse. And then that would be it. That I was just...too broken."

His throat worked as he swallowed back emotion. I squeezed his fingers. He did the same back. The rain fell heavier, a curtain around our intimacy.

"But I learned home is not something you earn," he said at last, cupping my cheek. "It's something you accept. A gift you take. And hold onto the best you can."

Rian searched my eyes. He wanted to know if I understood.

I did. I wanted—so desperately wanted—Dublin to be my home.

I wanted to tell him everything. What had happened. Why I left. The nightmare that was haunting me.

But my throat wouldn't work, my lips frozen. Instead of speaking I just nodded.

For a second, disappointment crossed Rian's face. I hadn't opened up. But that was replaced with acceptance.

"No matter what, Ry," he promised, "I'm here for you."

Rian pulled me into a hug and I let him, turning my head to the side to rest my cheek on his chest.

That's when I saw him. Collar turned up. Pale as a ghost. Alone in the rain, staring at us as if I'd betrayed him.

Lee.

LIAM

I watched Rian and Ry huddled close on their steps, letting the bitterness swill in my mouth.

I didn't think there was something romantic between them; I could see that their touches and stares were ones born from easy affection. Not passion.

What I coveted was how easily Rian commanded her attention and took up space in her life. Like he was entitled to it. The second he was back, there was no room for me.

I was on the outside looking in again.

Just like on the farm with Alan and his family.

I wanted what they had. I wanted to be accepted into their family. Accepted as part of Ry's and Rian's life.

But that would never happen unless I convinced Rian to forgive me.

But first…I had to admit my lies to Ry. And hope that she forgave me first.

My stomach jumbled into a knot so twisted, one I berated myself for because I caused it.

I should have told Ry weeks ago. I just got so caught up in *us*. I kept saying, *tomorrow, I'll tell her, tomorrow.*

Tell her that my name was Liam not Lee.

Tell her that I was her best friend's brother.

But tomorrow never came.

In the shadows outside Dublin Ink, I watched her through the windows, my heart aching at how close she was but so fucking far away. It killed me to brush off her messages, her requests for me to see her.

The worst of it all was when she glanced toward the door. I knew she was looking for me. Expecting me.

Fuck, hadn't I even told her I would be there after work? Hadn't I tried to tell her that with the steadiness of my eyes as she looked up at me from the kitchen floor that I would always be there?

I followed her and Rian home, hands in fists by my side, not caring that the rain was soaking my clothes, glaring at the way their heads leaned in together. Hating that her hand was wrapped around *his* elbow, that *he* got to hold an umbrella for her, that *he* got to jump puddles with her.

I crouched shivering on the rooftop, staring into their warm brightly lit apartment as they sang along to "Two Kids" by David Keenan and "This City" by Sam Fisher, as Rian helped her chop onions and open jars. I buried my rage as he took *my seat* next to her and stole her laughter from me and my olives off her plate.

I had to see her, to explain everything. I wanted it more than anything. But how would I even get her alone with Rian hogging her?

How could I tell her that the best friend who now spent so much time by her side was the very brother who hated the ground I walked on?

Could she still love me? Or would she join arms with Rian against me?

The pain that lashed through me at this possibility almost brought me to my knees.

It was clear that Ryleigh was part of *his* family.

Not mine.

If I lost her, I'd lose Rian, too. Forever.

~

The exhaust pipe slipped and I knew it was bad from the flash of pain and the sudden flood of heat between my fingers.

Blood dripped onto the floor in big drops as I cupped my hand and hurried toward the office. Out of the corner of my eye, Darren looked up at me from behind the wheel of the old junker he still thought he could bring back to life.

The rusted car door slammed as I did my best not to ruin the tidy stacks of invoices in my search for the first aid kit.

"Here," Darren said, wiping his grease-stained hands on a dirty rag before opening a metal cabinet door. "Just sit down."

My hands shook in my lap, jeans growing wet from my own blood. I cursed low under my breath. My toe tapped erratically on the old office carpet as Darren shoved a towel over my lap and set the first aid kit on the chair beside me.

He stood over me, arms crossed, eyes dark and assessing. I pressed the corner of the towel against the cut.

"Hospital?" Darren asked, his voice betraying just the tiniest concern beneath its typical crunch of gravel.

I inhaled to steady myself and lifted the corner of the soaked towel to peek under. Fresh blood filled the cut that stretched from the base of my thumb to my wrist, but I could see that it was shallow. I'd injured myself enough on the farm to know it didn't need stitches.

I shook my head. Darren let out a small exhale before sinking down onto the corner of the desk, arms still crossed tightly over his chest.

"I fucked up," I said, calm enough now to flip over the first aid kit and rummage for the disinfectant.

Darren grunted. "You've been clumsy all morning."

I sent him a quick glare. Kayleigh wasn't in, which meant the radiator wasn't on. The garage was as cold as it was outside. Colder even, given Darren's black hole of charm. No one could be expected to get a good grip on a wrench while fighting frostbite.

But it wasn't Darren's stoicism that got me sliced open. I was more than used to frozen fingertips and bone-deep cold out on the farm.

I sighed, rubbing my upper arm across my face, because I knew what had really caused my accident.

"I don't mean I fucked up my hand—"

"It sure looks like you fucked up your hand," Darren said.

He didn't move to help me undo the cap of the disinfectant. I was forced to use my teeth instead. I spit the cap at his feet. This earned me a grin. I still had one unhurt hand and its middle finger lifted just fine. Darren's grin got wider.

"What I mean is that I fucked up with this girl," I said, hissing as I wiped a disinfectant-soaked pad along my cut.

"The one who you let tattoo half your body already?" Darren asked.

I laughed darkly. "It's not like she forced me."

"Would that have made things easier?" Darren asked.

"She's my brother's best friend," I told him, eyes fixed on the washed-out wound, the pink flesh so easily ripped apart.

"My estranged brother. The brother who hates me. The brother who I came to Dublin to make amends with after years of not doing what was right for him. She is *his* best friend. And now he's back."

The office fell into silence as I pushed around different sized bandages, only half focused on finding the right one.

"And you want to…end things with her?" Darren asked.

I looked over at his sharp green eyes, narrowed at me.

"I love her," I said.

Darren exhaled. "That's worse."

The cut continued to bleed as I ignored it. Could I just be selfish and greedy for Ry? Could I be uncaring about what Rian thought? Getting Ry—*keeping* her—no matter what?

"Does he know?" Darren asked.

I shook my head.

"Does *she* know?"

My chin fell to my chest defeated.

He let out a curse. "And the bad blood between you and your brother—"

"Bad," I answered. "Wouldn't piss on me if I was on fire kinda bad."

Darren uncrossed his arms and rubbed the back of his neck. "You have to tell her."

"I know."

"*And* him."

"I know," I said quieter still.

"Are you sure you *love* love her?" he asked. "It's not just… ye know, lust?"

I watched myself bleed. The slow, steady line of my blood along my thumb. I'd bleed myself dry for Ryleigh. Without saying a word aloud, Darren seemed to understand my response. Know it instinctually.

"Kayleigh was with my brother first," he said. "And my brother loved her. Or at least, he thought he did. Got a ring and everything."

I'd never heard Darren say so much with such an open countenance. Somehow, somewhere, we'd become friends.

"Shite," I muttered.

Darren crossed his ankles, leaned back on the corner of the desk. Before continuing he drew a hand over his face. As if he could still remember the pain. Still feel its lingering scars.

"If I could have forgotten Kayleigh, I would have," he said, pushing up the brim of his baseball cap. "If I could have moved on from her somehow…hell, if I could have run away from Dublin… It would have ripped out my heart, but it would have been easier. Less painful."

Darren shrugged and I saw what I felt mirrored in his eyes.

"But you couldn't," I said in a soft voice.

"Not a chance in hell I could ever stop loving her," Darren said.

He pulled out a bandage and tore it open for me. Crumbled the packaging into the wastepaper basket. He left half a black thumbprint at the sticky corner of the bandage as he handed it to me.

I didn't need to thank him with words. In fact, I think he might have gone out for the pipe to cut me again if I did.

The wound stung when I pressed the bandage into place. But there was no way around it.

It had to hurt before it healed.

I took the stairs to Rian's door two at a time. My head was so thick from tossing and turning that I couldn't remember whether Ry normally left first or whether it was Rian. Or whether they left together. It was all a mad jumble.

I no longer cared. My desperation to see Ry, to hold her hands to my chest and spill my guts to her was so intense that I pounded on the door without any idea who would open it: the brother who hated me or the woman I needed to love me.

I heard footsteps just on the other side of the door. I accepted my fate as the door opened.

It was the first time I'd looked Rian in the face since our father's disastrous funeral.

That flame of hatred ignited behind his pale blues, the colour of our ma's eyes. Rian was too young when she died to know that her eyes never burned like his.

Rian stood there, chest heaving, fingers shaking on the handle. I stood there unmoving and let his eyes dissect me.

"Rian," I said. My voice sounded hoarse like I hadn't spoken for years. I supposed in a way, I hadn't. "Hey, I'm—"

"What the fuck do you want, Liam?"

This was what I had come to Dublin for. To have a chance to speak to Rian. To make things right. To clean a black soul.

But it felt like all I'd done was taken his place as the drug addict. My skin pale, my attention fading in and out, my head somewhere else. I needed Ry. I needed Ry like a needle in my vein. I was going through withdrawals from her. I couldn't see my brother through the fog. I could only feel my own fire-burning pain.

"You look great," I said, rambling. "Well, I mean better than—"

"Fuck off. I don't need your platitudes."

I couldn't do this with Rian. Not yet. I had to speak to Ryleigh first.

I tried to push into the apartment. "I thought I could come in—"

He blocked my path. "No."

What was I supposed to say to him? My thoughts raced. What had I practised on the long drive to the city, repeated again and again along those narrow, winding country roads? I couldn't focus. Couldn't think.

All my mind was Ry. All my heart was Ry. I needed to talk to her. She'd turned me into a junkie at a dealer's door. Desperate. And only growing more and more desperate.

"Rian…" I glanced past his shoulder, tried to see into the apartment a glimpse, any sign, of Ryleigh. "I know things aren't great between us right now and that kills me and I hope it can change—"

"I don't have time for this. I'm going to be late. So kindly fuck off."

Rian stepped outside before slamming the door behind himself, the lock clicking shut, cutting off my access to the apartment, to Ryleigh. It took everything in me not to lunge at the closing door.

"What are you looking at?" he demanded.

I glanced back at Rian and found him glaring at me. "I'm, um, no one…"

Shite.

Confusion bled across Rian's face.

I saw the moment when he put two and two together. My sudden appearance even though I was clearly not here for him. My desperate need to get past him.

Perhaps Ryleigh had told him about the "Lee" that she'd been seeing while he'd been in rehab.

His realisation was a knife to my own heart. A knife to my own back.

If I had any chance of reconciling with Rian, I'd just thrown it away. Just like that.

Fury bled across his face until it was all I saw.

"You go near Ryleigh and I'll kill you," Rian growled. "Do you hear me?"

I stumbled back as if he'd actually hit me. As if he'd lashed out physically, not just with his words.

"I'll fucking *kill* you."

RY

It'd been four days and seventeen hours since I'd seen Lee watching Rian and me from the steps of Rian's apartment.

His absence burned like a fever.

Before I could call out to him, he turned and in a blink, disappeared into the shadows. I realised how it must have looked to Lee. The closeness. The touching. My eyes misty as I locked gazes with Rian.

And us about to walk into Rian's apartment together.

Was that why Lee had stayed away? Was that why he was refusing to answer my text, to return my calls?

Had he seen me with Rian and misunderstood? Taken the love of friendship for the love we had?

"Rian, I'll be *fine*," I said as I buried myself further under my blankets. "*Go.*"

I winced against the lamp light as Rian lifted the corner of the thick comforter. The back of his hand came to rest against my forehead even as I protested and tried to push him away.

I groaned when he sank down on the edge of the mattress.

Rian grabbed my wrist. His thumb pressed against my fluttering pulse. I rolled my eyes.

"We went to *art* school together," I grumbled, tugging my hand away. "Not medical school."

Rian grinned. "I'm pretty sure I've seen more naked bodies than a doctor."

"Just 'cause you know how to draw them, doesn't mean you know how to heal them," I said, swatting away his hand.

"Exactly," he announced victoriously. "Which is why I should take you to someone who does."

I covered my eyes with my forearms.

"I'm *fine*," I whined, desperate for him to leave me alone. "And you need to get to Eithne."

Rian again went to feel my forehead. I hit him with a pillow.

"I swore I had a thermometer around here somewhere," Rian said, leaving the room.

Rian didn't know. Rian couldn't know.

"Look," I shouted after him, hearing him rummaging through the medicine cabinet in the bathroom. "I'm just going to guzzle some Benylin, turn up the heat, and pass out, alright? If you want to miss a date with Eithne just to catch my drool, be my guest."

Rian appeared in the doorway, his bottom lip between his teeth, his fingers drumming against the moulding. I knew how much seeing Eithne meant to Rian. How desperately he wanted to win her back. I wasn't hurting anyone by using that knowledge to my own means.

"Don't let her down because your roommate has some sniffles," I said.

Rian looked me over again. "Are you sure you—"

"Go on with yourself," I said, interrupting. "I'll be grand."

Because no, I wasn't going to be alright. No, I wasn't grand. And no, there was not a goddamn thing he could do for me.

I needed Lee.

But he was gone. Without a trace. Without a fucking explanation.

Rian kissed my forehead, reminded me I had his number in case I needed him and made me promise to call if I needed anything.

I nodded through it all, but I knew the truth.

I was alone. As I always was. As I always would be.

The front door closed and I drew the covers back over my head. My knees drew up into my chest and I closed my eyes.

One thing was for sure: my time in Dublin needed to end. I couldn't go on like this. It was killing me. Whether Balor had really found me or not, whether he was really following me or not, I was dying as long as I remained here.

I knew this city would break my heart.

Ironic that it would be Lee that would be the reason I left.

There was a knock at the door. I heard Lee's voice calling out my name, faint, but I'd recognise it in my sleep.

I didn't bother with pants. In just my thin t-shirt, I raced barefoot through the apartment, the rain on the roof sounding like the blood rushing in my ears.

I tugged open the door. My chest heaved as I stood there, staring at him.

He looked just as bad as I did. Maybe worse. Eyes somehow both dull and bright, a dog dying from a fever. His hair was matted across a pale forehead.

His shearling-lined coat looked like it had never been dry,

never held a shape other than his. It clung to him, to his stooped shoulders and heavily hanging arms.

Big drops cascaded from his eyelashes, his chin, his fingertips. If I didn't see the big sheets of rain thrashing in the wind behind him, I might have thought he was bleeding out.

"Where the fuck have you been?" I asked, my voice hollow.

He opened his mouth.

"No, I don't want to know," I cut him off. "I don't fucking care. You left me. you fucking *left me*."

I didn't know what to feel anymore. Angry? Used? *Relieved?*

"Let me explain." He lifted his hands and stepped forward. "Can I come in?"

"No." I blocked his path.

"Ry, please."

I shook my head as if that might send a message to my brain: close the door. Shut it now. Do not step aside.

Lee's eyes did not leave mine, even as I trailed over his body with my wary gaze.

"You've left me in a free fall," I said. "And I don't think I'll survive it."

He stepped up to me. His drenched chest came against the thin cotton of my t-shirt, soaking through.

My nipples hardened. I melted against him, every single cell aching for his touch after so long.

"This is me catching you," he whispered.

With one touch, he'd stripped me of all my remaining defences. The t-shirt felt like tissue paper over my stomach, quivering with every hard-fought breath.

His eyelashes dripped water droplets onto my uplifted face. One fell on my closed eyelid. One caught my cheek like a tear. I tasted the salt of his sweat on the dip of my Cupid's bow from a third.

He stepped us inside, his arms wrapped around me, me buried against his chest, body trembling against his, the door clicking shut behind him. His chest rose high. I rose with it. We fell together.

"Ry, I need to tell you something."

His arms tightened around me even as I tried to crane my head to look up at him. I thought he might crush me. The weight of him. The strength of him.

"I love you," he said to the crown of my head, his lips moving against my hair. "I love you, Ryleigh Elizabeth Carroll. You are mine. And I am yours."

His heartbeat smashed against my ribs as my head spun from his words. "Lee…"

"You are mine," he repeated, holding me, somehow, even tighter. "And I am yours… But there is one more thing I need to tell you."

"Lee, what is—?"

"Rian is my brother."

LIAM

"R*ian is my brother.*"

Finally, after all these months, the truth tumbled out. Once I started talking, I couldn't stop.

"My name is Liam…not Lee. Although," I tried a soft smile, "I've come to love that nickname. And I hope you keep calling me Lee."

What do they say? The truth shall set you free?

Except as Ryleigh pulled back from me, I caught sight of her face. The shock and confusion as she shook her head and stared at me with wide eyes…then the utter bone-shattering betrayal as my words sank in.

"No," she said, her voice shuddering. "No. No."

She shoved me away but I grabbed onto her wrists. I couldn't let her pull away.

"That's not possible," she said, her voice hollow.

"I'm sorry. I should have told you earlier," I said, my excuses sounding hollow, "but—"

"Rian doesn't have a *brother*."

I was so startled by her words that she was able to wrench

her hands from my touch. The loss of her sent an ache through me.

"He has a brother," I said. "You know he does."

"Rian has a demon," she said, her voice growing cold and cruel. "He has a monster. He has a cruel past that still won't let him go…but Rian has no *brother*."

She might as well have stabbed me with a knife, it hurt that much.

She fell back on her heel away from me, putting more and more distance between us.

Fuck. I was losing her.

"I can explain," I said, moving toward her, palms up and out. "There's more to the story that you—that he—doesn't know."

"Get out." She pointed a trembling finger toward the door. "Get out right fucking now."

"I'm not leaving, Ry," I said.

"Don't call me that," she shouted. "*Rian* calls me that. My best friend calls me that."

I was desperate. I had to make her listen. I grabbed her, pinning her arms to her torso.

"Let go of me!" she screamed as she struggled to get free.

"You have no idea how cruel my father was," I told her as she kicked at me. "How—"

"Let go!" She punched me in the stomach.

I let out a grunt and let her go. She scrambled away from me, her eyes darting between me and the door behind me.

"Ry," I begged, "he told me he'd kill Rian if I tried to help him."

"Oh God, I'm such an idiot," she said, spitting out the words with bitter laughter. "That's why you're in Dublin. Fuck, how did I not see it sooner? You being so interested in me. You asking all those questions. I *did* see you outside here that day. You *were* following me!"

If she could just hear me. If she could just understand.

"Okay, yes, I did come here to make things right with Rian," I admitted. I had to be truthful. I couldn't cover up my lies anymore. "I did follow you to Dublin Ink from this apartment. But then I *met* you and—"

"You were using me to get to Rian," Ry said, looking at me with renewed shock and horror. "None of it was real."

Anger flared up in my chest. She could call me all sorts of names, accuse me of all sorts of things. And I'd take them.

But not *that*.

I stepped toward her, my shadow looming. My voice dangerously low as I spoke, pointing my finger at her. "That's a lie and you know it. You fucking know it."

Ry glared at me, madness in her grey eyes. "I'm glad it was all a lie. Because I could never love who you really are. The man behind the mask. No, the *animal* behind the fucking mask."

I stalked toward her and she retreated, putting the couch between us. I moved to one side, she the other.

I was breathing heavily. Panting like the animal she accused me of being. I slammed my hands down on the back of the couch.

"This is *me*," I said, on the verge of shouting. On the verge of losing control. "This has always been me and you know it. I've never professed to be an angel and you've never professed to love one."

"He trusted you," Ry screamed. "*I* trusted you!"

"My father made me believe things I shouldn't have. My father stopped me from doing what I should have. And I'm here to make it right."

She needed to listen. She just needed to fucking listen.

"I opened up to you in ways I've never done before." Ry grabbed at her chest. "How you must have found it all so funny. Knowing what you knew. Being who you are!"

"That's *enough*!"

Frustration boiling over, I shoved the couch aside. It dented the wall with a crash.

Ry didn't even glance at the destruction. She just looked at the unencumbered distance between us and balled her fists. Ready for battle. Ready to fight.

"I told you to get out."

"And I told you I'm not leaving."

I'd pin her to the floor if I had to. I'd let her scream until she lost her voice if that was what it took. I would not leave. I was not going to lose her.

"I may have lied about my name," I said, "but I *never* lied to you about who I am. I'm still the man you *love*."

I was just as surprised by Ry's sudden tears as she seemed to be. She wiped at them with a vehemence. Like they'd betrayed her by welling along her dark lower lashes and falling down her cheek.

"I'll never love you again," she said, her words poisonous.

I was on her before she could even think to run, a dangerous mix of anger and fear burning in my veins. She stumbled back till she collided with the wall and I caged her in, no chance of escape.

It was not something a good man would do. It was wrong. Crossing a line. Going too far. But there was no universe where I wouldn't have done it again.

My fingers were rough on her delicate skin, my wet clothes against her body. Eyes locked on hers like I'd already thrown away the fucking key.

Her pulse thudded beneath my thumb, her lips parted, ready to suck in one last breath before I dragged her under.

I wasn't going to lose her. I was not going to leave.

I was going to make her listen. Make her understand.

No, it was not something a good man would do. But at last, I admitted the truth to myself… I wasn't a good man.

She didn't even have time to gasp in surprise before my fingers wrapped around her throat.

"You're going to listen to me, or I'm going to fuck you until you do."

RY

Lee—no, *Liam's* hand was around my throat, gentle yet firm, as his mouth closed around mine.

Instantly my world quieted. My limbs melted against his as they instinctively submitted. My wild anger swirled into burning lust.

For a moment I kissed him back, body aching from having been without him for so many days. His familiar masculine scent and his body against mine had my head spinning.

But then I remembered.

He was my best friend's brother.

He'd *lied* to me.

My hand came down on his cheek with a loud crack. I tore my lips off him and began to fight him.

"Fine." He scowled and caught my wrists, pulling them behind my back. "Your choice."

I let out a yelp.

"We do this the hard way." He pushed me toward the couch, bending me over the back of it.

"Let me go," I screamed as he held me down and ground his hard cock against my ass.

His hand came down flat on my ass with a smack. I cried out as pain flared through my body before a wave of pleasure replaced it.

"That's for not letting me explain," he said.

He smacked me again, the heat multiplying, but so did the pleasure.

"That is for trying to leave me."

Each smack made my core clench, forcing me to bite back any whimpers.

"That's for daring to tell me you don't love me anymore."

His fist tangled in my hair, yanking my head back before he spanked me again. My moans filled the air as I shuddered.

No. I had to fight against this, against him. I couldn't betray my best friend.

"Lee—*Liam,* don't," I begged. "I don't want you."

"Liar," he growled, pulling my panties down my hips and running his fingers along my soaking slit. "You're soaked for me and I've barely touched you."

His fingers circled my clit and a groan bubbled up from deep inside me.

I kicked out hard, my foot catching a lamp and it shattered.

Liam pinned my lower legs down with his knees as he continued to torment my clit.

"Stop," I cried, even as I pushed back against him.

What was wrong with me? I was so turned on I almost couldn't stand it. All my arguments flew out the window as my body betrayed me, as my back arched, begging for him to push his fingers inside me.

"You're going to take every inch of my cock and then tell me you don't want me."

I heard the sound of his zipper over my groans, my nipples strained against the thin material of my shirt.

I barely had time to breathe as he thrust his cock into me, impaling me. We let out twin groans as he reached around to hold the front of my neck.

"You can fight me, scream at me," he growled in my ear, "I'll still choke and fuck you until you come for me. This is how it'll always be for us."

I was at his mercy as he fucked me over the back of the couch. Liam kept my neck in a chokehold, and at times I could barely breathe as I writhed underneath him.

"Take it back," he demanded. "Tell me you still love me."

His hand tightened around my throat, his cock punishing my pussy in such a delicious way.

"No," I choked out, even as my pussy tightened around him as my head spun. God, I was going to come.

He growled and then he fucking stopped moving.

I let out a whimper as my orgasm remained out of reach. I just needed one more thrust. But he held my hips down with his weight, preventing me from getting my satisfaction.

"Tell me I'm yours and I'll give you what you want."

I let out a frustrated noise and tried to reach down to touch my own clit. If he wouldn't give it to me, I'd take it.

He grabbed my wrist and twisted it around my back, firm but not painful.

"No," I moaned.

I needed to come so bad. I needed to come around *him* so bad.

"Who do you belong to?" he said, sliding in and out of me

achingly slow, keeping me on the edge but not giving me what I needed. "Say it."

My resolve shattered. My heart swallowed up my guilt.

"You," I gasped. "I'm yours."

For a moment he remained still, as if he couldn't believe what I was admitting.

Then he pounded into me, hard, tilting his hips to find the angle that hit that sensitive spot inside me, his hand closing firmly around my throat.

I broke apart under him, pleasure and relief slamming into me like a dam burst.

He thrust into me and shuddered against me before he collapsed.

"And I am yours," he whispered.

~

Liam crawled onto the couch and pulled me on top of him, holding my head against his chest. I listened to his heartbeat as it slowed down.

"My father would beat us..." he confessed. "All of us. *Discipline,* he called it..."

For the first time, I saw the darkness that hollowed his eyes. For the first time, he let me see it.

Perhaps that's what had drawn me to him. Deep down, I knew he was like me: haunted by monsters.

"But Rian...he got the worst of it. I wanted so badly to stop what my father did to Rian. So badly. I *tried* to stop him..." His voice broke off in a choked sob.

He shuddered against me. For a moment I saw him as a young boy terrified of his father, so terrified he couldn't do anything to help the brother he loved.

Without thinking, I reached out and brushed my hands along his chest, soothing him, encouraging him to continue.

"My father said that Rian needed toughening up. And that if I helped him, if I defended him, I'd prevent Rian from becoming a real man. That Rian would end up like a lame horse that just needed to…to be shot."

I sucked in a gasp, my heart aching at his admission.

"Do you hear me, Ry? My father told me—he swore to me—that if I defended Rian, he'd *kill* him."

I squeezed my eyes shut as grief wrapped its cold fingers around my lungs.

I imagined these two frightened boys, Rian being forced to sleep out by himself in the cold barn night after night, and Liam, huddled in his bed and staring out his window to the dark barn, to the brother he was forced to ignore.

A sob broke from me. If there was a God, how could he let such monsters roam this earth?

He traced my cheek with his fingers. "I'm sorry I didn't tell you earlier. But I'm not sorry for pursuing you. And I am *not* sorry for falling in love with you."

I turned my face into his hand, aching for his touch. Even as guilt wormed through my insides.

"Rian won't ever forgive you for this," I said quietly. "If you had made up with him first, maybe…. But this…*us*…"

Liam rested his forehead on mine, his arms around me, holding me like I was his lifeline.

"As much as it would kill me," he said, "if I had to choose between Rian and you, I'd choose you. In every lifetime, in every way."

He pulled back, staring into my eyes as he confessed.

"I love my brother. But *you* are my world."

"I don't like it," Liam said as he held the top end of a thrifted mustard suede couch.

Grunting as I pushed from lower on the stairs, I frowned, "You don't like what?"

Liam checked over his shoulder for the last step before nudging the front door open with his foot.

"Watch your fingers there," he said before adding, "I don't like it at all."

We both sighed when we were finally able to set down the yellow second-hand monster in the centre of the tiny but cosy living room. Breathing heavily, I put my hands on my hips and stared down at the off-kilter cushions.

"I mean, you could have told me that before we lugged it up three flights of stairs," I said.

I looked up to find Liam frowning. His eyes bounced between me and the '70s relic and back again.

"I don't mean the couch, Ry."

"What do you mean?"

Liam came toward me, waving his hand vaguely. "All of this."

He wrapped me in his arms and sent us both toppling over the back of the couch. We landed in a tangled mess.

Liam brushed the hair from my face, eyes soft on mine. "I don't think you living here is a good idea. I think you should move in with *me*."

"We talked about this," I said softly.

Liam didn't understand why I needed my own place. The kind of place I liked: a temporary sublet. Paid in cash. No name attached. No trail to follow.

I was still fighting *staying*. A part of me still feared putting down roots. Still had one foot out the door just in case it became too dangerous. After all, it'd been what had kept me alive so far.

"And," he added, "I don't think it's a good idea that *you* are the one to tell Rian about us being together."

"We talked about this, too," I said with a gentle smile.

That one had been more contentious. Late night whiskeys. Half-naked arguing. Sex to blow off pent-up steam.

Liam wanted to be the one to tell him. He felt he owed his brother that much at least.

But I feared that Rian's hatred would blind him to anything Liam said.

I argued that at least if the words were coming from my mouth, he could at least maybe see *me*. His best friend. Someone he trusted.

Liam sighed.

"And you still haven't done it." His voice was soft but I could hear the strains of accusation in it.

"I will," I told him. "I just haven't found the right time yet."

Liam said nothing, but I could see the way he pursed his lips that there was too much he wasn't saying.

In truth, it'd been weeks since the night Liam finally confessed.

I'd had all the time Rian and I were alone in the apartment. All those moments at Dublin Ink when Conor and Aurnia went into the back storage room for a "break" or Mason left to watch one of Rachel's practices.

I'd had plenty of times alone with Rian. But I was afraid once I started speaking it would all come crashing down.

I noticed after several minutes lost in thought that Liam was smiling at me.

"Most importantly," he said, "I really don't think it's a good idea for us to ever get up from this couch."

I squirmed against him with a gleeful giggle. Felt the outline of his erection straining against his jeans on my thigh.

Our eyes locked and I knew: we were avoiding reality. We were falling back in ourselves, indulging ourselves in the lie that it was just the two of us. No one else.

It was a temptation we fell for time and time again. There on the couch was no different. The smell of engine oil on Liam's coat. The strength of his arm around the small of my back, sliding down to my ass beneath the waistline of my miniskirt. The circling of his thumb over my hardening nipple under my cropped black sweater.

The front door to my new apartment was still open. The March air was blowing in up the stairs from the lobby door we'd wedged open, icy on the skin Liam was exposing with prowling hands. But I didn't care.

It was warm against Liam.

"Ry!" I went rigid when a familiar voice called from the stairwell, "How many more flights is it? I'm dying here!"

Liam's eyes were saucers on mine.

It was Rian.

RY

"It's Rian!" I hissed. "Hide!"

I tried to ignore the disappointed look Liam gave me as leapt off the couch, my heart pounding. This was *not* the right time.

I tried a casual laugh as I pulled back down my sweater and shouted out the open door, "Conor would be taking the stairs two at a time."

Liam had just enough time to dart around the corner into the kitchen when Rian appeared at the top of the stairs. I straightened the pleats of my skirt as he collapsed over a tall stack of brown boxes.

"Insulting my masculinity," Rian said breathlessly, grinning up at me. "Thanks."

"I'm here to make sure your ego doesn't get too big."

Rian propped up his chin with his hand. "You know, I'm very secure in my manhood. And I don't define myself by the size of my muscles, but rather the size of my—"

"Brain?" I finished for him.

"Artistic talent." He grinned. "Obviously."

I laughed and went over to help him up.

"What are you doing here?" I asked as I kissed his cheek, hoping my voice didn't jump an octave or two. "You surprised me."

"But a pleasant one, right?"

I forced myself to nod and glanced toward the kitchen where I could see Liam peering out at us.

Goddamn. If Rian decided he wanted a glass of water, we were fucked.

"You really should have called before. I've not set everything up yet. I mean," I snuck another look at the kitchen, "I can't even offer you a drink because the glasses haven't been unpacked."

"Which is why I'm here, silly."

"*What?*"

"Ry," Rian said, gripping my shoulder, "you've done so much for me. I'm not sure I'll ever be able to repay you. When you insisted on moving out of my apartment, even when I begged you to stay… I mean, helping a friend move is seriously the absolute least I could do."

Oh shite. He was *staying*? Now what? I had to get him out of the apartment so that Liam could sneak out.

"I really appreciate it," I told him, guiding him toward the door. "But I only have a few things left at your place."

"Oh, that reminds me…" Rian said, running down the stairs two at a time.

"Reminds you what?" I called out after him.

He didn't answer, disappearing as he rounded the first landing. I nearly yelped when Liam appeared behind me.

"Tell him," he hissed, pointing downstairs.

"He's going to see you," I whispered back, shoving at Liam's chest.

"Tell him," Liam insisted as he turned to go back to hide. "Tell him now!"

I waved my hand at him and hurried downstairs to see a truck loaded with the rest of my stuff before Rian kicked it shut with his heel, arms piled high with mismatched thrifted pillows.

"Mason let me use his truck," he said. "He couldn't believe it when I told him you were getting a place."

"Why's that?"

"Said he swore you were out of here the second I got back," Rian explained stair after stair. "Said the open road called to you or something."

"Yeah..." I said noncommittally.

"Said something must have changed," Rian added, glancing over his shoulder as he stepped back inside my apartment.

I didn't realise until he was standing there, looking at me, that it was more of a question than a statement. I fumbled for an answer.

Rian dropped the pillows on the couch. "You're packing in your spinach, huh?"

"What?"

He tapped his finger on the big couch.

I felt my cheeks warm. There was no way I got this couch up those flight of stairs myself.

I could practically hear Liam saying, *"Tell him. Tell him now!"*

"Oh, em, a neighbour helped," I said, resisting the instinct to scratch at the back of my neck. Isn't that what liars always did?

Rian nodded. "Nice neighbours," he said a little distractedly, eyes drifting around the rest of the room.

I glanced toward the entrance to the kitchen. Liam had

hidden somewhere just out of sight. Surely Rian didn't suspect…

When I looked back at Rian his eyes were fixed on mine.

"You know, I told Mason that maybe you just remembered how much you liked Dublin," Rian said, sinking down to rest against the back of the couch. He crossed his arms and added, "But Mason said nobody really ever stays for a city. Said he would have left Vegas with us had it not been for Rachel."

I needed to tell him. I'd pushed it off long enough. He was even opening the door for me. Opening it wide open.

But I found my throat dry. My head buzzed and refused to form words. I couldn't lose my best friend.

"I told him it wasn't likely that you'd met someone," Rian continued, "because you would have told me for sure. If you'd met someone."

I swallowed back a knot.

Rian scratched at some dried paint on his jeans. His kept his gaze down as he asked, "Wouldn't you, Ry?"

Coming beside him, I grabbed one of the pillows and smacked him playfully on the back of the head.

"You know I've never been the commitment type," I said, struggling to sound casual, playful. The way friends sound when they're not hiding hurtful secrets from each other. "Mason of all people should know a one-night stand kinda gal when he sees one."

Rian caught the pillow when I went to hit him lightly once more.

"I can set you up with some guys, if you want," he said. "Nice guys. *Nice guys*, Ry. Guys that will treat you right. Good, decent men. Not bad guys."

Rian's eyes were drilling holes through mine. I was sure

that he knew every hidden corner of my heart. Could see every truth I tried to keep in the shadows.

"I don't want that, Rian," I said, relieved to be able to say something honest at last. "I've never wanted that."

Rian pushed himself up to standing. "Maybe you should."

I wondered if Liam could hear us, wherever he was hidden. I wondered if he could tell which parts I'd said were lies. And which weren't.

Rian and I brought up the rest of what he'd loaded up in Mason's car. I thanked him and the kiss he gave to my cheek was the same one he'd always given.

But a rift was opening between us. Rian could sense the rumblings underfoot even if he only had suspicions as to their cause.

I needed to tell him.

But I needed to trust I wouldn't lose him first. And I wasn't sure when I ever would.

If I ever would.

After closing the door behind me, I went to sit on the edge of the kitchen island. I kicked my feet back and forth in the silence.

A minute or two later, the pantry door creaked open an inch or two. My head fell back over my shoulder to catch Liam poking his head out.

"Coast clear?" he asked.

I nodded.

Liam came to stand between my legs.

"You didn't tell him," he said, stroking my thighs.

"I know," I said, not sure what else to say.

Maybe I should have told him how scared I was. Maybe, as he lifted his eyes through dark eyelashes to find mine, he already knew.

"So I'm just a one-night stand, huh?" he asked, fingers teasing my inner thighs. A smile raised playfully the corner of his lips.

I leaned back. Arched an eyebrow. "Oh, sorry, was that news to you?"

Liam pressed kisses along my collarbones before licking a hot trail up my throat. "A bad guy one-night stand."

I stopped him before he kissed my lips. My eyes met his.

"You're not a bad man, Liam," I said softly.

Pain filled his eyes and he glanced away, his throat working before he spoke.

"That's not what Rian thinks."

"Rian's wrong." I laid my hand on the back of his neck and played with the ends of his hair. "He'll come around. Because I need *you*. Whatever you are. Good or bad. Right or wrong."

I drew Liam to me and he kissed me.

"It's late," he said against my mouth. "Your place is still a mess. Come over to my place for dinner."

I shook my head. I felt I owed it somehow to Rian not to. My punishment for not fessing up.

I walked Liam to the door. He gave me one last goodnight kiss.

I waited for him to take the stairs. But he did not.

He walked to the door right next to mine, pulled out a key and with a whistle he opened the door *next door*.

"What the fuck?" I spat out.

He grinned at me over his shoulder. "Yes?"

"What the hell are you doing?"

He shrugged. "Since you wouldn't move in with me, I moved in next door."

LIAM

Ryleigh made it three hours before breaking. Three hours before the annoyed knock came at my door.

I opened it to find my grey-eyed hellcat glaring at me with fists on hips.

"What's the craic, neighbour?" I said.

"Stop. Smiling," Ry said as she stabbed me in the chest with her finger.

"I'm not," I told her, grinning like a Cheshire cat as I leaned against the frame of my front door, crossing my arms.

Ry pinched her bottom lip between her teeth as she stretched up onto her toes, craning her neck to try to peer past my shoulders inside.

"You want to come in?" I asked, trying not to enjoy this moment.

"*No.*"

I repressed a laugh. "Then how can I help you, miss?"

Ry shot me a glare. "'*Miss*'?"

"Are you in need of some *neighbourly* assistance?"

"I said stop smiling," she grumbled.

Ry glanced back toward the door to her apartment. The one right next to mine.

How many times had she come to stand where she was standing now? How many times had she raised her fist, hesitated, decided that she could wait a minute or two longer? An hour or two longer?

Did she press her ear against the thin walls dividing us? Was that what made it worse? Knowing I was just. right. there.

"Cup of sugar?" I asked, unable to hide my grin anymore.

Ry's eyes flashed to mine, a warning.

"Eggs?" I said, knowing I was going to pay for it but enjoying myself way too much.

I heard a growl of frustration and it was absolutely delicious. It was the same growl she made when I was ignoring her nipples, circling my tongue round and round her breasts without even a lick for those rosy, hard buds.

I'd heard it many a time when I stilled inside of her, loosened my hand round her throat, released her wrists I'd had pinned above her head.

It was the growl of frustration when she wanted something. When it was right there in front of her. When all she had to do was ask for it...beg for it.

"A scoop of laundry detergent perhaps?" I asked.

I drummed my fingers along my arms as Ry struggled against herself. She didn't like asking for what she wanted.

But I liked it. I liked it a hell of a lot. I loved hearing her ask, hearing her beg.

She sighed and glared up at me.

"Li-am," she said, emphasising my name like I was supposed to know what it meant.

I did, of course. But I wasn't done pretending I didn't.

"And you're Ry," I said, smirking at her.

God, she was adorable when she was pissed.

I stuck out my hand. "Nice to meet you, *neighbour.*"

If Ry was holding a tattoo gun, I would not have been the least bit surprised to have been stabbed by it.

When she did not make a move to shake my hand, I shrugged and tucked it back into my arm folded across my chest.

"What are you doing?" Ry finally asked.

"I was just going to eat dinner actually."

I thumbed over my shoulder casually as Ry's knuckles whitened over the crumpled grip of her miniskirt.

"I mean, what are you doing with this place?" she clarified.

I looked over my shoulder into the apartment, the layout a mirror image of Ry's.

I took my time studying it. I liked when Ry squirmed.

When I turned back to face her, she was about ready to explode.

"You mean like in terms of decorating?" I asked, tapping a finger on my chin. "I don't know, I kind of go for that minimalist sort of—"

The heel of Ry's palm packed more of a punch than I would have expected as she shoved me in the chest.

I stepped back half a step and she stormed inside, slamming the door behind her.

"Welcome," I said as Ry paced angrily in front of me. "Make yourself at home."

She pointed a finger at me as she spun on her heel and said, "For the last time, *no* smiling."

This, of course, made me smirk all the more.

"Can I offer you a glass of wine?" I asked, heading off toward the kitchen.

"Liam!" Ry shouted after me.

Even with my back turned to her, I could see those little balled-up fingers inked in black.

"Liam, what are you *doing*?"

Stepping inside the kitchen, I called back, "I'm deciding between a red or a white. What are your thoughts on Merlot? Or are you more in a Sav Blanc kinda mood?"

I returned with both, one in each hand.

She stood in my sparsely furnished living room, breathing heavily, fury wafting off of her in waves.

But I could see how she pressed her thighs together and the way her nipples poked out from her cropped sweater.

Oh, she hated me just a little bit right now. But she also loved me. And she wanted the shite out of me.

I grinned at her and held out both bottles. "You pick, *neighbour*."

"What are you doing, Liam?" she said through gritted teeth, her glare boring right through me.

I set down both bottles and walked right up to her as close as I could without touching her. My shadow loomed above hers on the floor, across the couch, up onto the wall.

This was important.

And she needed to hear me.

So I wasn't past using my size to intimidate her just a little.

"I'll tell you what I'm doing," I said, my voice darker than it was before. "You may be fine taking it slow, but I am *not*. You can stall with Rian, but I am *not* going to let you stall with me. Not anymore. I'm done waiting for what I want. I'm taking it."

Her chest still rose and fell too heavily as if catching her breath was difficult. Her pupils blown out so wide they were practically black with hate and need all mixed in at once, the most intoxicating combination.

"I want *you*, Ry."

Her shuddering exhales were hot around my jaw.

"If you sink in your heels, I'll throw you over my shoulder. If you pull your foot off the gas, I'll drag you out of the driver's seat. Throw you in the fucking trunk if I have to. If you think we're going to take this race at a nice, easy pace, I'm going to push you till your lungs are burning, screaming, *aching*."

Silence filled the apartment, except for the small fire crackling in my gas fireplace, making our stuttered breathing all too loud.

A full-body shiver coursed through Ry. I felt it like a pebble on a railroad track. Something was coming.

I grinned. Yeah, she would be coming around my cock.

I lunged for her, tearing her pretty cropped black sweater off her as she fought me. A pleased smile crossed my lips as I found Ry wasn't wearing panties as I ripped off her skirt too.

"No panties. Such a naughty neighbour."

"Liam," she cried out, slapping my arms. Shaking my head, I pinned her arms to her sides as I admired her naked beauty.

"Mine," I said before I pulled her against me, kissing her, claiming her.

I was fucking done waiting. I wouldn't be denied any longer.

She gasped when I shoved her forward violently, folded her over at the edge of the couch.

"You need to learn I'll always get what I want," I rumbled, releasing my cock and kicking off my pants. "I'm going to pump you so full of my cum you'll never run from me again."

"What? I'll fall pregnant," she cried out over her shoulder.

I tugged my shirt off me and advanced on her delicious ass up in the air for me.

"That is the point, baby."

"No." She clambered over the couch, struggling to get away from me. I grunted as she kicked at me. Scrambling away, she stumbled to her feet.

She glanced at the door behind me. But I was between it and her and she was naked.

I grinned. She was not getting away.

"I know you're scared. But deep down, you want to belong to me," I growled, stroking my cock as I stalked her across the room.

"No," she lied.

She backed up until she slammed into the wall. She let out a whimper as I caught her, pinning her to the brick as I ground my cock against her, enjoying her squirming as she writhed against me.

"Lying to me means I have to punish you."

She let out a whimper and I knew she was already ready for me, the threat of pain never failing to get her soaking wet.

But not yet. I was going to enjoy making this last.

I pushed her down and she slid to her knees, only half resisting now.

"Now open that lying little mouth."

She did. I slid my cock deep into her mouth until her head bumped against the wall. Fuck, she felt so fucking good, her tongue flat against the underside of my head.

I twisted my fingers into her hair and pinned her head to the wall as I fucked her mouth.

"Such a good girl," I said between groans.

Her lashes were wet as she stared up at me.

"Fuck, look at you, my pretty little liar. Tell me again how much you don't want to be fucked and filled?"

She sucked harder, her hands coming up to stroke at my balls and I rushed up to the edge.

I tugged my cock away from her and tsked.

"Naughty neighbour," I chastised, "trying to get me to cum into your mouth instead of that pussy. You obviously need more…education."

I picked her up and carried her to the rug in front of my fireplace. I pushed her down onto all fours. "I am going to enjoy putting a baby in you."

She let out a moan. I grabbed the gorgeous globe of her ass, spreading it wide to stare at her juicy cunt.

"Fuck, you are dripping at the idea of being filled with my cum."

I rubbed her clit with my thumb, I watched as she writhed like a cat in heat. She wanted it. I knew she did. She wanted this.

"You might say you don't want it, but your body never lies to me."

Flipping her over, I caged her in my arms, my hand on her throat as I kissed her softly.

I placed her other hand on my chest.

"Yours. I'm yours, Ryleigh, stop fighting me."

Ry melted against me, kissing me back. Lifting her leg onto my hip, I lined my cock up with her pussy and pushed inside of her.

I let out a groan as her pussy fit me like a glove, skin on skin.

"No more condoms," I promised, thrusting deeper inside of her. "Nothing left between us."

I squeezed her throat tightly as I fucked her, willing her to understand.

"It's you and me forever, baby."

As I ground the base of my cock against her clit, her strangled screams turned into whimpers and cries. Her eyes softened as I crowded her space, pouring out my love for her as I pounded into her.

"I won't ever let you leave me," I promised her. "Even when you get scared and want to leave."

Her eyes rolled as she got closer to release, wrapping her other leg around me as her body gave in. But her fingers scratched my back as her mind still warred against me, causing me to hiss.

She was so used to fighting, she saw danger where there was none.

Yes, I was dangerous. A boy didn't get raised in a house full of violence without becoming dangerous. But never to her.

"You will never be alone again," I whispered, feeling as her walls began to flutter around my cock. My girl was close to coming for me. "I am yours. I will fight the darkness with you. Alongside you. For you."

I released my grip on her throat just enough for her to gasp in a breath.

"Liam," she said on a sob and my heart clenched.

Not Lee. But Liam.

I know, baby girl. I know. I see you. I kissed her face, tasting her tears.

I held her tightly as I fucked her. As I claimed her.

Her body shuddered in my arms as she came. My balls

drew up tightly as I pumped her full of hot cum.

As we both came down to earth, I rolled her onto my chest and buried my face in her sweet-smelling hair.

I would love to have a little girl that looked exactly like her. Or a little boy. God, they would break some hearts.

It was a long time before Ryleigh pulled back. "It's getting late."

I tugged her back onto my chest.

"Stay."

She shook her head and pushed herself up again, scrambling to her feet and searching for her clothes.

"I've got to shower." She shot me a look. "And I want to sleep in my bed tonight."

"Alright," I said, getting up and tugging on my briefs.

We would sleep at her place then.

I snatched my keys and followed her out to her door as she opened it.

She stopped and held out a hand, literally holding me at arm's length. "I'm sleeping in my bed alone."

She slipped into her apartment and slammed the door in my face.

I wiped my face as I leaned against her doorframe.

Okay, maybe I got a little carried away.

But she was playing right along with me.

Until she wasn't.

I knocked on the door. "Ryleigh?"

She didn't answer.

"I'm right next door if you need me."

She still didn't answer.

It was only when I heard her shower running that I turned back to my apartment.

I lay in bed for a long time, listening through the walls for sounds of her moving around her room as she readied for bed.

How long was she going to keep this wall up between us? How long until she accepted that she was mine and I was hers?

How much longer did I have to keep fighting that part of Ryleigh that had one foot out the door?

What did I have to do to make her trust that I was not leaving her, ever? That I was her family. Would she ever let me in, fully let me in?

I was awake for hours, thinking about all these things, long after the creaks of her tossing and turning in bed stopped.

So I was wide awake when she started screaming.

RY

Balor held me down as he unzipped his pants, pushing them down to his ankles, his cloying oppressive weight pressing down on me, his vile touch slimy against my raw bare skin.

His fingers closed over my mouth as I began to scream.

I heard the shattering of wood, the dreadful moan of splintering boards, as he kicked through my door. I tore at the sheets and begged my sleep-heavy limbs to *run*.

He loomed tall and imposing in the doorway for only a second before lunging for me. Squeezing my eyes shut, I screamed and begged myself to disappear from this nightmare.

Instead I was pulled from the sheets. I fought the monster trying to pull me into his lap.

Liam's voice broke through, calling my name again and again.

"I'm here. I'm here, baby. You're safe."

I clung to him, my face buried into his neck, his familiar scent breaking through to me.

Liam was here.

I was safe.

The adrenaline draining from my body left me paralysed. My only movements were involuntary trembles as the tears streamed down the sides of my face.

"Liam?" I whispered, finding it hard even to move my lips.

My fingers curled into his hair, his torso bare, the heat rolling off him like a balm.

Liam pulled me in tighter against him.

"I—" Liam's voice came out as a hoarse croak.

If I didn't know any better, I would have assumed that he'd been the one who had been screaming his lungs out.

Taking a shuddering breath, he tried again, "I— Ry, I've never, *never*— I've had some of the darkest moments a person can have… I—I've felt like the whole world was hopeless, nothing but a black pit I couldn't possibly claw my way out of, but… Ry, I've *never* felt fear like when I heard you scream like that before."

He shuddered again. I wondered if he was feeling what I was feeling. Like he was thawing out.

"I thought someone was attacking you. Hurting you. *Killing* you."

My chest against his chest as I huddled against him, ankles crossed behind his back, arms stretched round his ribcage.

My sobs lessened as Liam ran his hands over the back of my head, smoothing the hair disturbed by my nightmare.

It was just a nightmare.

"Ry…" Liam whispered.

Only a nightmare.

"Ry…"

"It wasn't just a nightmare," I blurted out.

Liam's fingers stilled. I thought his heart followed.

I laid a palm against his bare chest. Willed him to breathe. Willed him to stay with me.

Liam shifted so that he could study my face. He looked so young in that moment.

I wondered what it would have been like, had I had him all those years ago. Someone I felt I could trust. Someone I felt I could…share my darkness with.

"Tell me," Liam whispered, as if he could read my very thoughts.

"I was fairly young when I discovered I liked it…a little rough," I said, noticing that my heart was no longer skipping painfully. "But I was old enough to know to be smart about it. To know that I wanted it from the right person. Someone I trusted. And connected with. Because that's what it was always about for me. That trust."

My fingers played at Liam's collarbone.

I continued, "I made a profile on a BDSM site. To find people who were interested in that kind of thing, too. I made sure it didn't have my real name or anything like that. Nothing that would let anyone find me. I vetted guys before meeting up. It was all fine for so long."

I fell into silence remembering how the night seemed to press down on my shoulders in that fateful moment. It felt so heavy. Like it had fingers to dig into my skin.

"Ry?" Liam asked softly.

I blinked and found his eyes searching mine. I swallowed down the emotion that was threatening to choke me.

And I began to speak.

He'd been charming. He'd done all the gentlemanly things at The White Room. I'd enjoyed him sharing it with me, the kind of exclusive club for millionaires that I could never dream of stepping inside otherwise.

He'd been thoughtful enough to select the table with the best view overlooking the city. We laughed over a fantastic meal with exquisite service. And, I reminded myself, he had been charming.

So why couldn't I shake the unsettling feeling in my stomach.

"Nightcap at my place?" he asked.

I knew the warning signs like the back of my hand. As he waited for my response while the valet fetched his car, I went through them.

Balor checked out. It was just the billionaire thing, I told myself.

That was the reason he seemed to be a little too natural, a little too casual, a little too...above it all. The distant, almost vacant look I caught a few times while we waited for a cocktail or the next course, champagne with dessert.

When you have an unfathomable amount of money, life itself must become slightly unfathomable.

He hadn't done anything that remotely came close to crossing a line. And he was interested in what I was interested in.

"A nightcap would be lovely," I said.

Balor didn't touch me in the car on the way to his mansion. In fact, he hardly looked at me. And he did not speak.

To reassure myself, I glanced at him from time to time. But whenever I thought I saw that blank, almost dead look, he blinked and I saw a normal guy.

I was just being paranoid. I settled against the seat as Balor steered his whining sports car around the hairpin turns in the pitch-black dark.

But I couldn't stop myself from glancing again. Searching. Searching for what I missed.

Massive wrought-iron gates swung open and Balor pulled his car around a stunning stone fountain.

I should have found the sprawling mansion beautiful.

But it was well past midnight and every window was lit up a garish yellow. I don't know why exactly, but it made my skin crawl.

"Expecting guests?" I laughed, my nerves jangling.

Balor was already out of the car, crossing in front of the hood, opening my door, I thought, a little too roughly.

But his smile as he leaned down to offer his hand was gracious.

Still, I didn't like how much I had to hold onto his arm as my ankles wobbled in my high heels.

"No tour," I joked when Balor moved directly toward the stairs when we entered the grand foyer, my arm falling limply from his.

Balor spoke to the top of the stairs instead of me when he said in a strange voice, "We both know there's only one room you want to see, Ryleigh."

The pretence of the nightcap was completely forgotten as he led me up one side of the split grand staircase toward his bedroom. I was once again unnerved by how he didn't glance behind him to make sure I was still following.

There was no playful brush of fingers on the marble staircase, no pressing me against the wall in the too brightly lit hallway to nip at each other's wine-stained lips, no knowing smiles exchanged at the closed door, his hand hesitating on the doorknob to allow me to consent.

Balor swung open a door and stepped aside with a sweep of his arm. I glanced to the front door. I shook off my paranoia and walked toward Balor. The rasp of my heels sounded strange in my ears.

What I discovered was apparently the only room in the mansion not fully illuminated.

"Go on," Balor said, almost breathlessly. "Isn't this what you wanted?"

I checked his eyes once more. His pupils were wide. But we were there for sex after all, right?

I stepped inside. Balor flipped a switch and low lights came on along the floorboards. Horrible, contorted shadows looked like monsters.

I gasped. This wasn't a bedroom.

Black padded leather lined every wall and everywhere were whips and chains, metal barred cages and paddles, electric cattle prodders and adjustable tables with straps for wrists and ankles.

I retreated back a few steps and collided into his chest. I hadn't heard him come into the room.

"Wait..." I said, trying to step around him toward the exit.

He caught me by the throat. The suddenness of it startled me.

This wasn't how this worked. There was supposed to be talk around boundaries. Clear consent. Respect. A safe word.

I tried to push Balor off of me, but he just grinned. I clawed at his fingers as he groped at my breasts.

"We don't even have a safe word yet," I gasped. "Let go."

He laughed. "It's better without a safe word."

He kicked the door shut with his heel.

Fear spiked in my chest seeing my way out blend in seamlessly with the wall, with all the walls. When Balor began walking me backwards, I panicked.

"Please," I said. I thought I could bargain for time. "Balor, we haven't started yet. Just— I'm not ready yet."

He slammed me roughly against the table which was positioned perpendicular to the floor.

He tore at my dress as he said, "We started the second you posted what you really wanted online."

I gasped when he slapped my bare breast. There was no pleasure with this kind of pain. I could see it in his eyes: he wanted to hurt me. It had nothing to do with getting me off.

He got off on violence, pure violence.

"I'm leaving," I said, but he pressed himself against me and rubbed his erection into my thigh.

"Yes," he groaned, licking my throat. "Try and leave. I like it when they fight."

He stuck his hand under my skirt.

I shoved him away. "I said stop, asshole."

At first all I heard was the crack of his knuckles against my cheekbone. There was nothing at all as I fell to the cool metal floors.

But my vision went in and out. I gingerly touched my face, the hot pain came out of nowhere and left me breathless. I gasped for air, struggling to understand what the fuck just happened.

He wrenched me back by my hair. My scalp screamed as he pulled till I was forced to look into his insane eyes.

Leaning over me, his foul breath hit my face. "Disrespect me again and I'll kill you, bitch."

I believed him. Balor was rich enough, powerful enough that women like me were expendable for his fun. I should have known when I saw that look in his eyes.

Rules didn't apply to him. If he went too far in this playroom of his, there would be no consequences for him.

Balor shoved me down roughly and was on top of me before I could squirm away. Pinning me down, he grabbed a whip from the stand.

I screamed when he brought it down hard on my exposed chest. I covered my face as he did it several more times.

When he crawled off of me, I looked around for something to fight back with. I reached for a thick chain, but he dragged me across the floor by my ankles.

The floor scraped my back and my dress rode up, my skin burning from the carpet.

He was heading toward a cage. Bile rose up in my throat. If he got me locked up in there, there would be no escape. Ever.

I kicked out and took him enough by surprise for him to drop my legs. I scrambled away into a corner of red velvet cushions, but he straddled the backs of my thighs before I could get away.

"Bitch," Balor snarled.

My dress up around my waist, he shoved my panties aside and shoved a finger into me. I screamed at the pain of his violation.

I heard him unzipping his pants behind me.

No. I couldn't just let him. I had to fight.

I flailed my hands out, reaching for something, anything. I knocked the table over with a crash, glass shattering and heavy metal toys rolling across the carpet.

Balor flipped me over to face him.

"I like a little fight. But not this much."

His cock was out, big and angry red. Fear burned bitter through my blood.

"I'm going to fuck all your holes raw," he said laughing, and then began to choke me.

This was not a love-necklace. His fingers crushed my windpipe, bruising my skin, cutting off all my air.

He was trying to knock me out.

Or kill me.

Either way, I would not survive whatever he had planned if he succeeded.

I scrambled around on the carpet, ignoring the sting of broken glass. I grabbed something heavy and cold: a giant metal butt plug.

With a scream, I sent it crashing down atop Balor's head.

He blinked slowly and toppled off of me. It was all I needed to make a run for it.

I didn't know whether I'd just stunned him...or killed him.

But I wasn't waiting around to find out.

I fled the mansion in the middle of the night, clothes torn, body bruised and bloody.

Fear shivered down my spine as I heard him yelling after me as I ran.

I hadn't killed him.

I'd just pissed him off. Pissed off a sadistic billionaire who knew where I lived.

"I'll fucking kill him." Liam's voice echoed through the silent room, shaking with rage. "Tell me where he lives. Where he took you."

I shook my head. "I don't know. His car had tinted windows and I wasn't paying attention to where we were going.

"That's why you left Dublin."

Tears filled my eyes as I nodded. I blinked them open and Liam caught the first falling drop with his thumb.

"I made the cabbie stop at my apartment just long enough to shove a passport, cash and clothes into a bag. I cleaned myself up at the train station. Got on the first train to Belfast. From there, I took the first flight out. I made up some lie to Rian. Some bullshite about needing to see the world."

Liam pulled me in tighter.

"I never wanted to leave," I admitted. "Dublin was my home."

"And you didn't ever tell Rian?" Liam asked.

"I couldn't."

"Why not?"

It was a complicated question. And an even more complicated answer.

"I...he would have told me to stay," I said slowly. "He would have believed he could keep me safe. I...I couldn't risk his life."

Liam was silent for a moment. Then he kissed the tears off my cheeks. "I understand why you took so long to tell me. But

Ryleigh," he said, his voice growing fierce, "you are mine to protect now. You don't keep things from me anymore, you got it? You don't carry this shit alone."

Inside, a little part of me dared to hope he was right.

Liam drew me to him. I felt the racing of his heart as he pulled off my top and pressed my breasts against his warmth.

He lowered me onto his length and tried to teach my heart how to beat in time with his.

"Mine to protect," he said over and over again as he fucked me, as he made unbreakable promises to me with his body. "I won't let anyone hurt you."

I almost believed him.

But Balor was still out there.

Rian was still so far out of reach.

Nothing had changed.

And yet everything had. Liam and I had tied chains around each other.

The tattoo of the couple wrapped round in iron was our future.

I'd dreamed of it then. Fantasised about it in the pink glow of the tattoo parlour.

But now I was afraid that we might be too close.

When I was dragged into deep waters, how were we to swim? Chained up tight, chest to chest, how were we to do anything other than drown?

LIAM

It wasn't just about me anymore. Wasn't even just about Rian.

It was about the woman I loved. Her life. Her safety. Her trust.

After her nightmare, I carried Ry into my apartment and tucked her against me. But it was hours before she stopped trembling and her breathing finally evened out.

My heart ached as I curled around her like armour.

I couldn't be by her side every single second. I needed an army to keep Ry safe, and I needed to start recruiting. And Rian was first in line.

I wrenched open the front door of Dublin Ink, something I'd avoided doing for weeks. But now I had a purpose.

It was no longer about me and that black pit in my heart. It was about keeping Ry safe in Dublin until I could fix it, permanently. I had one purpose, one focus as the little bell rang above my head.

But that didn't mean seeing my brother's eyes morph into pinpricks of hatred didn't feel like a punch to my gut.

Rian pushed out of his chair so violently that it crashed back, toppling over and tearing against the brick wall behind him. He was alone in the shop, but I was fairly certain he would have shouted even if there had been a client in each chair.

"Get the fuck out!"

He advanced on me like he was going to shove me right out onto the sidewalk if I didn't move. Like I didn't have half a head on him. And a good thirty pounds of muscle.

"Rian, we can talk like adults, can't we?" I tried, holding up my hands as if that alone could prove my innocence.

Rian wrenched open the front door and jammed his finger out into the deepening dusk.

"Paying customers only," he said, chest heaving.

The little bell's echo faded and then died. A car passed in the street outside. Its headlights fell on us and then that too moved on. We could hear its tires for a block or two and then nothing. We stood there and only the occasional snap and pop of the neon sign on the wall above the stairs marked that any time was passing at all.

"Well," I said, "it seems I'm in luck."

Rian's eyes narrowed suspiciously.

I held up my hands in a loose shrug. "That's what I am."

Rian's hand had yet to fall from where he pointed outside. It did then. Just an inch or two.

"You're what?" he asked.

I think he already knew the answer. I think he already resented it.

But there was no avoiding it. No escaping it.

Hell, he already hated me. Why not let him hate me a little more if it gave me a chance?

"A paying customer," I said.

Rian scoffed. He still thought there was a way out of this. Some way that I would just leave.

"*You* want a tattoo?" he said, spitting the words.

I nodded.

I didn't think this was the right moment to show him all the ink under my clothes that his best friend had marked me with.

Rian shook his head, laughing bitterly. "Little goody-goody farm boy wants a *tattoo?*"

"This is a tattoo shop, isn't it?"

The sides of his jaw twitched as he looked outside. Dark was falling fast.

He looked back inside the shop. The black leather chairs. The metal tools flashing in the neon light.

"They're permanent, you know," he said, eyes filled with hatred as he looked at me. "They're a stain you can't wash out. A sin there's no forgiveness for. There's no coming back from it. Once it's done, it's done. I'm not sure you understand *that,* Liam."

I didn't flinch from Rian's death stare. Not even when hurt flashed behind his eyes like lightning in a turbulent grey sky.

That's what stung my heart the most; the hurt I knew was hidden beneath the fury.

I kept my eyes fixed on my brother. "I understand."

Rian's arm fell from the door like a domino. It set everything in motion. The door slamming shut. The clanging and clattering of tools as he prepared. "Fuck," muttered angrily under his breath. Him pounding his fist against the seat of a black leather tattoo chair.

"Well?" he shouted at me, barely keeping control over himself.

I slipped off my jacket as he watched me like a hawk.

Careful to keep my shirt covered over the tattoos Ry gave me, I rolled up my sleeve to the elbow.

I lowered myself into the chair next to my brother carefully. Afraid that any jerky movement would send him running. Or stabbing. I knew tattoo artists weren't afraid to turn their tools into weapons.

Rian looked like he wanted to spit onto my inner wrist much more than he wanted to tattoo it.

"Why do you want a tattoo there?" he asked, keeping his eyes shadowed.

I ran a thumb over my skin. My calluses caught on that papery flesh over blue veins.

It sounded like my voice got lost in the height of the atrium ceilings of the parlour as I said, "They remind me of the rivers on our land."

Rian was silent for a moment. "That's not my land anymore."

"It's not mine either," I said, unable to keep the sadness from seeping into my words, as few as they may be. "Not anymore."

If Rian was surprised by what I said, he hid it well beneath his stormy brow. He pulled on black latex gloves, snapping them loudly.

"I don't understand," Rian said, setting a fresh needle into his gun. "Do you want it covered up or highlighted? These 'rivers' of yours?"

The rage hadn't subsided in him, though it burned lower. But even a fool knows embers hold their heat.

"Do you want to forget or remember?" he said.

"I don't think forgetting is possible," I replied.

Rian switched on the tattoo gun. The low rattle it gave

was a welcome relief to the crushing silence of the tattoo parlour.

"I don't think remembering is either," Rian said, his eyes avoiding mine.

"I remember," I said quickly.

Rian laughed darkly. "No, you don't."

I grabbed Rian's wrist as he went to pierce my vein with the needle.

"I remember," I said in a low hiss.

Rian slowly but calmly peeled my fingers away from him. My hand resembled a dead spider, its legs curled in. He shook me off. My hand fell heavy.

"Paying customers only," he reminded me.

I hissed when the needle found my skin. I knew then that Ry had been gentle. Gentle with her pain.

Rian, on the other hand, was not. He gave me no mercy. I understood there would be no breaks. No checking that I was doing alright. He would tattoo me at a punishing pace, take my money, and be right back at the door, finger pointing into the dark.

"I need to tell you something," I said through slightly clenched teeth.

The skin of the inner wrist was delicate. More nerve endings there than on my back. The body wanted you to feel there, at the hands. In the fingers. It wanted you to experience the pleasure of touch. The slick of soft wetness between a woman's legs. A droplet of sweat in the arched small of a back. The wet heat of a mouth, tongue curling round.

But where there was pleasure, there was pain.

And I was feeling it.

"This isn't a shrink's office." Rian didn't bother to look up from his work. "I'm just getting paid to put ink in you. Nothing more."

Looking up at the ceiling, I sucked in a breath.

Rian might not want to hear me. But he would. As long as that tattoo gun hammered against my veins, he would.

"There's so much I didn't see at the time. I don't know why I didn't see it…" I shook my head as I stared up at the ceiling. "No, I won't say that. I did what I did. Or didn't do what I didn't do."

Time to own up. To everything.

"I—I've been a bad brother. I've made terrible mistakes. There's no excuse."

I couldn't be sure, but I thought that Rian dug the needle in even deeper.

I glanced down at my wrist. Blood pooled and my brother didn't even bother wiping it away as he worked, bent over like madman.

I resisted the urge to hiss. To groan.

"That land, that land that used to be ours," I said, my heart rate accelerating. "It's hard land. Taxing land. It demands all of you. Body. Mind. Soul. And it changes you. It makes you hard. Cruel, even."

I held my breath for a moment as sweat broke out across my brow.

"Our father was cruel. He was. He was a hard and cruel man. And…and he raised us to believe you had to be. That it was the only way. To survive. To keep hold of the land. To not let it break you."

My fingers trembled as I drew the back of my hand across my forehead. I wanted to unbutton my shirt. It was constricting. Making it hard to breathe.

But Ry's tattoos were there. And I hadn't finished what I came to say.

"For Alan it was easy," I continued. "That hardness. That cruelty. I had to learn it. I had to conform to it. It was unnatural, but I thought it was the unnaturalness of learning to ride a horse. You'd get used to it. You were *supposed* to get used to it. And so I did. I became what our father wanted. I became what he was. What Alan was. What you, too, were supposed to become."

"You're tensing your arm," Rian said, his words as sharp as the needle gouging my skin.

I sucked in a rattling breath and tried to relax. But the pain and the memories were a poison and I was forced to keep swallowing them.

"But you didn't learn like I did," I said, really breathing heavily now and not knowing how to get my lungs back under control. "You never conformed or broke or got in line or whatever the fuck you want to call it and when Ma died—*Shit*."

"You have to stay still," Rian said, his voice ice cold.

My wrist was on fire.

"When Ma died," I said, "Dad came to me and he told me that it was time that you grew strong. We were alone now and we all needed to be strong. I believed him because I was weak, too. I cried every night for Ma. And I was tired of being weak. I wanted to be strong like Dad and Alan. To not cry. To not feel pain. I thought that's what it meant for you, too. To not feel pain. I didn't know he would beat you, too."

I hissed when Rian dragged the needle across my skin. It cut me open and the blood dripped onto the floor, but he just kept going. His own brow wet, his eyes laser focused on my wrist, his hands shaking.

"Rian, please," I said, not sure whether I was begging him to hear me, believe me or stop. "Da said he'd kill you if I interfered. He said if I stopped him, I was accepting that you were weak. That you'd always be weak. And we put down weak animals, so he'd do the same to you. Rian, please. I never stood up for you because I thought he would *kill you*."

The metal tray of tools clattered to the floor, banging noisily as Rian stood and screamed at me to shut up.

My brother's eyes were wild. It looked like he wanted to destroy the place. Tear it brick from brick.

My blood continued to drip to the floor. I shook like I was in the grips of a bad fever.

"Please," I whispered. "I was just a kid."

"*I* was just a kid!" Rian shouted. "*You* were my older brother!"

"I know," I tried, but it was wrong, the wrong thing to say.

"No," Rian's cheeks were flushed as he shook his head. "No, you *knew*. You knew the whole time. You always knew it was wrong. And you did *nothing*. You never stopped them. You never stood up for me. This—this excuse you're telling me now, this—this *lie*...it's just to clear your conscience. Da never said any of that. Because I was never the one who was weak. It was always you, Liam. Fucking *you*!"

With a scream of rage, Rian stormed out.

A light bulb shattered when he shoved over a floor lamp. The little bell fell from above the door he slammed too hard.

I could hear him shouting out on the sidewalk. A deranged man, people would say. Stay away from him, mothers would tell their children. He's a danger, they'd all think, crossing to the other side of the street.

But it was me.

I was the danger.

Rian had cut me open, but the wounds I gave him were deeper.

With trembling fingers, I reached for a tissue to blot at the blood.

I'd failed.

I no longer felt the pain. I was numb.

When I swiped at the fresh tattoo, raising the already raw skin, I saw what my little brother had found fit for me: a snake. Half finished. Its mouth open to consume itself, had he had enough time.

My blood-soaked cash I left beneath the still humming tattoo gun.

I left Dublin Ink a shell of myself. Empty. Cold. Feeling more alone than ever.

RY

I might have been afraid of the intense pounding at my door had I not heard Rian shouting my name from half a block away.

Liam had fixed the door that he'd broken in. Now as it rattled under the hinges, it seemed in danger of being kicked open again.

I flipped the lock. I jumped back just in time to get out of Rian's way as he stormed inside. I closed the door against the fierce wind and nosy neighbours already leaning out of their windows.

"Are you *with* Liam?" Rian asked, his voice shaking, as he stalked back and forth like a caged animal in front of the cold hearth.

I licked my lips. This wasn't how I wanted this conversation to start.

"You don't even have a coat on," I said. "You must be freezing. Come in front of the fi—"

"Answer the fucking question, Ry." Rian's hands balled into fists.

"I should get you a blanket." I turned away. "And something warm to drink."

For a second it felt nice to think that I could delay the inevitable with tea.

I never thought that Rian would ever hurt me. Not even touch me save to press a kiss to my cheek or playfully tap his knuckles against my shoulder.

But I flinched as he grabbed my arm and whipped me around to face him.

"Answer. The fucking question," he snarled. "Are you *with* him?"

I swallowed heavily. A part of me wanted to retreat. Take a step back. Feel safer.

A part of me wanted to smack my best friend square upside the jaw.

But he deserved the truth. The unashamed truth.

"Yes."

I kept my gaze steady on him. Unflinching this time.

He searched my eyes one more time as if he were trying to find a different answer.

"So I open up to you when we're in art school. I share my living nightmares with you. The abusive father. One brother joining in. And one brother who could have saved me. Who *should* have saved me because unlike the other two, he had a soul."

Rian's face began to crumble. "I tell you, Ry, my best goddamn friend, that *he* is the one I hate most of all. Who I blame most of all. And you, what?"

Rage burned brightly in his eyes.

"You *fuck* him?"

The windows rattled with the volume of Rian's voice.

"It's… It's not like that."

"Not like what? Tell me with a straight face that you haven't sucked my brother's dick."

I flinched. "Stop it."

"You spread your legs for the one who caused me to turn to drugs, who practically signed my death warrant," he hissed. "You guided him inside of you? Come on the fuck in, Liam!"

"That's enough, Rian," I said in a low voice, just as dangerous as his.

Rian's face was as pale as the ash that fluttered off the consumed logs.

"Did you scream his name, Ry? Did you scream it real pretty for my bastard of a brother as you came for him?"

"I *love him*."

Those three words hit Rian harder than I ever could. Harder than Liam ever could.

Rian's face contorted with confusion. And anger. And hurt.

"I didn't know he was your brother at first," I said, seizing upon his stunned silence. "I don't know if things would be different if I had. But I do know that I can't change how I feel about him now. This isn't just some fling. He isn't just some fuck. And neither am I. He loves me, too."

Rian just stared at me. His voice was hollow as he said, "And that's supposed to be better?"

"It's the truth."

Rian stared at me like I was a stranger. Like he didn't know me. Like he'd never known me.

"You could love a man like that over *me*?" he asked, his voice seeming to shrink. As if he were already getting farther and farther away from me. "Knowing who he is? What he let happen to me? You could *love* a monster?"

"Rian, you don't know everything," I said. He just needed

to know the truth. If he did, then maybe there was a chance at burying this bitter seed. "I want to explain."

"Explain?" Rian said, high-pitched and strained. "*Explain*, Ry? I was fucking *there*."

"You don't know it all though," I tried.

Liam had wanted to be the one to tell him. But I had to be the one. And hope he'd forgive me for spilling his secrets.

Rian had to know. I had to make him see. Once he understood, it'd all be okay.

"You don't know what your father said to Liam. What he—"

"'Da told me he'd kill you if I intervened'," he said in a mocking voice. "'Da told me I was saving you by standing by and watching you get bruised and bloodied. Da promised if I brought you a blanket in the barn, he'd leave you out there till you *really* died this time.'"

It was my turn to be stunned. "Liam talked to you?"

"Clearly he talked to you too, Ry," Rian spat out. "But you seemed to have fallen for it a bit more than I did."

"Rian—"

"Unless..." He started breathing heavily once more. "Unless you helped him come up with it. This tidy little tale. This oh, so convenient lie. Did you two put your heads together last night? Did you convince yourself this was your best shot at brushing a lifetime of pain under the rug? Did you fuck to celebrate your brilliant fucking story, Ry?"

He was screaming again. I stood there, cold down to the marrow of my bones.

Liam had told him. And it didn't make any difference.

"You—you didn't believe him?" I muttered.

I don't know whether Rian heard me or not. It didn't seem like it would have made much of a difference either way. He was back under the control of blind rage. Not hearing reason. Not seeing me or anyone else. Not feeling anything but pulsing, throbbing heat.

Liam was right. His brother didn't believe him.

"All the times I was there for you," Rian ranted, storming back and forth in front of the fireplace. "All the times I had your back. And all you had to do was say no to one dick. One fucking dick, Ry!"

"You should have believed him," I said, suddenly so nauseous I couldn't care whether my voice got to him or not.

"I was always there for you," Rian continued to shout. "Always fucking there for you and you do *this* to me!"

Not always.

With another growl, Rian looked away. His head fell. Chin to chest. His breathing remained ragged. Enraged.

"It's me or him," he said so softly I could hardly hear him.

I clutched at my chest as my heart felt like it was seizing. "What?"

Rian kept his gaze fixed on the floor as he said, no more loudly than before, "It's you and me, Ry…or it's you and him. I won't stick around if you choose my brother."

His words were like a knife to my stomach.

"You'd…abandon me?" I asked, hurt making my voice come out strained. Weak. Thin.

Rian walked toward the door without answering.

"Rian?" I called after him.

Before he slammed the door, he glanced halfway back over his shoulder.

"As far as I'm concerned," he said, "*you* did the abandoning."

I'd just finished brushing my teeth when another wave of nausea sent me right back to the toilet. The porcelain was still warm from where I'd gripped it just moments before. It was little comfort as I gagged and struggled to breathe.

A minute later I was sagged against the bathtub, feet out long in front of me like a broken doll. I hadn't even bothered getting up. I figured at that point it would just be a waste of toothpaste.

I considered reaching up for a hand towel to wipe the sweat from my brow. But the distance to the little golden ring seemed impossible.

I groaned when I heard the doorbell. I forced myself up.

After half crawling, half stumbling against the wall toward the front door, I pulled myself up into a mostly upright position. I dragged my sleeve against my mouth. It was the least I could do for my friends.

"Hey there," I said as cheerily as I could manage as I swung open the door.

Aurnia, Eithne, and Rachel stood in the light outside my door with armfuls of bottles of wine, bars of chocolate, and a stack of pizzas three high.

Their smiles fell and their arms sagged the instant they saw me. Cries of 'Happy housewarming' died on their lips.

"Oh, Ry," Aurnia said, adjusting the snacks so she could reach out a hand to my forehead, "you look terrible."

I brushed her away, though the clamminess of my fingers was clearly just as much of a giveaway.

Rachel pushed her way inside like an investigator on the hunt.

I turned around to watch her eyes travel over the apartment, in search of the crime.

Aurnia and Eithne followed soon after as I tried to pull myself together for my housewarming party.

"I'm fine," I said, not really sounding all that reassuring.

All it took was flipping open the first box of pizza to send me rushing back toward the bathroom. I kicked shut the door as best I could while wrangling up my hair, but it did nothing to stop my friends from clambering in around me.

"Thanks," I mumbled as I sat on the tiled floor in the cramped space.

Rachel flushed, Eithne served up a dollop of toothpaste onto my brush, and Aurnia patted down the back of my clammy neck with a washcloth.

I didn't fail to notice their meaningful glances to each other over my head.

"What?" I grunted as I stuffed the toothbrush into my mouth.

I scrubbed roughly at my tongue and looked from girl to girl. I got avoided eyes. Downcast glances. Lower lips bit between teeth.

"What?" I shouted, toothpaste splattering my shaking knees, "What?!"

Twenty minutes later the four of us stood in a circle. Silent. Waiting. Eyes fixed on the little window of a pregnancy test.

The pizza was cold on the kitchen counter. The wine bottles were abandoned on the couch. Only the chocolate was unwrapped, though it tasted like cardboard in my mouth.

"What do you want it to be?" Aurnia whispered after checking the little clock on the stove.

Maybe she could remember how long ago I peed on that damned stick. I certainly couldn't. Time seemed to both stand completely still and rush forward out of control. I hardly even knew where I was as I bit off another chunk of tasteless chocolate.

Before I could answer Aurnia, Rachel sucked in a breath as two little lines appeared.

Liam had gotten his wish.

I was pregnant.

RY

I could feel my friends' eyes on me. I knew they were waiting for my response.

Should they be happy for me? Draw me into an embrace and jump for joy as we squealed like teenage girls?

Or should they start on the reassurances. Next steps. Promises that everything would be alright. Tight hugs that try to communicate the incommunicable: unwavering friendship.

I knew they were searching my face, judging every blink, scrutinising every beat of my heart. But all I could do was stare.

There it was. The future I'd feared. A tether. A new life chaining me to Dublin. A baby I didn't know how to keep safe.

My friends collapsed in on me like a wave. The weight of their arms and chests and cheeks felt so real that I clung to them as the tears came faster.

For so long I'd moved through foreign cities like a ghost,

kept away like I was something haunted, that I'd started to believe that maybe it wasn't even possible to be embraced.

But at that moment, wedged in tight in my tiny bathroom, my friends were solid. I was solid.

They held me as I laughed and cried.

When I finally pulled away, we all had to wipe our eyes. My own fingers shook as I dragged them under my eyelashes.

"I guess… I guess I need to tell the father."

Aurnia grinned. "Mr Tattoo?"

I raised an eyebrow at her. "'Mr Tattoo'?"

"It's our name for the mysterious client who keeps coming in for only one artist," Aurnia said. "And only when the shop is empty."

Obviously Rian hadn't told them. But I'd expected this. Admitting that his best friend and his estranged brother were fucking around together behind his back was too painful to say out loud.

"Aurnia thinks he's a spy," Rachel said, rolling her eyes.

"And *Rachel* thinks he's a celebrity," Aurnia retorted.

Only Eithne chewed her bottom lip, her silence telling that she knew. She knew but she was my friend anyway. She knew but it wasn't her secret to tell.

"So it is Mr Tattoo then?" Aurnia said, eyeing me excitedly.

I almost lost myself in the moment, in the fantasy of this playful girls' night in. Gossiping about lovers and fights and fucks. Playful teasing, the way only family can. I felt for a second like I really was one of them. A part of the group. A member of the family.

I even fell into the trap of imagining Aurnia bouncing Liam and my baby on her hip, Rachel squeezing its tiny toes and fingers as she sang, Eithne painting its nursery.

But then Eithne asked carefully, "Does Mr Tattoo…have a name?"

My smile fell as I looked to her. She was giving me an opening. A way of admitting the truth.

But I panicked as her soft eyes bounced between mine. I wasn't ready. For any of this. I wasn't ready to admit the truth. I wasn't ready to be a mom.

I scratched at the back of my neck. "What? You don't like Mr Tattoo?"

Rachel saved me by saying, "Mrs Tattoo does have a nice ring to it."

I held up my empty ring finger. "I think we're getting ahead of ourselves."

"Oh, we're already way ahead of ourselves." Aurnia waved the positive pregnancy test.

We all laughed again and I tried to hold onto that feeling.

Things were only going to get harder from there. I'd thrown a wrench into a gear that was already a mess.

Later, I promised to call if I needed anything at all.

They shouted congratulations in the stairwell and I could even hear their happy shouts out on the sidewalk.

I tried not to feel like it was all a charade I was going through. I tried to convince myself that this could all be real: a safe, cherished, supported family.

But I needed Liam to be there, to smile with me, to hold me in his tight embrace to truly believe.

I know he said he wanted a baby for us.

But since he'd confronted Rian, he'd been…distant. He seemed so removed, so unsettled. His hopelessness rocked me. I was used to him being the rock.

The thirty minutes it took for him to drive back from the garage were filled with anxious pacing, constant hand wringing, and flinches at every creak and moan outside the apartment.

When he unlocked the door to my apartment—he had a second key cut for himself when he repaired my door—and stepped inside, his eyes searching for me, I saw my future.

I saw him bending over a crib, huffing on his hands to warm them before lifting our child to his broad chest. I saw him pressing a kiss to my forehead, the smell of engine grease mixed with the last bit of shampoo he used that morning. I saw us tired and bleary-eyed in the middle of the night, but together as we cooed and hushed the baby back to sleep.

I saw it all.

But Liam just saw my tears.

"What's wrong?" he asked, fear obvious in his voice as he rushed to me.

His hands were all over me. Checking me for wounds or broken bones. I shook my head, muttered something incoherent as emotion constricted my throat.

"What happened? Ry, what happened?" Liam asked as I took his hand in mine and pulled him toward the bathroom.

"It's okay," was all I managed to tell him in the dark, narrow hallway. "It's all okay."

Liam's eyes were wide and darting in the bathroom mirror when I switched on the light. My happy laughter only made him more confused as I wiped at my wet cheeks.

"Look," I said, but when I went to show him the pregnancy test I found it missing from where I'd left it on the counter.

Liam closed the cracked open window as I checked the small trash can on the side of the sink. Nothing but our balled-up tissues and some cotton balls darkened with mascara.

"Why is it freezing in here?" Liam asked. "Ry, baby, aren't you cold?"

I lifted the trash can. Searched around it. Ducked behind the toilet to see if it had fallen behind there somehow.

"I'm not cold at all," I told Liam distractedly as I spun around in the tight space. "I'm… I'm…"

It had been right here. Where the fuck did it go?

Liam's hands cupped my face and held me still. I pulled at his wrists to continue searching, but he resisted.

"Ry," he said, his voice stern, still struggling to hold onto his composure, "you texted me that you needed me right away. What's wrong?"

"I can't find it."

I looked to the window Liam had shut. Had I opened it? Had one of the girls? But if the wind had moved it, it would surely just be in the bowl of the sink…

"Can't find what?" Liam asked. "Ry?"

"Maybe Rachel accidentally threw it in the trash with the box."

Liam looked like he was about to lose it. His concern was on the verge of boiling over.

"Took what?" he asked. "Ry, are you alright?"

Liam's impassioned eyes fixed on mine drew my attention back to him.

I smiled. Tears began anew.

"Took what, baby?" Liam begged.

"A test," I said, bottom lip trembling.

Liam hesitated. "A test?"

I took in a shuddering breath. My hands gripped Liam's wrists.

I could feel his pulse thundering. Despite the cold, his skin was on fire.

"A pregnancy test," I said, searching his eyes as I spoke.

I felt his heart leap beneath my fingertips.

"A pregnancy test?" he repeated in a much quieter voice than before.

"A positive pregnancy test," I whispered. "I'm pregnant."

LIAM

Ever since I'd finally confronted Rian, my head had been a mess. I'd known it and Ry had known it. For days I'd wandered around her apartment like a ghost, hardly eating, barely sleeping, sometimes just sitting in the chair next to her, watching her toss in her sleep.

She'd told me that Rian had confronted her.

She'd told me about his ultimatum: me or him.

I forced myself, as I traced her sleeping form with my gaze, to consider that perhaps Ryleigh was better off with Rian and the Dublin Ink family than me.

I forced myself *not* to think selfishly. Isn't that what they say, if you love something let it go?

That had been the stupidest thing I'd ever heard, until now.

I'd even confided in Darren at the garage, asked him if he thought I needed to leave Ryleigh. That maybe as a form of penance, I had to let my brother have her.

That I should disappear into the night like Ryleigh had so

many years ago, so that she could carve out a better life for herself without me.

Just look at what my selfishness had done: I was a bomb that exploded her fucking life with my lies.

Darren slapped me on the back of my head. "Don't be fecking stupid."

Still, my questions echoed in my head. Round and round like a broken record. Until she'd said those words.

"I'm pregnant."

Light tumbled back into my life, purpose shining like sun's rays.

I'd been so stupid. I'd let my guilt over my brother cloud my heart.

Ryleigh was my world. And she was going to have our child.

We were a family.

I drew Ryleigh into my arms and with her forearms on my shoulders and her hands cupping my uplifted face, spun her round and round and round that tiny bathroom. The fluorescent lights blurred like a halo around her dark curtaining hair and the glare of the streetlamp streaked into a shooting star as I twirled us till I was dizzy.

The icy floors bit at my bare feet, but I did not feel the cold.

I was going to be a father.

Ry watched me even as I set her down, her lip in her teeth.

"Are you happy?" she asked softly.

I drew my fingers shakily through my hair. My chest heaved as I sucked in a stuttering breath.

"Happy?" I repeated. "Ry, I'm so beyond happy. I'm... I'm..."

Ry shut me up with a kiss.

"I am, too," she admitted with a giggle against my mouth.

"This is a new start," I told her. "A fresh start. This is... it's..."

Again Ry, so calmly, so assuredly, completed my exact thought, "It's exactly what we need."

I clasped her to my chest. Held her so tight I thought surely she'd wince in pain; she did not.

"I'm going to do things right," I vowed to her. "This baby, *our* baby... I'm going to teach it love and kindness and...and everything that I failed to do for Ri—" I cut off, unable to say his name out loud.

The urge to move, to do something, to start on making a crib or ordering diapers or reading ungodly amounts of baby books almost seemed to overwhelm me.

But the serenity on Ry's face soothed me like a warm fire. She was half my size but she kept me steady.

"Our baby won't even know my da's wretched name," I told her. "She'll never go to that godforsaken plot of land. She'll—"

"She?" Ry asked, a smile at her lips.

I ran my hand over her stomach.

"Of course I don't know," I said in a quiet whisper. "I'll love *him* just as much."

"We don't know anything."

In her voice I heard a soft warning: don't go giving your heart away yet. Don't set yourself up to be hurt. Don't make the mistake I've already made.

"We know everything, Ry," I said confidently. "We know that this is a cruel, dangerous world. We know that we've hurt and been hurt and we know that's not the last time either. We know that there are people out there who want to harm us, take everything from us..."

Rage nearly sent me fleeing again from the heat of Ry's body. The idea that some man was out there, seeing my woman every time he closed his eyes…

I squeezed my eyes shut and pressed my forehead against hers, continuing in a whisper, "We know that we've had to survive and we know that we've learned the wrong things—to run. To stay silent. To suffer alone."

Breathing in deeply to steady myself, I pulled just far away from Ry so that she could see me and I could see her.

"And we know that our baby will never have to learn those things. We know we'll do anything and everything to keep our baby safe. We know that it will be loved and protected and allowed to grow up with kindness and warmth in its little heart."

Ry teared up as she stared at me. The trust she showed me with her unwavering gaze made my chest tight.

"We know *that*," I said, and Ry nodded vigorously as she fought back tears. "So we know everything."

"We know everything," she repeated.

I squeezed her tight to my chest. I could feel her little hands balled up into my shirt. She was just as ready to fight for our baby as I was.

"Move in with me," I said after we remained silent for several minutes, hearts beating against one another's.

At first Ry didn't say anything. Then I felt her head moving against my chest, her hair sliding across my bare skin.

"Yes?" I asked. "Are you saying yes?"

I heard her muffled response, felt her little puff of hot breath.

"Yes."

I exhaled against her.

For all the times she'd let me choke her, this was the moment where I knew she truly trusted me.

She was going to let me protect her. Watch over her. Keep her safe.

She'd never allowed that of anyone. Not even Rian.

"Your heart is racing, Liam," Ry said, tilting her chin up to look into my eyes.

I pressed a kiss to her forehead.

"I felt this way outside of Rian's apartment," I told her. "The day I first saw you. I stood at the bottom of the stairs and I wanted so terribly to do what was right. I wanted the chance to prove that I was a good man. It nearly ripped me in two, that desire…and that's the way I feel now, too. I have a shot at redemption. I can be a good man for you. You and our baby, Ry."

Ry nestled in close again. Her fists uncurled and her hands smoothed across my pecs. Travelled up to slide along my neck. Fingers twisted into my hair.

I listened to her breathing.

"Liam," Ry whispered. "Maybe I—*we* don't need you to be a good man. Maybe we just need you to be *our* man."

Her lips moved against my skin. "Maybe I was never meant to be with a saint."

"Maybe I'm tired of being a sinner," I whispered.

Ry's hand slid between my legs as her lips found mine. My cock responded to her hand.

"Are you tired now?" she asked before tugging at my lower lip with her teeth.

"And here I thought you were an angel," I said as I lifted her up and carried her to the bed, laying her across the mattress. "The mother of my child."

Dark hair spread out around her head, she grinned at me.

"I'll be an angel tomorrow," she said.

I pushed up her shirt and circled my tongue around one of her nipples.

"Please don't," I said, and then she pushed my head down to her pussy.

From just the sound of one of Ry's whimpers, I knew she was right: I'd be whatever she needed me to be.

I'd sell my soul for her. I'd throw away my chance to redeem myself. I'd crawl into the belly of the beast for her. And for my child.

I'd do wicked things for them. I'd *be* a wicked thing…

RY

I heard the door to the apartment open as I went to the bathroom to grab a hair tie before cooking dinner.

"Hey, baby," I called to him. "How does pasta sound?"

As I rifled through the drawer, I heard Liam drop off his bag of tools at the door. I imagined him slipping out of his steel-toed boots and rubbing his grease-stained hands together: hungry for dinner, hungry for me.

It was nice, I thought, the little domestic life we'd already begun to make for ourselves. Liam had moved in here with me the day after we found out I was pregnant.

"Baby," I said, returning to the kitchen, "I asked if—"

I found Liam at the counter cutting the onion I'd just laid out on the cutting board. He was awkward with the knife, clearly not an expert at home cooking. And he was crying.

"Liam, honey," I laughed, coming over to touch his back. "Let me do it."

"No. *I'll* do it."

I bit my lip. "You're honestly kind of making a mess of it. What did that poor onion do to you?"

He sniffled. "It's not a mess…it's rustic."

He hadn't even taken the time to take off his shearling coat when he came inside. Had he *run* to the onion?

"Okay, now," I said, reaching gently for the knife. "You've had your fun."

Liam turned to look at me and the tears in his eyes were so fucking adorable. With his wind-tousled hair and dirty cheeks from the garage, he looked like a little kid.

"Please, let me do it for you," he said, melting my goddamn heart. "I have to."

It was either the onions or the pregnancy hormones that were making me tear up as well.

"You mean you want to," I said.

But Liam, tears streaming down his cheeks, shook his head.

I slipped my hand under his coat and plaid flannel to rub circles at the small of his back. I could feel the muscles, strained and tight.

"You've been working all day," I said softly.

"*I* chop your onions."

I laughed at his seriousness. "You mean *this* onion."

"No. I mean I chop *all* your onions from now on forever."

I frowned. Was this some kind of misogynistic shi—

He reached out his hand to push back a strand from my face and smiled. "I don't want anything to make you cry."

I softened instantly. Melted right into a puddle, actually.

He could chop all my onions.

I turned on some music.

As Liam saute the onions, I boiled the water for the pasta. I retrieved the jar of sauce from the cabinet, I closed the door to find Liam suddenly there. I looked between his stern face and his hand held out to me, palm open.

"Give it."

Laughing, I said, "I can open it."

"But you don't have to," he said, wiggling his fingers at me. "I'm here."

I narrowed my eyes at him but plopped the jar into his hand.

He couldn't know this, but I always struggled with those damn things. Banging them against the counter and grunting to try to pry them open.

With a quick pop, Liam had it open and done.

I rolled my eyes at the pride in his eyes as he placed it back into my hands and kissed my forehead.

Really I found it quite charming. I kinda liked having a big, strong man in the house.

When Liam had finished cooking and was plating the pasta, I came back over to help him carry the dishes to the table. He wagged his finger at me.

"I've got it," he said, tossing the kitchen towel over his shoulder. "Sit."

"I can help," I protested.

"You can sit and get served by a hot baby daddy," Liam replied.

"Oh, is he coming soon?" I asked, glancing toward the front door.

Holding two heaping portions of pasta in each hand, Liam kicked me playfully in the butt.

We sat together at the table and it was so natural, the way Liam's hand came to rest on my knee as we ate.

The idea of domestic bliss might have made me laugh before, but in that moment it made me want to cry.

It was all just so sweet and simple, Liam asking about my day, oblivious to the little bit of tomato sauce at the corner of his mouth. I dabbed at it with my napkin.

When I finished, Liam took my hand gently in his. From the way he massaged my palm, hesitant eyes focused on the task, I knew he was going to ask about it. I'd been purposefully avoiding it, because I hated the pained look on his face when I mentioned his brother.

It had been so nice to just shut out the world for a little while, to just share this meal together. I was tempted to go on playing pretend forever. Why not, when we were clearly so happy, just the two of us?

But Liam couldn't let it go. As happy as he did seem there at the table, I knew it was just an illusion. His fragmented relationship with his brother tore him apart inside.

In a slightly strained voice, Liam said, "When…when do you think you're going to tell Rian?"

I knew it was coming, I did. But just because you see a train coming down the tracks doesn't make the impact hurt any less. My pasta soured on my tongue.

"Soon," I said. "I just…couldn't today."

I hoped he didn't ask why not, because I didn't have an answer. Or, at least, not a satisfying one.

Since Rian had confronted me, he'd basically ignored me at work. Barely looking at me when I came in. Refusing to come to lunch with the crew if I was going. Choosing to sit at the table farthest from me.

But at least he hadn't told me to leave. Hadn't fired me straight out. That's why I held hope.

And telling Rian that I was pregnant with his brother's baby wasn't going to go down well. Not while things were still tenuous between us.

I'd begged the girls to keep it to themselves for now, saying that I needed time to tell the father *first* before I told Rian and the boys. But I could tell their whispers and giggles were becoming suspicious to the boys.

"Maybe tomorrow then?" The look in Liam's eyes stabbed my heart as he glanced up at me from his plate.

I twisted more spaghetti around my fork, aware of his patient gaze on me the whole time. I couldn't give him what he wanted. And it killed me.

"Maybe tomorrow," I said, before stuffing my mouth full of food.

I felt Liam's hand on my knee. It had been there the whole time, but now I fixated on it as the silence went on. Had his palm gone damp? Was he squeezing me harder than he'd been just before? Looser?

I chewed and chewed and couldn't seem to swallow. I feared Liam removing his hand altogether. I was quite sure he would actually.

But he didn't.

"Ry," he said softly. "He's going to find out soon when you can't hide your belly under loose clothes anymore."

I nodded. Of course I knew this. Sometimes it felt like it was all I thought about. Anguishing through the hours of the day, checking myself in the mirror constantly, begging Liam to come home and make all those worries just fade away.

"I know." My voice broke. Tears I hadn't intended pricked at my eyes. "I'm sorry. I know I have to— I know I *should*— I just—"

"Shh," Liam cooed. "I know you know, baby. I shouldn't have brought it up."

"No, Liam—"

"Hush," he said, running his thumb over my lips. "Wait here a second, alright?"

I'd wanted to reassure him that I was with him. That despite my love for Rian, I was *his*.

Telling Rian was going to be devastating. But I would do it. I would.

For *him*.

Liam returned, smiling like nothing at all had happened. He placed a black velvet jewellery box beside my plate of pasta and my heart leapt at the sight of it.

I watched him take his seat once more, lips parted stupidly.

"Go on," Liam said, scooting back in and nodding toward the box.

I suddenly had the ridiculous thought that I wished I'd done my hair better, put on a little lipstick, fuck, at least changed out of this stained sweatshirt I'd been living in.

It was ridiculous because it wasn't what I should have been thinking at all. I should have been thinking that marriage to Liam meant no more running.

I should have been panicking. Fear should have been creeping up my spine. I should have been glancing round my shoulder at how far away the front door was.

Instead I was worried about how I would look when I said, "Yes"?

I reached a shaking hand toward the box. It was harder to pop open than it should have been, the lid snapping open almost violently.

There on a plush silk cushion was a bracelet.

It wasn't a ring.

Disappointment hit me like a truck. I quickly hid it with a smile, knowing that Liam was searching for my reaction.

"Liam," I whispered, not yet trusting my voice. "You shouldn't have."

Liam laughed and his tanned, weathered fingers entered my shimmering field of vision. He took the bracelet out and indicated for me to give him my wrist to try it on.

"You can't say that every time I get you something nice, baby. Because I plan on doing nice things for you a whole hell of a lot of times."

I laughed, too. Laughed at myself for being so silly. Laughed at myself for getting upset. Laughed at how I'd somehow ended up with such a great guy despite myself.

"It's beautiful," I said.

Liam finished clasping it in place and I twisted it around in the light above the table.

"It's a sonogram bracelet," Liam said with a smile at me.

"Is it?" I asked.

I fumbled with the charm and blinked back tears when I saw it was set with a tiny image of our first ultrasound.

"Ry…" Liam said, pulling his chair around toward mine. He drew my head toward his chest.

"It's too perfect," I said.

"Promise me you won't take it off," Liam whispered against the crown of my head.

"I promise," I said, as my tears wet his flannel shirt that smelled of engine grease.

Liam ran his hands over my hair and shushed at me.

I meant it. I meant it more emphatically than I could put into words.

But he didn't understand just how much my guts twisted. Because it *was* too perfect. *He* was too perfect. Attentive. Supportive. Kind.

He went to all my doctor's appointments, surprised me

with treats and gifts, made sure I was completely taken care of.

That sort of perfection couldn't last. I knew it couldn't.

Fear weaved through me, seeming to increase by the day along with the size of my little baby. I felt *watched* all the time now, and shadows seemed to jump out at me more and more.

It wasn't just *my* life I was afraid for anymore.

LIAM

The balled-up receipt for Ry's pregnancy supplements rolled across the floor mat on the passenger side as I took a turn a little too fast. It jostled against the other receipts I'd tossed aside.

I wanted Ry to have the best of the best: doctors, nutrition, comfort, ease. There was a receipt for a new mattress, a specialised pillow, a delivery of organic fruits and vegetables, and a whole slew of other things my wallet wanted to forget.

It wasn't that I wasn't happy to pay for anything and everything. Fuck, I'd have purchased the moon for her.

I was doing well at the mechanics; my work was always good and I'd started getting customers coming in and asking for me by name.

It was just that I still wasn't earning enough to give her *everything*.

But that wasn't why I took the turn a mile or two (or ten) above the speed limit. It was because Ry had texted me that Rian was on an extended lunch break from his shift at Dublin Ink.

The tattoo parlour was empty. The tattoo parlour was *ours*.

The little bell over the door announced my arrival.

I loved watching Ry lift her head from her work, recognition bringing light to her eyes. To have her run *to* me and leap up into my waiting arms.

Her hair smelled like the special pregnancy-safe oatmeal shampoo I'd bought her. She'd sworn it was too much, unnecessary, but her protests died off rather quickly when I'd massaged it into her scalp in the bath last night.

"Well, hello there, gorgeous," she said, smiling broadly.

Amongst all the chaos and uncertainty, she was happy. For a second I forgot about my money stresses. All I really needed in life was Ry's happiness.

"That's quite a greeting," I replied.

Ry smirked as her toes came back into contact with the floor. She pointed at the takeaway bag in my hand.

"I meant the burrito."

I held the bag back when she reached for it and held out the bag from my other hand instead.

"Business first," I said.

"More supplements?" Ry asked, rifling through the pill bottles.

"It's everything the book recommended," I said, taking a seat in one of the black leather tattoo chairs.

Ry came over to me and I hoisted her up onto my lap. Her elbow came to rest on my shoulder.

"I thought we already got everything the book recommended," she said, cupping my cheek.

"Different book," I said.

Ry laughed. "I'm going to start glowing like that neon sign if I keep taking more stuff. You should see my pee already."

"Should I?" I frowned.

Ry chuckled. "Everything is going to be fine. The doctor said I'm perfectly healthy, remember?"

I twisted around one of the bottles I'd bought. "Maybe just this one, too?"

Ry shook her head and held up the burrito.

"Definitely *this* one," she said before taking a massive bite.

With hot sauce smeared all over her lips, she went in for more.

"Have I told you how beautiful you are?" I said.

Ry stuck out her tongue.

I laughed. "How gorgeous you are?"

Ry licked her lips, managing to further smear sauce around her mouth.

I groaned deep in my chest. "How fucking *hot* you are?"

Ry sucked on a refried bean-smeared finger as she gave me pouty eyes.

"Goddamn," I whispered, shaking my head.

Ry laughed and the sound was glorious. She gave me her laughter so freely now, I almost forgot about the ever-present darkness, about the man that I was still hunting in the background—and failing to find.

Not that I had many avenues, being new to Dublin.

I knew Rian had a friend who worked for the Garda but... I couldn't exactly ask him to help.

"If I wasn't so busy pleasuring this burrito right now, I might give you a little reward for all your sweet nothings," she said, tapping the tip of my nose.

My cock twitched beneath her ass. I nipped at her neck.

"I have time," I murmured to the hollow of her throat even as she took another bite.

"So you're saying I should chew slower?" Ry asked, pulling away to assess me with a cheek of food like a chipmunk.

"I'm saying I thought you liked burritos you could choke on," I said, pulling Ry's hips down tighter on my swelling cock.

Ry's eyes became hungry for something other than Mexican food. She threw her burrito aside just as the little bell rang.

I heard her startled gasp before I turned to see who it was.

In her haste to get up off of my lap, she knocked over the bag of supplements that were at my side. A bottle rolled across the floor and stopped beneath the raised toe of an all too familiar boot.

Rian's boot.

Wiping her hand across her mouth, Ry said in a hollow voice, "I thought you were going to lunch."

My brother's eyes burned still with hate-fueled fire as he glared at me.

"I figured it would be nice to bring you something back," he said, his voice low and dangerous. "You know, since we used to be friends."

He knelt to the floor to pick up the bottle.

The parlour was washed in a deadly silence except for the clatter of pills as he shifted it around in his palm to read the label. The words were right there on the front. Unavoidable.

"You're...pregnant?" Rian said, breaking the silence as if with a hammer.

It was like shattering the window of a car submerged in a lake. All I heard now was a violent gushing of blood against my ears.

"Rian," Ry said, taking a step forward.

I came to stand beside Ry, shouldering in front of her, fists balled my sides, eyes focused, ready to defend her if Rian attacked, if he even dared to raise his voice.

Rian lifted his head.

But there was no fight in Rian's gaze. Rather he looked emptied. Like he'd lost too much blood too quickly.

My guts twisted. I was prepared for a fight. I wasn't prepared for this.

His voice was hollow. "The way Aurnia and Rachel kept whispering and touching your belly... And Mason would jump every time you had to carry the smallest thing. Even Conor wouldn't let you hold the damn door yourself..."

Fuck. I watched as Ry's face fell apart.

I grabbed her hand and squeezed, letting her know I wasn't letting her go through this alone.

"They all knew..." Rian said. "Everyone knew except—"

"We were going to tell you..." I said, because I had to say something.

Ry's face was already tracking with tears, her eyes round with guilt, her hand trembling in mine.

Rian made a choking sound.

"Him, I expected something like this from. But you..." He turned his eyes to Ry and lanced her with his stare. "*You...*"

"That's not fair," I said, defending her.

Rian ignored me as he stumbled back, shaking his head. "By the time I get back I want you gone."

"Rian, please," Ryleigh cried.

"You are dead to me."

He turned and fled into the streets, the little bell clanging violently above the door before it slammed shut.

"Rian!" Ry shouted.

I caught her wrist when she went to dart out after him.

"You need to give him time," I said.

Ry stood there staring after him. She stood like that for a silent minute; I counted the seconds by the now sluggish thudding of my heartbeats.

When Ry finally turned back to me I could see the cracks around her eyes, at the redness already on the tip of her nose, at the clench of her jaw as she tried not to cry.

Ry pulled her arm from my grasp. She walked past me and collapsed into the chair we'd been so happy in just moments ago. Before the world came pouring back in. Before the little bell woke us back up from our dream.

I sighed and dragged a tired hand over my face.

"Everything is going to be fine," I said, repeating the words she'd told me a few minutes ago when the question of which supplements to take seemed like our biggest challenge.

"How is everything going to be fine?" she cried, collapsing her face down against her knees. "*How* is everything going to be fine? I've lost my best friend. If that wasn't bad enough, I'm going to lose all of his friends, too. Rachel, Eithne, Aurnia. Mason and Conor. They've been the only family I've had and I'm going to lose them, too. We're going to be *alone,* Liam. Alone. With Balor still hunting for me and my job gone and—"

"Shh," I said, drawing her toward me. "Shh."

Ry wrapped her arms around my waist. I smoothed my hand over her hair in calming strokes even as my own heart raced.

"Don't worry about your job," I told her, trying to keep my voice steady even though my chest tightened so much it felt hard to breathe. "I'll find a way to make some extra money. I'll talk to Darren. Do overtime. Start taking side gigs. I'll figure something out."

Money problems seemed to be the easiest to tackle.

I swallowed thickly before continuing.

"And as for Rian," I said, hesitating. "As for Rian..."

Ry bunched her fingers in my jacket. She understood that there might not be an answer.

Gently I lifted her chin, guided her eyes to mine.

"I do know that there's no such thing as alone as long as we're together," I said. "Us. You, me and our baby."

Ry nodded, but I saw the pain still lingering in her eyes.

"I didn't want to hurt him," she whispered.

I understood that more than Ry knew.

All my life that was all I wanted: not to hurt Rian.

It was why I stood back when he took my father and older brother's abuse. It was why I waited in the wings, believing that it would end and Rian would emerge stronger as promised.

It was why I allowed Ry to delay telling him about us when I should have done it months ago.

"*I* hurt him," I said to Ry. "Not you."

"That's not true."

"Your only fault was in loving me."

"Or in loving both of you," she said softly. "It's like trying to hold onto the east and the west...it's tearing me apart."

I kissed the top of Ry's head and begged time to rewind to the bath yesterday evening where she let me wash her hair.

I promised I'd do anything to protect Ry and the baby, to keep them happy and healthy. But what if the thing I needed to do just that was the one thing I couldn't accomplish?

To reach Rian.

To get his forgiveness.

~

Darren's garage was empty, which seemed like its own special kind of curse. I needed to fucking fix something. Because the truth that was creeping up on me like a goddamn shadow was that I couldn't fix anything.

I sorted and resorted my bills on the desk in the little back office. I'd taken to hiding bills from Ry. Sneaking them from the letter box to the garage like they were drugs.

I prayed an old rattling engine would come sputtering down the street. I told myself that's all I needed. A little time with a wrench. A smear or two of grease across the brow. The sweet purr of a healthy, thriving motor.

Then I'd come back to the desk and find a solution for how I was going to pay for the ever-increasing cost of having a child, let alone raising one. But as it stood now, papers shuffling, heart fluttering, there was no solution. I mean, at the end of the day, it really was pretty fucking simple: if you don't have the money, you don't have the money.

But it was my problem to fix. The only problem with my problem was I didn't know how. How to fix it. How to give Ry the life she deserved. How to give her *everything*.

My phone rang and Ry's name flashed up on screen. I let it ring twice more to give myself time to clear my voice, rid it of the strain of stress and the brittleness of panic.

I forced a smile.

"Hey, baby," I said as I answered.

Ry's sigh told me everything.

"Same thing?" I asked as my stomach dropped.

"It's such bullshite," she said.

I covered my bills with an order for spare parts just so I wouldn't have to look at them while I was talking to her.

She was angry, but not as angry as the first few times this

had happened. She was wearing down, too, like brake pads slammed on a few too many times.

Ry continued, "It's hopeless. This is like, what, the three hundredth tattoo shop I've talked to?"

I repressed the urge to correct her estimation of Dublin tattoo parlours. It didn't matter how many parlours there were, only that it *felt* like three hundred to her.

"They look at my belly like it's a grenade," she said, her voice filled with bitterness.

I squeezed my eyes shut. Yet another thing I couldn't fucking fix.

Ry had been trying to rent a chair at one of the other tattoo parlours for weeks now. No one saw her art, her talent. They just saw baby, baby, bun in the oven. It was apparently not worth it to let her work for a few months. Even though those few months would make all the difference to us.

"Ry, honey, you don't have to work," I said as softly as possible. "I can support us."

It didn't matter that it wasn't the truth. I'd do anything to *make* it the truth. My heart sank when I heard sniffling on the line.

"Ry," I whispered.

"It's just the stupid pregnancy hormones," Ry snapped before I heard a fresh wave of tears.

I let her cry for a moment. It's what she'd told me she needed when she was like this: not comfort, not kind words, not even assurances that everything would be alright. She just needed me to be there. Hear her. Know that things were hard and not leave.

Finally Ry drew in a stuttering breath and said sadly, "It's just that—you know this is hard for me. For so long I've been completely independent. And I saw that as my safety, my weapon even, me not needing anyone. And now… I'm helpless, Liam. I feel so helpless and, and…"

Ry sniffled and let out several deep breaths as she fought back more tears.

Fuck. I should be with *her*.

Instead I was in this dirty fucking garage when there weren't even any customers.

What use was I? I couldn't give Ry what she wanted, a chair in a tattoo parlour, work to ease her mind, art to soothe her soul. I could barely keep up with our bills now that we were down to my single income.

I wanted to punch something. To kick the shite out of something.

"Ry," I said gently, wrapping all my frustration up and swallowing it like a bitter pill. I would never—could never—let Ryleigh see me like this. "You're not helpless. In just a few months, our sweet little girl is going to look up into your eyes for the first time and she won't see helpless. She'll see strength. Power. Goodness. Love. Security. Protection. Utter devotion."

Ry sniffled and I smiled knowing that she'd heard me. That I'd given her at least a tiny bit of peace.

Gravel crunched of someone pulling into the driveway. I glanced through the office blinds to see a sleek black Mercedes rolling to the driveway. The door opened and a man got out.

"I've gotta go, baby, a customer just showed up."

And from the looks of it, a customer with money. Hope lifted my spirits.

At the edge of the open garage door stood a tall silhouette against the glare of the hazy afternoon sun.

I weaved through the toolboxes and stripped frames on

shadowed winches. I blinked against the sun as I came to stand in front of him, shielding my eyes with one hand.

"What can I do for you?"

The man stepped forward, came into view and his expensive cologne hit my nose, sharp and woody.

The second thing I noticed as he shook my hand was a smile. It seemed a little too big. A little too warm. It seemed to linger a bit too long as I asked what brought him in today.

He pointed at me with a beefy finger and eyed me with that same smile. "I like you. Yes, I think I'm getting just the right impression from you. I think you're *just* the man for the job."

"I appreciate the vote of confidence," I said. "But I'm not sure I can in good faith agree with you since you still haven't told me an iota of what exactly that job is."

The man clapped his hands together in front of his chest, the single gold signet ring on his pinky winking in the sun.

"I want what every man wants. I want something beautiful. Something rare. I want something…" he laughed, "I want something that I probably shouldn't have business at all wanting."

His wink turned my stomach.

The stranger snapped his fingers and then slipped them into the breast pocket of his tailored jacket. He handed me a glossy page with a picture of an old classic Harley and below it, a mocked-up custom restoration, a royal blue beast I could hardly see past the theoretical dollar signs.

"She is a beauty," I said, nodding.

The man had that same big, childish grin on his face when I looked back up at him. His beefy finger tapped the drawing, the idealisation, the future "after" photo.

"I need your help getting to her. Making her mine. You

can tell the old girl is stubborn, but I think you hold the key to transforming her into exactly what I want."

I stared across at him. He licked his lips.

"You have no idea how long I've waited to ride her," he said. "How many nights I've dreamed of only her. Tearing her apart, putting her back together. Hearing her purr. Hearing her scream. Knowing I have full control of her."

His choice of words was…strange. There was something about this guy that seemed a bit too slick.

"And you want me to handle the restoration?" I said slowly.

"Exactly," the man said. "I need you. I want you. In fact, you're the reason I came here in the first place. I need a man who knows these machines. I'll pay a lot of money for *you*."

He could have said just about anything and I would have turned him down. Politely suggested he try somewhere else. Insisted that I could be of no use to him. But he spoke that magic word.

Money.

And what was more: a *lot* of it.

I hesitated for only as long as it took to smack my lips. "Let's go talk in the office."

In the office his eyes darted everywhere. He lingered before sinking into the chair opposite mine.

I figured it was fair enough: you want to make sure you're dealing with someone who has his shite together.

I hastily cleared my space. Pushed aside coffee and my phone and keys.

"I didn't get your name," I said as I scooted in toward the desk.

The man moved his eyes slowly from my little mess at the corner. "Peter."

"Peter," I repeated. "I'm—"

"Liam Merrick." He nodded. "I know."

I studied his face for a moment, trying to dissipate my unease by reminding myself how much we needed this guy's cash.

"Because you looked me up online?" I asked.

Peter inclined his head. "You are impressive. You've done what I know a lot of people over the years have not been able to do."

Again…what a strange choice of words.

I couldn't shake the sense that something was off him. But before I could figure it out or get the nerve to say fuck it to the money and fuck it to him, Peter drummed his fingers on the edge of my desk.

"So," he said, "here's the gist: this Harley is down in Cork. It's in bad shape according to my sources, but that's where you come in. And that's where my million euros also comes in."

"Excuse me?" I choked.

Peter tilted his head to the side. "You don't think it's a fair price?"

I stammered as I tried to process a single coherent thought.

A million euros. For a Harley transformation.

I mean, I'd heard of a 1908 Harley going at auction for over a million. I'd heard of a Harley transformation that cost several hundred million, so really, a million wasn't unheard of.

But for what he was after, I made some calculations in my head, it'd leave me with a profit of at least a few hundred thousand.

My head spun. That would cover all the pregnancy costs and more.

Peter waved his hand. "Fine. Make it two."

"*Two* million euros?"

Peter's smile unnerved me once more. He leaned forward. Too close.

"You get me what I want and I'll give you all the money in the world."

Fuck.

I could buy Ryleigh a house, a practical mansion with a giant nursery. I could hire a nanny to help her. I could buy her her own tattoo parlour. She'd never have to worry about anything again.

We discussed particulars till he glanced at his beeping phone. He picked up his phone and scowled at it.

Pen in hand, mid-sentence, I stopped. "Everything alright?"

"Of course," Peter said, adding, "though, I wonder if I might inconvenience you for a drink."

"We have some Cokes in the fridge out back?"

I left to get the Coke and when I returned, Peter was gone.

On the desk was a note that he'd been called away on business after all, but that he'd be in touch and he very much looked forward to working with me.

I told myself that he was eccentric because he was rich. Because that much money could make anyone a little weird.

But I couldn't ignore unease as I remembered that tiny detail that had been buried by the staggering amount Peter offered.

I had to go to Cork to retrieve the bike.

Which meant I had to leave Ryleigh in Dublin, alone.

LIAM

I think it was fate that Eithne was running late the evening I'd arranged to leave for Cork.

As the little bell above the door for Dublin Ink rang, Eithne was still sitting at Rian's side on the sagging floral couch.

It was so easy to imagine what would have happened if she'd already set off to my place to meet up with Rachel and Aurnia for their girls' night in.

Rian would have stormed at me. I wouldn't have been able to get even a word in. Would he have hit me? Would his knuckles have cracked the delicate bones along my cheek?

I could see that. I could see the scar he would leave me. I could see it in the mirror, in a different future, my fingers tracing over the jagged white line. It would be the last gift from my brother. My only remaining memory of him.

It would have all fallen apart if Eithne hadn't seen the lightning bolt of rage surge through Rian and placed her hand on his knee…

I heard her say to him, "Just think if I hadn't heard you out. If I'd not let you utter a single word to me."

Rian did not look at Eithne as she spoke, his glare was only for me.

"Rian, please," Eithne continued, her hand now flat against his chest, pressed tight against his heart, "you *need* to listen to him. If only because I listened to you."

Her lips were light as a butterfly's wing against his cheek. It was enough to break his rage as he grabbed her roughly and kissed her back.

I lowered my gaze to give them some privacy.

"Good luck," Eithne whispered like a soft breeze as she passed me.

The door clicked shut behind her, her footsteps swallowed by the noise of passing cars. The softness left Rian's face along with her.

"It's about Ry," I said before he could advance on me.

Eithne was Rian's saving grace.

Ry was mine.

Her name alone brought me more leniency than any apology I could manage to perfect over years, decades. By invoking her name, I'd cashed in my final chip. There it rolled to a stop between us: our mutual love for the woman who'd chosen me.

Rian carded his fingers through his hair as he leaned forward, fixed his eyes on the frayed rug beneath his rapidly tapping toes.

"You're the only other person in the world who loves her as much as I do," I said from where I remained, upright and firm footed by the door.

Rian scoffed. "What good that love did, eh?"

He lifted his eyes to me. His pupils burned in rage. But

they were ringed with the redness of exhaustion. It was tiring to carry this much hate.

"It didn't have to be that way. None of this had to be like..." I waved my arms vaguely at the empty shop, its pink neon glow flooding over Ryleigh's empty tattoo chair, "...like *this*."

"Don't talk to me about how things could have, should have been different. I'm all too familiar with thoughts like that. They've been chains around my ankles nearly all my life."

I tried to ignore the sting his words brought to my chest.

Rian and I had unfinished business. There was no denying that. A reckoning was coming. I could feel it like I felt the hairs on my arms before a thunderstorm.

But I was here for Ryleigh.

If Rian just heard me out, I was hoping he would be, too.

"I'm leaving town for a night or two," I said, pushing aside the urge to run to Rian and shake him, hug him, hit him. "And I'm here because I want to ask you, as her best friend or at least as someone who was once her best friend, to look after her."

Rian pushed himself up from the couch. He walked toward a desk at the back corner of the parlour and riffled through the contents. "Ry's a big girl. I'm sure she can look after herself just fine."

"Do you really see nothing?" I snapped.

Rian looked back at me in surprise from where he stood holding a bottle of whiskey.

"What?" He took a swig from the bottle then narrowed his eyes at me. "If this is some kind of trick to—"

"You have no clue what's going on," I hissed. "Do you?"

My chest heaved, my vision going unsteady. How could he be so blind?

At the first glance I could tell something was haunting Ryleigh.

How could *he* not see it?

I wanted to hit him. To smack him until he saw sense.

I strode across the tattoo shop towards him. "You've been so obsessed with your hurt, with your pain, little brother, that you've blinded yourself completely to anyone else's. You think you're the only one in the world to suffer? The only one in the world to be scared of the dark?"

"I think you need to leave," he said in a low, dangerous tone as he stalked toward me. "Right fucking now, Liam, before this turns bloody."

"Do you know she has nightmares?" I said, as his chest butted against mine, a physical fight on the brink. "Do you know she screams herself hoarse in the middle of the night?"

This wasn't how I wanted this conversation to go. I wanted an ally and I was making an enemy instead.

But I was so afraid for Ry.

"Do you really believe she left you all those years ago to 'see the fucking world'? Are you really that *self-centreed*? That clueless?"

I was being selfish. I knew that. I was using Ry to hurt Rian.

But he needed to *see*. I needed to scare him into protecting Ry while I was gone. I needed someone else in Dublin to *care*.

Because as much as I told myself all that Ryleigh needed was me, she needed a *family*, too.

She needed Rian.

"There's someone after her."

Rian blinked at me, stunned into silence.

My heart pounded, blood rushing against my ears, breath panting like a rabid dog. "She's in danger. She's been in danger ever since she ran five years ago. She hasn't had a moment of peace all this time. All this time you thought she's been having a party on some goddamn tour bus. She's been running scared. She's been *alone*."

The bottle fell from Rian's limp fingers. It rolled across the rug, whiskey pouring from the open top before it thudded to a stop against the leg of the couch.

"She would have told me," Rian said, but there was little conviction in his voice.

He stared past me, his gaze somewhere far away from Dublin Ink. Was he seeing that night she left? Was he replaying their conversations on the phone all those years? Was he trying to find the moments he missed?

"She… She would have told me." Rian shook his head and looked at me with a raw pain in his eyes. "Why wouldn't she have told me?"

It was the most I'd felt like Rian's older brother in a long time. He was looking to me for answers the way a little brother should.

"Sometimes," I said slowly, "sometimes people don't reveal a hard, painful truth if…"

I sucked in a breath and exhaled through my nose.

I'd opened up to him, told him the truth I'd kept like a knife in my heart for my whole life. And he rejected me. He called me a liar. He swore my truth couldn't be the truth, or at least not his. Never his.

That was Rian's problem: there was only ever room for *his* pain, *his* truth.

Looking my brother straight in the eye, I said, "Would you

have believed her, little brother? Would you have been able to see past your pain to help her with hers?"

I left without another word. The pieces of our broken relationship had edges that were too sharp.

I'd failed Ry. I'd gone to Rian for her sake. To make sure that she didn't go unprotected through the night. And I'd made a mess of it.

If anything I'd driven a further wedge between them. Rian would callous his heart toward Ry. I was sure of it. There wasn't a mirror Rian could face. And certainly not the one I'd shoved in front of him.

No one was coming to Ryleigh's aid if she needed help and it was my fault.

The guilt plagued me as I drove out of the city as I thought back to our goodbye.

I had hesitated at the door.

"I don't have to go," I said to Ry. "I'll find another way to make some money."

She smiled and came up onto her toes to kiss me. "Go."

"Maybe one of the girls can stay—"

"Go!"

She shoved me out the door and closed it on me before I could stop her.

I'd pressed my hand on the painted door and chewed my lip.

"You'll be grand," I whispered.

It was just a night. She'd be fine.

RY

Weren't goodbyes between friends supposed to take all night?

Weren't Aurnia, Eithne, Rachel and I supposed to stand around by the front door for another fifteen, twenty minutes? Why was it that the night I prayed they'd stay forever, my friends seemed to be gone in the blink of an eye?

I closed the door hesitantly behind them. In one hand I held a near-empty glass of alcohol-free champagne, in the other I held a taser that Rachel's American friend had smuggled illegally through the post to her.

That was all that I had left of the night. That was all I had left of the sense of safety and protection the girls had temporarily given me.

Now I was alone. Really alone.

I'd considered asking them to sleep over. To please not leave. To please, please just *stay*.

But my pride had won out. That kind of pathetic, panicked begging would inevitably lead to questions. And what's more, answers. Answers I kept like a canary in the cage of my chest.

Besides, our apartment was so small, so cramped. There was no room for them here.

Come on, silly, I can survive a night.

Liam only left me to secure the financial future of our baby. It made sense. It was the right thing to do. I would be fine.

A long bath helped. The relaxation of flickering candles. Soft music. My hair spread round me like river weeds as I stared up at the lights dancing across the ceiling.

I touched myself the way Liam did. My breasts. My nipples. The warmth between my legs.

With my eyes closed I could almost convince myself he was there, his knees knocking against the porcelain tub. His brow wet from the steam. His hands firmly on my throat and my hips as he fucked me.

Our bed in the glare of the streetlamp looked particularly empty. But I imagined it in a few months' time full. Practically overflowing. Me and Liam and our baby.

We'd lie on our sides, a thumb for each of our baby's perfect hands. We'd look into each other's eyes over the downy fuzz of his or her head. We'd discuss a new mattress. A bigger one. In a new place. And we'd have the money for it.

Once Liam got back…

I thought sleep might run from me like the end of a rainbow. I'd been expecting a long, drawn-out battle for rest.

But when I tugged an extra pillow toward my chest and breathed in deep the musk of Liam's shampoo and the lingering hint of engine grease, I found myself calm.

My thoughts grew heavy. I squeezed the pillow toward my

belly. Felt the pressure. Trusted Liam would give anything in the world to have his hand right there, right now…

I smiled sleepily, halfway dragged under when I heard the front door unlock. He'd decided to come home.

That was okay. We'd find the money some other way. Liam, here, was all I needed. All I wanted.

But his footsteps sounded…heavier than usual outside the door.

He hesitated just a little too long before he turned the bedroom doorknob.

As I lay with my back to him, snuggled beneath the blankets, ready for him to slip in behind me, it was not his satisfied hum that caused the hairs on the back of my neck to rise.

It wasn't Liam.

I spun to face the intruder.

Fingers clenched around my choked scream like iron shackles.

"Well, aren't you just all that I remembered," Balor cooed.

LIAM

"Strange," I muttered as the dial tone rang out.

I'd tried Peter's number three times now to let him know I was on my way to Cork, but he still wasn't picking up.

It was weird because he'd practically called me every hour on the feckin' hour in the days leading up to it to make sure I was still going, what time was I leaving, what time did I expect to be in Cork by?

The way his voice had trembled with excitement, you'd think that bike was a fucking woman he was in love with. And he'd transferred a 50,000 Euro non-refundable deposit into my account without blinking.

So why had he now just...disappeared.

The yellow lines of the road dashed by, getting swept under the wheel like fall leaves. The silhouette of the trees blurred past the windows against the low-hanging moonlit clouds. I'd driven plenty of times at night before, but never had the road seemed so endless, the destination so far.

Why couldn't I shake the feeling that leaving Dublin was wrong?

I rolled down the window a crack and tried to breathe in the country air. I thought it might revive me. Maybe it was just too hot in the car, the air too stifling.

I just needed to think straight for a moment or two. I was doing this for a reason. Leaving Ry. Driving across the country. Hauling back our future.

Two million euros was a sum I never could have imagined before Peter happened, as if out of the blue, to walk in the door of the shop.

My stomach turned despite the cascades of icy air across my outstretched face.

"We need this," I told myself as I forced my foot down harder on the pedal. "Ry needs this. Our baby needs this. I am doing what is *right*."

At night, with the glare of the headlights casting the surroundings into an even darker black, it was easy enough to imagine familiar hills. Long stretches of desolate land I could call to mind with perfect detail by just closing my eyes. *Home.*

I wasn't near my father's farm. But in my mind's eye I saw the fence that needed mending. I saw the birds diving into the pond circled in reeds, the only place of happy memories, like a single ray of sun between the clouds. I saw the house in the distance.

Just one light on.

And the silhouettes of a little boy and his father.

"I'm only doing what's right."

Isn't that what my father had said? The night he told me he'd kill Rian if I interfered.

"You'll protect him by not protecting him, d'ye hear?"

I'd left Rian unprotected to protect him. Was I making the same mistake with Ry?

I couldn't stop seeing her, the fear in her eyes that she tried to hide as I was leaving, the little step forward at the door before catching herself.

She might have said "go" but she didn't want me to go.

I heard Rian's voice as if he were sitting beside me. Not a man like he was today. But nine or ten. "Do I have to stay?"

I looked over at the passenger seat. It was, of course, empty. But it didn't matter. He was *there*. Rian. Hands wringing. Black eyes ringed with purple.

I knew he didn't want to sleep in the barn. He shouldn't have to. He wanted to come into the house with me and I wanted him to. The cold of the night would teach him nothing compared to the heat of our shared bed.

Cruelty has no lesson. It is love that transforms. I knew this now.

"You'll be grand," I whispered as I struggled to maintain control of the wheel. It was what I whispered to him that night I left him alone in the barn. It was what I assured Ry with one last weak smile.

I turned my attention back to the dark horizon.

And tried calling Peter one more time.

RY

Perhaps if I had started fighting sooner, it would have made a difference.

But it took me a second to get over the shock. A few seconds where I just lay there, stunned, limbs frozen, gripped in fear as I stared up at the face of my nightmares.

I'd faced Balor so many times in my dreams. Each dream was different but the same.

Sometimes we were in my tattoo parlour, often we were back in his playroom. The worst nights were when he'd show up in my bedroom.

I'd try to force myself to wake up, *wake up*.

Just like now.

Except this time, it wasn't a dream.

And this time, I wasn't just fighting for *my* life.

I clawed at his cheeks and chest. I threw elbows, drove my knees up, kicked with my heels. Every single martial arts move I'd learned I threw at him.

Balor just laughed. Using his grip on my throat, he

smashed my head back against the headboard, stunning me into momentary submission.

For a moment, all I could see was his smile as the rest of the room blurred.

"You know, I was slightly worried that I'd hunt you down all these years…the *one that got away*…and it wouldn't all be worth it in the end. That my romantic idea of you would far outmatch who you really were."

Balor stroked my cheek.

I snapped at his hand with my teeth, bit his finger to the point of bleeding. But he snatched his hand back and *beamed* at me, eyes flashing onyx.

"But you're *everything* I dreamed you would be," he said, shoving my shirt up to expose my breasts. He laughed, almost in disbelief as I tried to push his hands off me, as I struggled to cover myself and to fucking *breathe*.

"Is it possible that you're *more* than I dreamed?"

His cock grew hard against my belly where he held me down with his weight as he closed off my airways. "What do you think?"

I choked, scratching at his hands as the corners of my periphery closed in.

Oh God. This was it. I died this way. My baby died this way. No.

He released my throat. I gulped in air and coughed.

I screamed and Balor groaned loudly as he closed his hand around my throat again, cutting off my cry for help. His cock twitched, and my stomach rolled. I swallowed down bile and eyed the bedside table as Balor's hips ground against me.

The taser. Where was it?

A slap to my face brought stinging tears to my eyes.

"There is, of course," Balor said, spit flying from his mouth, "your recent behaviour, young lady. *That* was most disappointing. How, I thought when I found that little pregnancy test of yours on the bathroom counter, can I love a whore?"

He slapped me again and I cried out in pain.

Through the tears I saw it, shimmering like a mirage: the taser peeking out from under the pillow.

"But then it just started sounding nicer and nicer in my head," he said, chuckling. "Now there's two of you to play with..."

Over my dead body. I lunged for the taser. I managed to brush the edge of it just as Balor's fingers twisted in my hair and he dragged me from the bed.

The taser rolled off the edge of the bedside table as he tossed me like a rag doll to the floor.

I curled over my stomach instinctively. My shoulder erupted in pain as I slammed down hard on it.

Somewhere on the side table my phone began to ring.

Liam.

Standing above me, Balor sucked in a ragged breath. Carded his fingers through his slicked back hair. The glare of the streetlamp sliced his face in half, making him look like the crazed Joker.

"My boyfriend's on his way home," I said, trying not to let my voice tremble as I scrambled back across the carpet. "He had to work late. He'll kill you, know you."

The yellow light shifted to illuminate both of Balor's eyes as he grinned down at me.

"You mean...Liam?" he asked sweetly.

He snatched up my phone and showed me the screen.

A photo of Liam's smiling face along with the word ***Hubby*** flashed up on the phone.

"He's much more gullible in person." Balor tossed my phone aside.

My blood ran cold. I curled in further upon myself, over my baby.

"No." Balor shook his head, "I don't think your boyfriend will be coming home anytime soon. I think he'll be miles away, actually, on his way to Cork. And getting farther by the second."

I crawled for the taser. Balor's boot caught me in the ribs. I heard the crack over my cries of pain, over my phone ringing again.

He pressed his heel into the small of my back. I felt the compression on my stomach and tried to squirm away. No.

He just dug in deeper, harder. The carpet burned my naked skin, but I thrashed nonetheless till Balor leaned down to grab a handful of hair. I thought he was going to snap my neck, the way he wrenched it back.

"I thought that little lovebird of yours would never leave you alone," he hissed. "Every time I'd get close to you, there he'd be. Following you, watching you from the shadows, and then eventually worming his way into your life."

My skin prickled. I reached for my phone as it rang again, Liam so desperate to reach me. He must know by now something was wrong. But it didn't matter.

He was too far away. Tricked into leaving me.

"Oh, didn't you know? Your stalker was thwarted by..." he chuckled, "another stalker."

I sucked in a breath.

"It was fun, for a little while. Our little game of cat and mouse. But there's only so long a cat can play with its food."

White light exploded behind my eyes when Balor slammed my face down onto the floor.

I heard him cackling, the echo of my phone ringing.

Then nothing.

LIAM

It was impossible to describe the relief I experienced when I saw *Call incoming: Wifey* on my phone.

Thank God.

She was okay. She'd probably just been in the bath when I rang…twelve fucking times. Fuck, I was paranoid.

I waited a ring or two to answer so I could steady my breath. I didn't want her to hear the remnants of the panic that'd been choking me at her not answering. I didn't want her to have any idea at all that I'd been worried. Terrified. Sure that something irreversible, irreconcilable, unreturnable had happened.

I was practically laughing as I answered. "Baby, it has never been so good to hear from you."

The hesitation on the speaker was unexpected, the silence echoing through the car.

When it stretched on for the count of two breaths and then three, it was unavoidable: a black cat across my path, a broken mirror, seven years' bad luck.

"Ry?" I said, fear slipping back in. "Ry?"

"It's me."

The words were right. But the voice was not. Deep, masculine and…usually so full of hatred for me.

"Rian?"

Another pause. Another agonising silence. Another counting of my stuttering breaths: one…two…three…

"Rian?" I repeated more harshly this time. "Where's Ry?"

Rian gathered himself together with a ragged exhale, and finally said in a hollow voice, "I'm so sorry, Liam."

I struggled to keep the car on the road, the lines of the road were suddenly not so straight.

"I should have believed you," he said. "This is all my fault."

I didn't want to ask it. I almost didn't dare.

Oh God, how bad was it? What had Balor done?

"Just tell me she's alive," I begged before I lost the nerve.

"Liam, you've got to get back here."

I saw red, the car swerving out of control. I swerved the car back between the lines, having drifted dangerously toward the shoulder.

"I'm already driving back to Dublin," I said. "What's going on?"

I'd done a U-turn the very second Ry's phone had rung out the first time.

"I just had this feeling, ye know. After you left. I just couldn't shake it. So I came over to her—*your* place… she…" He choked on a sob.

Dear God, please don't say she's dead.

"Rian." I gripped the steering wheel, fighting the urge to rip it out from the column. "Just fucking tell me…is she *alive*?"

"I…I don't know."

"What do you mean, *you don't know*?"

"I...I'm sorry."

No. No no no no.

"Rian," I warned. "What the fuck—?"

"Ryleigh has been taken."

RY

"Look at her," Liam's voice was soft as we watched a tiny figure running across the grassy field. "She's as wild as the winds that sweep across those emerald hills."

I nestled closer to Liam even though I couldn't put my finger on what exactly was wrong with this picture.

He pulled me into his lap where we sat on the grass. His strong arms closed around me and knew that no matter what, our baby would feel protected, secured, loved.

He whispered, "I'll teach her that the land is beautiful if you know her secrets, cruel if you treat her like a stranger."

I imagined these were things he wished he could have taught his younger brother. Had his father allowed him. Had his father had different ideas about the land. About strength. About beauty.

Liam kissed my forehead. "She'll learn love from you and there's no way to buy that anyway."

How I would have loved to see him as a little kid, dirt

under his fingernails, mud across the cheek. Bright-eyed and pink from chasing the wind.

His father had been cruel. And what was worse, showed him how to be cruel.

But Liam had learned a different way to be. The one with me safe in his arms. And our child…

My hand reached up to my belly.

Our child…

I stared around as the green leaves crumbled into black, as the earth shook underneath our feet.

"Liam, what's happening?" I begged, clutching onto him.

He just gazed into my eyes, his thumb brushing along my cheekbone, as if the world wasn't crumbling around us.

"You have to be strong, baby," he said with a sad, knowing smile. "We need you."

"I need you, too," I cried out, reaching for him.

Blackness swallowed me whole.

A cold sweat covered my body, panic gripping my chest. My body was reacting, but my mind could process nothing more than that I was awake, but I didn't want to be.

My baby.

This thought was like a dam breaking.

With a horrible gasp I came to full consciousness.

I was on a bed, but it was not my own. My sweat-covered back arched off the sheets like it was all just a nightmare I'd awoken in the middle of, screaming.

But there was no sound from my chapped lips.

And this *was* the nightmare.

I was splayed across a firm mattress. I tugged at my wrists, but they were each tied to a post of the iron-frame bed, this position making it difficult to breathe through my panic. My ribcage seemed unwilling to expand and I was left with tiny, gasping inhales of musty air.

A fresh wave of horror swept over me when I realised how widely my ankles were tied apart at the end of the bed. No matter how hard I tried, I couldn't turn my knees in far enough to force my thighs together.

Beneath Liam's oversized t-shirt I was completely exposed in my panties. Cold air wrapped around my exposed skin so that the hairs stood on end.

If there wasn't my baby to think about I might have succumbed to the temptation of just closing my eyes, blocking out what tortures awaited me.

But I needed to find a way to escape.

I forced myself to look around me.

The bed was in what looked like a massive warehouse. The size of the space with its industrial lights, only a few lit up, high above me was not just intimidating, but dehumanising.

Everywhere I looked in that huge space just sent my heart racing faster. Racks, toys, whips laid out on the cold concrete floor, covering the corrugated metal walls.

I imagined Balor planning their arrangement and thought I might throw up. Before, his playroom had been in Balor's home.

This was a slaughterhouse.

I could not see or hear anyone else. Wherever Balor had gone, he wouldn't have left me alone for long.

I imagined him approaching the layout of his sick warehouse in the same practical, cold-blooded way he would his office, his boardroom. Rearranging things for months. Perfecting. Getting hard as he ran through all the ways he could hurt me in his mind.

Tears welled in my eyes despite myself. It would be one thing for me to go through this bastard's revolting games. But to know that my baby would have to be right there with me filled me with unbearable rage.

If I was still on my own, I could have taken some solace in knowing I wouldn't survive. Balor had clearly been planning his revenge for so long there was no way he would let me live.

My tears were as hot as blood on my cheeks. It hurt to imagine Liam pulling me to his chest amongst the reeds of some filthy river outside the city, my bones broken, my face bloated and bruised.

But it was unbearable to think of our helpless baby dead in my belly. Liam's hand pressing the cold skin of my stomach.

He could have survived losing me. But not both of us. That would kill him.

My life wasn't just mine anymore.

I felt my heart harden with purpose. Liam's love wrapping like steel around my nerves. I had to fight even if I died trying.

I had to get back to Liam. I needed him to hold his baby.

I had to survive.

I tested my bindings again. They were rope, made of slick unnatural fibres in a thick twist. The kind of fibre that would melt if a flame was applied to it.

It scraped my skin as I tugged. But there was the slightest bit of slack in the knot because of what it was made of.

If I could just wriggle my hand out, if I could just get one hand free… I could untie the knots on my other bindings. I had a hope of getting out.

But I had to do it before Balor came back.

I repressed my cries as the rope scraped my skin bloody,

as my joints screamed as I tried to contort my hand in a way that would let me slip loose.

Come on. *Come on.*

I was so close. So close…

“Finally…” the voice came from the shadows, “you’re awake.”

LIAM

Funny how life seemed to slow down the moments that should be sped up. Like the drive back to the apartment I shared with Ryleigh seemed to last several lifetimes where she was taken from me over and over again in every single one.

And vice versa. All those perfect moments with Ryleigh, shining in my memory like porch lights in the dark, had sped by too quickly.

We needed more time.

I'd only just found her. We were only just starting a life together.

This couldn't be all the time we had left.

It just...couldn't.

My car jumped the curb amidst a deafening screech of brakes. I wrenched the hand brake on, not bothering to turn off the engine before I leapt out in the downpour.

My headlights glared in my eyes as I ran past them as icy rain beat at my head, a snare drum to the smashing of my heart against my ribs.

The slick railing slipped in my grip as I took the stairs two at a time. It felt like I was climbing quicksand.

Rian stood just outside the doorway of my apartment, silhouetted against the lights glaring from inside.

"Liam…" His voice broke, grief already forming in the lines around his mouth.

No. He could *not* be grieving. She could *not* be gone. I wouldn't let her be gone.

"We're going to get her back," I said, trying to convince him, to convince myself.

There had to be hope inside our apartment. Right? A piece. A crumb. A drop.

If there was, I would find it.

I pushed past Rian. The door was open but the lock was undamaged, a key hanging from the outside of the front door lock.

"It was like that when I got here," Rian said. "And the door was wide open."

I drew in a shaky breath. He'd used a key.

My fucking key.

I thought I'd lost it in the garage somewhere. But he must have stolen it.

My mind flashed back to the meeting with "Peter", at how I'd left him alone in the office. I swear I'd had my keys on the desk there.

How could I have been so fucking stupid?

I entered the apartment, my brother following me. Nothing in the living room looked disturbed. I strode to the bedroom in the back, hesitating at the doorway, the bottom dropping out of my stomach.

The drive home had been long enough to imagine dozens

of different scenarios. In some there was blood on the walls, bloody torn clothes, tangles of ripped-out hair in others.

There was none of that. The sheets were messy, a few things knocked to the floor from the bedside table, the rug askew on the floor.

Ry's attacker had come with the express purpose of taking her somewhere else. This had just been a means to an end.

Not the end.

Ry was a doll and this room had merely been her shelf. He was taking her to where he was going to play with her.

A shiver ran down my spine as I stood there just inside our bedroom in the lamplight. My hair was wet from the rain, my jacket damp at the shoulders. But this was a deeper kind of cold that sent my skin erupting in goosebumps. This was the cold of fucking *evil*.

In my nostrils I could just make out the same expensive sharp cologne I'd smelled at the garage.

"Peter" *was* Ryleigh's stalker.

I'd shaken his fucking hand. Let him sit in my office chair. Took money from him.

I'd let him trick me into leaving Ryleigh alone.

My stomach turned, and I shivered as if I were burning up from fever.

I imagined his hands on Ry, his beady eyes daring to trace over her skin, his breath like a foul, hot wind on the hollows of her throat.

I stoked the blood lust inside of me.

Suddenly, I was no longer breathing heavily. No longer feeling panicked or sick. My fingers didn't shake when I righted the lamp in the bedroom. I was calm. Focused. Determined.

I'd lived on the farm long enough to know you can't let something rabid live. When you got your barrel between its mad eyes you didn't fucking hesitate.

And I wouldn't hesitate.

I was going to kill him.

Rian was there when I turned around. His eyes searched mine and I wondered what they saw amongst the shadows.

Did he still recognise me as his brother? Or had I already become something else?

"I called Mason and Conor and left messages for both of them," he said, gravel in his voice.

I nodded. It felt robotic, unnatural.

But I reasoned that everything was going to feel that way till she was back in my arms.

"Maybe we should call Diarmuid, file a missing persons with the Gards—"

"No cops," I replied darkly, already moving back toward the door.

Rian was fast at my heels.

"Liam, I think we need as many people as we can get to figure out who this stalker guy is that's taken her."

"I know *exactly* who took her."

"*What?* Who?" Rian asked, anger entering his voice.

I ignored him. There was no time…

I was surprised by the strength of Rian's sudden death grip on my upper arm.

Rian had always been the smallest of us boys. Or at least, that was how my father wanted me to see him.

But I could feel in his fingers and see in his eyes that I wasn't going to escape without giving him answers.

"Where are you going?" he demanded.

My brother looked older than I'd ever seen him. He was

no longer the scared little boy in the barn, begging me not to leave him alone. He was a man. He deserved to know, not to be shielded.

"I'm going to get her back."

"How?" he asked, his voice going dark.

My stomach flip-flopped. He might be a man, but Rian was still my baby brother. I couldn't protect him then, but I could protect him now.

He didn't need to get involved. Blood was being shed that night.

But there was no reason it needed to stain both of our hands.

"Go home, Rian," I said carefully, infusing my voice with meaning. "Go back to bed. You *don't* want to be a part of this."

There. I'd released him from the duty that he'd felt obliged to.

I tried to pull my arm free from Rian's grip. But he held me tight.

"No," he said in a firm voice. "I'm a part of this. I'm coming."

I shifted my jaw.

Rian never liked the slaughtering of the animals on the farm. He didn't have it in him, that ruthlessness. That savage instinct. That deep, unspoken craving for it. *Blood.*

He was better. He was always better. Than me. Than Alan. Than Da. Than all of us.

"It's going to get…messy," I warned him.

"For Ry?" Rian's eyes turned cruel, for a moment I saw a flash of our dead father in them. "I can do *messy.*"

Suddenly it felt like he was gripping my arm not like an enemy, but like a brother.

I nodded. "Let's go."

I would find Ryleigh. Even if I had to burn the world down to get her.

I only hoped I wasn't too late.

RY

"Do you like my playroom?"

The shadows distended and out stepped Balor, the overhead light cutting across his features with dark shadows making him look almost supernatural.

He grinned. "I built it just for *you*."

In Irish mythology, Balor was the leader of a race of evil creatures that came up from out of the ground and under the water to attack the innocent.

He was always described as monstrous, sometimes with one eye like a cyclops, sometimes several eyes with petrifying abilities if you were unlucky enough to be caught in his stare.

In the warehouse, Balor's gaze was pinned to me and fear turned my body into stone as if the myth was real.

The only thing that broke the spell was the flash of metal in his hand.

A knife.

I thrashed involuntarily on the bed, tugging on the bindings around my wrists and ankles, my blood soaking the rope fibres.

He smiled at me as he began to approach. Like a panther who could see their prey was caught and going nowhere, he took his time, fingering his blade.

"You made me work so hard for you, little slut." His voice was hard yet it simmered with anger. "You made me chase your breadcrumbs all over fucking Europe. Every time I thought I had you, you'd fucking disappear. Until my prodigal sweetheart returned to Dublin."

The grin he gave me sent shivers down my spine.

I glanced back up to my wrist. If I could just get my hand free. I ignored the sting as I wrenched my wrist.

The bed creaked as he kneeled beside me. A blade was at my throat seconds later.

I froze at the cold metal. My stomach turned as he leaned in, his sour breath against my cheeks.

"Did you forget that you were *mine*?"

"I am not *yours*," I spat out.

I belong to Liam.

Balor's features hardened. "By the time I'm done with you, you will be."

He slashed at me with the knife. A cry broke free of my lips but there was no pain.

Balor cut the material of my oversized shirt, the ripping sound echoing throughout the warehouse, until the strips fell away from my breasts.

Cold air slapped my nipples. I tugged at my wrists again, trying so desperately to cover myself, but I couldn't.

He let out a low groan as he stole the sight of me with his dirty gaze, a sound that made my stomach turn.

"You're more exquisite than I remember."

He leaned down and licked across one nipple. It hardened involuntarily even as a sob broke free of my throat.

"Go on. Cry for me, baby," he said. "Scream. It makes me hard."

I swallowed down my panic and set my jaw. *Stay strong, Ry. Don't let him break you.*

Balor chuckled darkly as he licked his lips.

"I soundproofed this whole fucking warehouse just so you can make all sorts of pretty noises for me."

He grabbed my panties and cut them off my hips, exposing me, making me dirty with his stare.

"Such a pretty little cunt," he said as he dragged the flat end of the blade across me.

I suppressed a sob and turned my face away.

"No?" Balor asked when I kept my trembling lips sealed. "How about now?"

A line of burning fire appeared across my upper thigh as he cut my skin. Hot blood slid over my inner thigh to the mattress.

I swallowed my scream and squeezed my eyes shut.

"Just a little scream," Balor said, his breath hot on my leg. "A little scream for daddy."

I gagged as he licked at my wound and growled low in his throat, his face so close to the most intimate part of me.

"I really thought I would get a scream that time," he said, sitting up. "Shall we try again?"

He sliced over the swell of my breast, just enough to pierce the skin, not enough to kill me. I grabbed fistfuls of the sheets as fire raced across my skin.

It's like getting tattooed. You can handle being under the needle for hours at a time, you can fucking handle this.

I didn't have to look down to see blood stains seeping across Liam's t-shirt.

I fought against the sudden lightness in my head. As lovely as it would be to pass out, the horror of what he might do to me—to my baby—while I was under kept me grasping for consciousness.

"You're being stubborn," he muttered as if I were a child refusing to eat my peas.

He continued to trace the knife tip across my skin, drawing lines into my flesh, pain burning everywhere.

He was making a mess of my body, hot blood dripping along my rib cage to seep down into the mattress.

I didn't want to scream. I wanted to stay strong for Liam. Strong for our baby.

But I just couldn't hold it back.

A scream tore from my lips and I poured my fear and horror into it, echoing around the warehouse.

Balor chuckled.

"So pretty," he said, palming his cock.

His knife lashed once more, causing me to flinch. The rest of my shirt fell open on either side of my stomach.

He scowled as he glared at my seven-month pregnant belly. If I thought having my breasts and pussy naked to him felt exposed, nothing felt more vulnerable than having him staring at my belly, my arms and legs stretched out, unable to cover my baby.

"There it is," he said, "the fucking epitome of your betrayal to me."

He held up the knife, glinting in the downlights.

"I'm going to cut that cunt's baby right out of your belly."

LIAM

"Left up here," Rian said.

I turned the wheel hard, the tail of my car fish-tailing as the tires screamed for grip on the road.

Rian let out a curse and grabbed the "oh shite" handle above his passenger side door as the force slammed us both into the side of the car before we righted. In his other hand he clutched my phone.

We were driving through an industrial area on the outskirts of north Dublin near the airport. This late at night, it was deserted. Thank God. I was not above running over people to get to my girl.

No Garda out on these roads to slow me down either.

"I'd love to install a tracker on Eithne's phone, too," Rian said. "But she wouldn't let me."

I kept my stare on the road, even as I felt his eyes on me.

"Ry didn't exactly…let me."

To my surprise Rian let out a low laugh. "You demented fuck."

I let out a low snort. "You know how abandon-happy she

was. She had one foot out the door the whole time she was in Dublin."

"So you put a tracker on her without her knowing?"

I shrugged. "I couldn't lose her."

"Right up here," Rian said, grabbing the handle.

I turned hard again, the screech of my tires loud over the engine.

"Wait a minute," Rian frowned at the app open on my phone. "I thought Ry's phone was back in the bedroom."

I pursed my lips, eyes scanning the dark warehouses. Ryleigh was in one of these metal boxes.

"How the hell did you get a tracker on her then?" Rian asked.

"Just...keep your eyes on the app," I muttered.

I'd always expected Ryleigh would bolt at some point, her instinct to flee when it got too hard getting too much.

I figured her pregnancy might tip her over and she'd try to run from me.

But I was never letting her go.

Not her or our baby.

I never expected I'd be using it to track her down from being kidnapped by a psychopath.

The truth that I wasn't about to share with Rian was I'd had a tracker inserted underneath the sonogram charm.

I'd have to hope that Ryleigh forgave me when she found out what I'd done.

If we weren't too late.

RY

Balor lowered his knife to my belly.

No!

I struggled again, thrashing uncontrollably, as panic gripped me.

"Wait! If you cut my baby out then I'll die of blood loss, and..." I swallowed down the bile collecting in my mouth, "... you wouldn't want it to be over so quickly, would you?"

Balor stared at me for one long moment.

"I mean," I continued, hating every word I said, "you spent all this time and effort to get me back."

He laughed and waved the knife tip at me. "I do so like a whore with a sense of humour."

"I'll...do whatever you want," I said, trying to trade the only thing I had left, my compliance. "I'll be...*good.* Just let me give birth to my baby. Let them live."

Balor let out a noise of annoyance. "I want you to beg for *your* life. This selfless shit really does make me soft."

Grinding my jaw, I said, "Sorry to disappoint."

"However," Balor said, "you make some valid points..."

He tossed the knife onto the bedside and walked over to a display of monstrous dildos, each bigger than the next. Even the smallest one would have torn me open.

Twirling a ball gag around his finger, he said, "You know what? I *could* let you have this baby. And I could raise the innocent little thing. Slight diversion from your plan, I know."

He bit down on the ball gag, eyes flashing madly at me. "I could teach him or her to be everything you weren't. A good little subservient slave."

Horror filled my mouth with bitterness. That was a fate worse than death.

I would kill him before I let him hurt my little baby.

I tugged at my restraints, trying to slip my hand out. That knife was by the bedside. I just have to get one hand free.

"If she was a girl, I'd name her after you," Balor said, distracted by a wall of whips and clamps. "Little Baby Ry."

I tugged at the rope, wincing as it scraped my skin. I was almost free.

"Of course, she would have some of another man's DNA in her," Balor said, clicking his tongue in disappointment as he batted a sex swing around like a cat playing with a toy. "Already tainted. Already filthy."

Balor picked up something heavy and metallic.

"New plan," he said, creeping toward me. "I kill your baby. And replace his seed with my own. I make something that is truly all mine."

"*No*," I cried, tugging harder at my wrist, my fingers screaming as the rope squeezed them so hard they felt like they were going to break. "You bastard. You disgusting animal."

"Darling, you wound me."

Balor crawled onto the bed and straddled me.

"Remember this?" Balor snarled.

He dangled something metallic above my face.

I saw flashes of Balor's face. Younger. Contorted and red with uncontrollable anger. I felt my fingertips on a cold metal floor, grasping for something hard. I heard a crack against bone like thunder from my memory.

It was the butt plug I'd hit him over the head with.

He'd never forgotten that. Never been able to move past it. I'd embarrassed him. Thwarted him. Hurt him back. He was going to make me pay for that.

He was going to have his nasty fun with me.

Then he was going to kill me.

He lifted the butt plug high over his head with both arms.

"We're just going to have to hope you survive the miscarriage."

Balor swung violently down at me.

My hand came loose from the ropes. I curled in on myself on my side to protect my baby. When the metal collided with my ribs, I heard a sickening crack.

"Such fight in this one." Balor chuckled. "Not that it's going to help you."

He yanked my left arm away from where I'd wrapped it protectively around my baby and pressed it out to the side.

I fought against him so hard I thought my shoulder would dislocate. But it was no use. He was too strong and he was using his weight to pin my arm down.

He lifted his metal weapon again.

"Goodbye, baby Ry."

RY

It felt like forever, behind my squeezed lids, as I waited for the metal plug to descend. As I waited for the pain to erupt in my belly.

Despite how much I fought, I was pinned down, the most vulnerable part of me exposed. The scream tearing from my lungs felt like an exorcism, as if the horror of what was about to happen ripped forth from me like a wraith.

It was a wraith with no worldly powers though. The depth of my rage could not stop him alone.

For one long moment, I *hated* being a woman. Because I hated that being a woman meant being prey. Unable to stop one single man if he felt like he wanted to take something from me, no matter how many hours in the gym I'd done, no matter how many fucking martial arts classes I'd taken.

The unfairness of it consumed me so I felt like I burst into flames hot enough to burn this world down.

I'm sorry I couldn't protect you.

The last of my scream heaved from my lungs.

But the pain didn't come.

A deep, enraged roar caused my eyes to fling back open. Balor was pulled off of me, my arm now free.

Through blurry vision, he was lifted into the air and slammed back against a rack.

I gasped as the hulking figure, more shadow than man, unleashed a violence against Balor that might have shaken me with terror if not for the relief coursing through my body.

Black-gloved fists pummelled Balor's face into a messy red pulp, his cries gurgling against a mouthful of blood. Teeth rattled against the floor. It was like a toy in a dog's gnashing teeth as it whipped mercilessly back and forth, spittle flying.

Liam.

Somehow he had found me.

I felt fingers at the rope around my still bound wrist.

"Rian." I exhaled heavily.

My best friend wouldn't look at me as he worked on the knots. His fingers trembled as he fought with the knots, his eyes wide with a frightening intensity, reminding me of when he was high.

I grabbed Balor's knife from the other bedside. I pushed the handle into Rian's hand.

"It'll be faster," I whispered, my voice hoarse.

He finally looked at me. His eyes were blown wide, making them childlike. "Ry… I thought…we thought…"

Yeah. Me, too.

He hacked at the ropes and one by one, my limbs were returned to me, pins and needles stinging my hands and feet from the blood rushing back in.

He helped me sit up.

The sight of Liam took my breath away. He'd never looked wilder. He was practically feral with blood splattered across his stubbled jaw and his teeth bared like he was rabid.

"Liam!" I cried out. "That's enough."

I could only imagine the blood rushing against his ears, the pounding of his heart. Even though my voice had been weak and raw, he stopped and looked up, rage-blind eyes searching me out.

Only when he finally saw me did it seem like he could actually see.

I saw the bloodlust in his eyes which he fought to force back beneath the surface as he stared at me, panting harshly. Then he rushed to my side.

Balor collapsed to the floor like a limp doll, his head cracking against the floor.

Rian helped Liam take me up into his arms.

His lips were all over the crown of my head as his fingers tried not to squeeze too tightly.

"You're alright," he murmured. "You're safe now. You're safe."

A wave of white-hot pain crashed over me. I let out a cry, curling over my belly.

"Something's *wrong*."

LIAM

On the farm even at a young age, Rian and I would be tasked to herd the cows or roll hay bales together. We learned how to anticipate each other's movements, weaving around each other in silence.

Even after all this time, Rian and I fell into working together like no time had passed. Like we were still brothers.

He pulled open the passenger door as I carried Ry out of the warehouse. I laid Ry down as gently as I could in the seat and he reappeared from the boot holding a blanket.

I took it from him and unfolded the blanket as he hurried around to the driver's side to get the car started, switching on the headlines which illuminated the side of the warehouse through the late-night mist.

Something's wrong with our baby.

Ry shook uncontrollably as I laid the blanket over her, her body burning up to the touch even as her teeth chattered. Shite. She was going into shock.

"It's going to be okay, baby," I whispered, pushing her hair from her clammy forehead. "It's going to be okay."

Was I trying to convince her? Or me?

The threads of the fury that had consumed me were still there on the periphery. But this was not the time to indulge them. I had to stay calm. Focused. I had to get Ryleigh safely to the hospital as quickly as possible. I had to get my family to the hospital.

Only this singular purpose kept the beast inside me in check.

I paused at the driver's side. Rian had his arms crossed over his body, chin against his chest. We'd both seen what we couldn't ever unsee.

The woman we loved naked and bound to a blood-soaked bed, her beautiful body marred with cuts. I didn't know exactly what she had endured before we'd arrived. I didn't know whether she'd be okay.

I could only hope.

The misty night air smelled like the coppery tang of blood as I inhaled deeply.

"*This* isn't over," I said to Rian.

He looked up, purpose renewed in his eyes, his features turning from grief to stone.

"I'll…*tidy up*," he said, his dark tone betraying his real meaning.

He turned to the warehouse but I grabbed his forearm.

"Leave him for *me*," I said.

Rian nodded and clasped my forearm back, sealing our bloody pact.

"Meet us at the hospital," I said before climbing into the driver's seat.

In the rearview mirror, in a glow of red from the taillights, I saw him disappear into the warehouse and close the door behind him. I trusted Rian would do what needed to be done.

Up until tonight I would have called Rian the "good one", me the "bad one". But it seemed even my baby brother hadn't escaped the reaches of our violent upbringing.

Perhaps we were all equally good and bad. Or perhaps we were all equally neither.

Evidence would need to be destroyed. Balor would need to be punished.

But right now, I had to get Ry and our baby to the hospital.

I accelerated, gravel kicking up into the mist behind me. Keeping one hand on the steering wheel, I reached across for Ry. She grabbed ahold of my hand with both of hers; they were crusted with dried blood.

"Liam," Ry whispered, "what if—the baby—"

I pushed the pedal down harder and lied, "Everything's going to be alright."

RY

The lights of the ER were harsh against my stinging eyes as Liam barged in through the entrance with me cradled in his arms.

"Please," he yelled, "my wife was attacked. She needs help!"

Even as the nurses shouted, swinging doors crashed open, the rattle of a gurney's wheels across the pale linoleum floors, all I could think for a moment was,

He called me his wife.

They pulled me out of his arms and onto a gurney.

I reached for him even as they started wheeling me away, panic choking me at the loss of him. "Liam."

"Ry."

He tried to follow me past the swinging doors but he was stopped. I caught a glimpse of his worried face twice more before the doors stopped swinging.

My stomach hollowed out at the thought that this would be the last time I ever saw him.

A nurse took my head in her hands and held it still.

"Don't move till we figure out the extent of your injuries," she said, as the overhead lights passed one after the other like the lines on the highway.

"I'm okay," I tried to tell her. "It's my baby."

As we entered a room I heard the sound of curtains being drawn around me along metal bars. Claustrophobia made my chest even tighter.

There were hands all over me and panic threatened to consume me. I struggled not to fight against the strangers' hands.

Thick gauze was wiped across my cuts, stinging my skin. I moaned as hands forced my arm away from where I was holding it over my belly, and they forced a blood pressure cuff up to my bicep.

"Please," I begged, "my baby. Just see if my baby is alright."

They placed ECG dots on my chest for *my* heart rate and slipped a clip on my finger for *my* vitals. I wanted to tear them all off of me to finally get their attention: not me. My *baby*.

My baby was all that mattered.

Hearing the rapid, erratic beat of my heart only made me panic more. Yes, I was alive—barely. But what about my little bean?

Another face came to peer over me, a serious-faced doctor in a white coat. He peeled up my eyelid and shined a light that stabbed straight into my brain. More tears streamed down my already damp cheeks.

"Urgent CTG," the doctor said. "Intravenous access."

A moment later a nurse pricked the vein in the crook of my elbow for a catheter, but I didn't even feel it. I was already in too much pain.

There was too much chaos around me, too much fear

making my blood thud against my ears, and far too much pain in my belly.

"My baby," I choked out. "Is my baby okay?"

Everyone was ignoring me. There were half a dozen people working around me and not a single one answered.

"Shh, shh," voices cooed.

A hand pressed against my forehead, but I pushed it away.

Why didn't they understand? If my baby died it didn't matter what they did to try to save me. It was over.

I stilled when I felt someone wipe down my stomach and then place two dot monitors. I held my breath as if that would help them get a good reading.

Nurses still tended to my cuts, but I ignored the sting as I looked desperately between the monitor and the doctor's face as he studied it.

Time seemed to stretch as I waited for something to happen, not even sure what it was that was supposed to happen.

Everything still bustled around me, but the doctor was so still. My eyes darted with increased frequency between his face and the monitor.

I begged for him to sigh in relief, to turn and smile at me. I prayed that I wouldn't see him slowly close his eyes, preparing himself for a moment before delivering the hard news that would break me forever. It was nearly unbearable, that waiting, waiting, wait—

A second heartbeat.

For a moment the relief wiped away all my pain.

But then the doctor, eyes still fixed on the monitor, said, "Baby's heartbeat is fast...ultrasound."

The flurry of movement his words triggered made me panic. My head rolled, eyes searching for some sort of answer to what was going on as someone smeared a cold gel over my belly. The doctor swiped the ultrasound wand over me and cursed.

"Likely a uterine rupture."

More activity around me. None of it comprehensible to me. In fact, no one even seemed to notice that I was there, something more than just a body on a table.

"What does that mean?" I begged. "Please, just tell me what that *means*!"

I screamed as a sharp agony cut across my belly like I was being split in two.

Through my haze, I heard a nurse's shout: "Doctor, she's bleeding!"

I pressed my fingers against the hot slick on my thighs. I lifted my hand up and even as it shook in front of my eyes, my fingers stained red. So much blood. Too much blood.

I couldn't breathe.

"What's happening?" I gasped. "Is it the baby?"

I looked up and saw the doctor's face filled with dread. I opened my mouth to beg him to tell me something, *anything*, but at that moment another lashing of pain tore through me. My vision greyed out as I screamed.

The beeping on the monitor grew faster and faster. Was it my heart rate going out of control or was it my baby's?

An alarm went off, loud and sharp against my ears. My head began to swim. I blinked my eyes open but saw little through the edges of foggy grey.

"Her blood pressure's dropped."

"Emergency C-section. Go!"

"If it's a choice," I tried to say before I drowned in black, "save my baby."

LIAM

Of all the instruments of torture, there was none more brutal than time itself.

I sat in a flimsy plastic chair only to decide I wanted to stand. I'd close my eyes only to wrench them open at any sound that might be the doctor pushing through the swinging doors of the ER. An unbearable heat had me tearing at my jacket just seconds before I was tugging my collar tight to my throat, shivering from a feverish cold deep in my bones.

The possibilities of what was happening to Ry while I was away from her tormented my exhausted mind. I saw her screaming my name, reaching out for me, only to find I'd abandoned her once more.

I imagined her body hard as marble, laced with icy blue veins, dead because I hadn't gotten there fast enough. Grief and helplessness howled like a fierce storm inside me for what felt like years.

When the doors of the ER finally swung open I could barely see the doctor through the burning of my eyes, an older man with small glasses and a mint green cap over his mostly grey hair.

I had no sense of time anymore. I had even less sense of myself. I wasn't even sure how I was standing, or rather whether I was standing at all.

"Family of Ms Carroll?"

It took me a second to register that he was talking about Ryleigh. I'd come to know her only as Ry. As my wife. As *mine.*

I lifted a hand which felt like it weighed fifty pounds. The doctor gave a curt nod of his head and moved toward me. My heart leaped wildly in my chest. I might have been hyperventilating.

"The husband?" the doctor asked.

"Yes," I said without hesitation. It didn't matter that we hadn't officially said the vows, I was *hers*. And she was mine.

He indicated for me to take a seat beside him.

I slumped into the chair, black spots already creeping in at the edge of my vision. "Just tell me she's okay."

Placing a hand on my knee, the doctor said, "Ms Carroll is out of surgery and is resting now."

I struggled to process his words. That meant Ry was alive, didn't it? Why hadn't he just said that? Why did he have to make me read between the lines when I hardly even knew my own name at that point?

"Take me to see her."

I stood, blood rushing to my head and making me stumble back a half step.

The doctor remained sitting, looking up at me with his palms flat on his knees. "Visiting hours begin at nine a.m. tomorrow."

"No," I said.

"I'm afraid those are the rules, sir."

"*Rules?*" I shouted.

There was no steady progression from in control to not. I snapped like a rubber band stretched too far.

It all happened so fast that even I was startled by the loud crash of the plastic waiting room chair against the wall. I was capable of violence, but usually it was a choice when I snapped.

"Take me to her. Right. Fucking. Now."

The lobby of the ER had gone silent. Out of the corner of my eye I saw waiting patients inching away. The nurse behind the desk had a phone halfway to her ear.

The doctor held up his hands from where he'd remained seated. "You need to remain calm, Mr Carroll."

Calm. *Fucking calm?*

I kicked away the chair next to him. He flinched, his face going white.

"Where is she?" I jabbed a finger toward him. "Where is *my wife?*"

He stumbled back out of the chair. "Security? Security!"

I punched a wall. I could barely feel the pain, plaster crumbling around my fist like crumbs.

"Where. Is. My. Wife?"

I stormed toward the swinging doors to the ER as a security guard stepped into my war path.

"Ryleigh!"

The guard came for me, joined by another, beefy hands already on the handle of their batons at their hips. I ducked their swinging arms and pushed one to the ground.

I felt a crack against my ribs from the other's baton. I let out a grunt and threw back my elbow, hitting the guard behind me.

He let go of me with a loosened grunt.

I was free. All I could see were the swinging ER doors just ahead of me.

Somewhere beyond them was my wife. My baby. My family.

I was pumped up on adrenaline, dripping with sweat that stank of fear, and exhausted to the point of insanity.

I reached out an arm to shove through the doors.

"Liam. Stop."

A hand grabbed my shoulder.

I thought it was a security guard, up for another round. I whirled around with crazy eyes and a lifted fist.

It was Rian.

My brother.

I was certain that nothing in the world would have kept me from ploughing through those doors to get to Ry. They could have sent a dozen more security guards after me and I would have fought through them all.

But just one look into my brother's eyes had me frozen in place. The deep sympathy in his steady gaze made it difficult to stay standing. I wanted to collapse into a heap. Everything felt so heavy. I was so tired.

"Liam," Rian said, his voice firm yet gentle. "Everything's going to be alright, okay?"

Rian dropped his hand from my shoulder and turned around. With the doctor and the security guards close behind, it felt like he was protecting me. My little brother. The brother who hated me. Protecting *me*.

The air in the ER was still electrified, an uneasy silence ready to spark back into violent chaos. I could almost hear the growls, see the hackles raised on the guards ready to strike.

"This man that you just saw is not my brother," he began, speaking firmly. "My brother is kind and loving and devoted. This is a man who almost lost his family tonight. The man *all of us* would be if we were put in the same position."

I saw the eyes of the doctor slide from Rian to over his shoulder. To me. His gaze softened and he exhaled slowly.

It was like he was seeing me in a different light. Even though I was still hunched over and fuming like a rabid dog.

"He needs to see her," Rian said. "To touch her. To hold her. Your words mean nothing. He needs to know for himself that she is alright."

Beneath Rian's wet shirt, slick to his back, I saw his muscles roil. His fingers curled into fists. He might be talking calmly, but I knew he'd be fighting there alongside me if it came to it.

A piece of my heart swelled.

"You need to let him see her."

The security guards behind the doctor looked at each other and then the doctor: they'd take their cues from him now that I wasn't an active threat.

I felt my heart smash against my chest as the doctor shifted his jaw from side to side.

Finally he nodded. "Room 307."

Rian thanked him and took me by the arm. He pressed open the swinging doors and guided me through before I had the time to do the same. Not that I would have been capable of thanking the doctor in my state. I still wanted to bash his head in, the need for violent release still simmering in my blood.

The lights were dim outside the bank of elevators down the hall. Nurses worked quietly under the yellow light of desk lamps across the way. It was almost eerily silent after the noise of the waiting room.

Rian didn't even trust me to get into the elevator without his arm on me. I let him hold on to me as the door hissed closed. I don't think he knew how close I was to leaning against him.

"Where in the hell did you learn how to *do* that?" I asked in the silence of the elevator.

My throat was raw and I winced from the pain of speaking.

Our mother, before she died, was kind, soft spoken, but it wasn't in the Merrick blood. We were brutal, violent savages. We didn't know how to settle a fight other than with our fists.

Glancing up at the flashing numbers overhead, Rian smiled a little.

"Eithne may have taught me a thing or two. Like often it's better to lead with empathy than violence."

"You love her," I said simply.

"She is proof we can't choose who we love," Rian said, his voice distant. "Lord knows if that were true, Eithne would have never chosen to fall in love with me."

"She sounds like an amazing woman," I told him as the doors opened on the third floor.

"She is a better woman than I ever fucking deserve," he admitted, stepping out and pulling me along after. "I'm going to spend the rest of my life trying to deserve her."

Our solitary footsteps echoed down the quiet hallway of sleeping patients and the machines they were hooked up to.

I understood what he meant: he was changing. Certainly not all at once and certainly not without his fair share of growing pains.

Eithne was making him a better man.

Ry had done the same for me.

We could be better men, despite our family's blood.

Outside Room 307 I could just make out Ryleigh's figure in a bed through the slanted blinds over the window. Rian was silent for a moment as he paused for a second.

"I'll be waiting at Dublin Ink when you're done here," Rian said quietly.

"You don't want to come in?" I offered.

He loved Ryleigh, too, in a different way. He must need the relief of feeling her pulse underneath his fingers for himself.

He shook his head.

I wanted to hug him. But I didn't know how he'd react, not sure my heart could take it if he rejected me now.

I hesitated and Rian slipped past me without another word. I glanced back at his retreating figure, his shirt sticking to his sweat-damp back. I regretted not reaching for him.

But I had Ry and the baby to worry about for now.

I steadied myself, drawing in a few even breaths. And then entered the room.

Whatever calm I'd managed to achieve got swept away as if in a flood the second I saw Ry in that hospital bed.

The lamp in the corner made her too pale skin look jaundiced, especially compared to the stark white of the bandages that covered large swaths of her body. My blood boiled knowing what was beneath them.

All over again I saw those cuts across her body, congealed with blood the colour of rust. Rage threatened to overtake me again. Her fear, her helplessness. Her pain.

For a moment, all I could think about was chasing after Rian so we could get our revenge.

But then Ry called my name.

It was weak and needy and it was all it took for me to rush to her side.

Drawing her into my arms was like breaking the surface of the water. Like I'd been drowning for every second I'd been without her. I gasped for air.

"Liam," Ry cried again, burying her face into my chest as her fingers, all caught up in wires and tubes, grasped around my neck.

She broke down again with emotion as she tried to speak.

"Breathe," I told her softly, rubbing her back. "Ry, baby, breathe."

"Our baby…"

My stomach twisted into knots as I pulled back. That's when I noticed her belly was smaller.

Oh God. I turned Ry's face gently toward mine, holding back a fury of emotions at the dark circles around her eyes, the cut on her lip, the bright flush of a fever on her cheeks.

"Tell me," I whispered, sounding braver than I felt.

There was nothing anyone could do to prepare me for the news that our baby hadn't made it.

Sitting there, with her face in my hands, between not knowing and knowing felt like that moment right before you tipped over a chasm. Would I rock back to safety? Or would I fall into the abyss?

"They had to get the baby out," Ry whispered, fresh tears falling.

My eyes darted between hers, trying to decipher her message. What did that mean? What did that fucking mean?

"Ry," I whispered. "Is he—she—is the baby…"

She bit her bottom lip, shook her head.

"I don't know."

LIAM

I slipped into Dublin Ink, the little bell affixed atop the door jangling harshly.

Rian's red-rimmed eyes met mine from across the room.

Could he tell from across the dimly lit tattoo parlour how erratically my heart was beating? Could he see the way my hands curled and uncurled from white-knuckled fists? Did he know, just from looking at me, the darkness in my heart? Did it seep out like spilled ink? The evil? The murderous desire?

"Where is the…unfinished business?"

Rian put down his pencils.

"What are you going to do?" he asked.

"I'm going to make sure he never touches Ryleigh ever again," I vowed as I strode toward him. "Where is he?"

"You know, that can mean a lot of things."

Rian closed the sketchbook he'd been bent over and folded his arms, watching me closely.

"It could mean getting the police involved," he continued. "A trial. A conviction. Jail, for a few years at least."

I snorted. Rich white men didn't get "jail", they got "probation" or a short stint at a minimum-security prison, practically a holiday.

"It could mean getting Ry out of Ireland," he said further. "Out of Europe, if necessary."

I remained silent but my heart seemed to crack with every beat. Like I was stuck beneath ice. Punching to get free. To breathe.

Rian looked up at me, his eyes searching mine.

"Which one of those do you mean?" he asked, barely a whisper.

I didn't flinch.

"I don't mean any of those."

"Liam," Rian said slowly, "you can still come back from this. You haven't done anything...*final* yet. You can go straight back to Ry."

I shook my head. "You know that's not true."

The parlour was silent. Even the neon in the sign that cast my shadow long across the tattered rugs seemed to cease its popping, its steady humming.

"The law was created to keep us safe. But the law can't hold powerful wealthy men like Balor to justice. Sometimes the law isn't enough. So...we must make *our own*."

Rian nodded, acceptance softening his features.

"Sit first," he said. "I've got some unfinished business of my own."

The sudden buzz of the tattoo gun was loud in the studio.

"I don't have time for this."

"Sit," he said in a tone that brokered no arguments. "This won't take long. Then I'll tell you what you need to know."

The only person I knew more stubborn than Ryleigh was

my brother. I decided doing what he asked of me was faster than arguing.

I sat.

"Roll up your sleeve."

I curled up the hem covering the unfinished snake.

This time I didn't hiss as the needle punctured the sensitive skin of my inner wrist. I was sure I couldn't have felt a knife twisting in my chest at that point.

After the pain of seeing Ryleigh like that, knowing that someone had hurt Ry… I was numb. Ice cold. And yet ready to burn. To fucking take the world down with me.

"I'll give you what you want," Rian said, when he'd finished, switching off his gun. "On one condition…"

The fresh tattoo on my inner wrist was a snake, with its mouth open to consume itself, held in the talons of a hawk.

A new family crest.

"…I want in."

The dark warehouse stank of iron as I stepped inside.

For a second I saw Ryleigh lying on the blood-soaked bed, strung up to the posts.

I blinked.

And Balor appeared instead.

It seemed Rian had seen fit to chain him down, ropes were not enough to restrain this vile creature.

"You've signed her death warrant," Balor said as we approached. "With you two in prison, who will be there to protect the whore? Who will be there to stop me when I carve that bastard child from her stomach?"

I stared down at Balor as I snatched the knife he'd used to cut her from the side of the bed.

"No," I said, "you have signed your own."

I had forced myself to sit there in the hospital room as Ryleigh confessed everything he'd done to her, forced myself to be a silent witness to her pain.

Now I got to be her avenging angel.

Blood splattered my face, tasting like copper in my mouth as he screamed.

"Go on," I said through my teeth, repeating the vile words he'd said to Ry. "'*Scream for daddy*'."

Rian had grabbed his own weapon, the metal plug from the floor. When he struck, the crunch of bones reached my ears as if through water, muffled and muted. So did Balor's gagged screaming, his incoherent pleas, and cries for mercy, and finally for death.

As I'd learned on the farm, animals had their own law.

Perhaps I should have felt a seed of remorse.

But I didn't.

Perhaps this made me a bad man.

But like I'd told Ryleigh, I never claimed to be a good one.

A dark righteous pleasure filled my crooked little heart with every violent strike, with every one of his sobs. I didn't stop when I'd matched cut for cut, I gave him tenfold for what she'd suffered.

Rian's hand gripped my arm. "That's enough, Liam."

I lowered my hand, the knife clattering to the ground.

Balor's face was nearly unrecognisable. Slices of skin replaced his cheeks. Only the glimmer of an eye peeked through bruised and swollen skin.

"End it," Rian said on a hiss.

"You won't kill me," Balor said. "You don't have the balls."

Rian started toward him but I held out a hand.

It had to be me.

I winced as I lowered myself to the bed beside Balor, as if I were sitting beside an elderly relative. A weariness deeper than any I'd ever experienced made my bones ache.

I did feel pity for him at that moment.

He really thought we would leave him alive. He actually had the arrogance to think we'd leave him to the police. That the world still worked for him. His money. His power. He really saw in his future a trial, slick-suited attorneys, a paid-off judge declaring not guilty.

He really, truly believed that nothing could touch him.

I smiled at that slice of eye. That last remaining hint of a human.

I closed my hands around his throat and squeezed, wrapped justice and judgement around his neck until I felt his hyoid bone break in my palm, and then I held.

I leaned in close. I wanted the last thing this monster to see was the face of his judge, jury and executioner, *my* face.

I saw the panic in his eyes when it dawned in on him that I was no longer afraid to be evil. That if it took evil to kill evil, I would be evil. That I would turn into Satan himself if that's what it took to protect Ryleigh and our baby.

"You will *never* touch her again."

He gave one last futile gasp for air, then he stilled.

~

I could still hear the roar of flames behind as I drove us away from the warehouse. Soon the glare of fire trucks would add to the orchestra of death, but not yet.

We sat in clean clothes, showered in the onsite bathroom

Balor had installed in the warehouse, all evidence left behind to burn into ash.

My brother and I sat in silence, the violent pact now tying us both together.

It wasn't until the glare of fire upon the horizon was gone from the rearview mirror that he spoke.

"You love her, don't you?"

In his voice was a sort of acceptance. There was still hurt, still regret, still even a sort of longing and hope for an answer he knew he wouldn't get, but most of all there was the dull but steady ground of acceptance.

I said simply, "More than my own life."

A moment or so later, I heard the crinkling of paper. I glanced over to see Rian pull a folded letter from his back pocket with one hand.

"Ry left this for me," he said, guilt in his voice as he tapped it against his thigh before holding it out between two fingers. "When she left Dublin Ink."

It unfolded easily, the edges of the letter well worn, clearly folded and unfolded untold times. Rian cleared his throat.

"'Rian,'" my brother began as I drove us into the night,

"'You have no idea how difficult this is to write. Not because I don't know what to say. I do. I think I've known for a long time, like the words were written on my heart.

Liam came to Dublin for you.

I wasn't the reason he was in the city. He wasn't searching for me when he found me.

It was you.

If Liam loves me, and I believe he does, it is only because he loved you first."

I gripped at the wheel, my knuckles turning white. I didn't

dare glance over at Rian. I was afraid he might stop. Afraid that I'd start crying. Afraid that I'd see him cry.

Afraid, most of all, that the words weren't real. That I'd look over and realise in my exhaustion I'd been hearing voices. That Rian was asleep, cheek against the icy glass. That Ry never wrote the words that were saving my blackened soul, one after the other.

Drawing in a breath, Rian continued,

"'That is all there is to say, Rian. Your brother loves you. I know that love might feel like a dagger right now. I know you may not want to hear it. Or trust it. Or believe it. But he loves you.

Because if he doesn't love you it is impossible that he loves me. And I know he loves me.

Liam loves me.

If you don't believe him, believe me. If you don't trust him, trust me. Because, whether you like it or not, I have always loved you, too.

Your best friend always, Ry.'"

I felt my brother's eyes on me but I kept my eyes on the empty road. For once, it wasn't raining. I could scarcely dare to breath, waiting for what Rian might say next.

"It's going to take me a little while..." he said.

I let out the breath I was holding.

It wasn't acceptance. But it was a start.

"Okay."

"I'll need some time."

"Okay," I repeated.

Out of the corner of my eye, Rian refolded the letter. He slipped it back with the ease of movement that told me he'd carry that letter for years. The letter had a home in his back pocket. It'd be a weight he'd grow accustomed to. A scar he hardly felt though never forgot.

"If you're willing," Rian said, glancing at me, "I mean, if you're willing to try, you could attend one of my therapy sessions."

"Yeah?"

"Yeah."

I swallowed down the knot in my throat, let the tiny ball of hope settle in my chest.

"Yeah," I said. "I think I'd like that."

RY

I woke up and for a moment I was back there, tied to that bed. My heart rate soared as that familiar sick fear gripped me.

"No." I gasped for air, lashing out with my hands as an alarm sounded through my fog.

I felt a small hand on my shoulder.

"Ry, Ry," a soft voice said near my ear. "You're okay. You're in the hospital. You're safe."

Peeling my heavy eyelids back, I blinked slowly at the tubes winding along my arm. I studied the monitor beside me with foggy thoughts. I turned to the figure at my bedside.

"Liam?" I croaked.

Aurnia smiled sweetly and said, "I'm afraid not."

She massaged my shoulder to comfort me.

I tried to get up.

But two more sets of gentle hands guided me back down to the propped-up pillows. Rachel brushed my damp hair from my forehead and Eithne brushed down the sheets.

"Liam," I said again, still feeling the effects of the drugs.

I was vaguely aware of glances exchanged above me. I still wasn't entirely sure whether I was even awake or not. So I couldn't be certain. And the ache all over my body took what little concentration I had.

Aurnia lifted a cup of juice with a straw to my lips. "Drink."

The sweet liquid soothed my throat. I sank back after drinking, once again exhausted.

From the doorway, I heard a deep familiar voice ask, "How is she?"

Was that...Conor?

At first none of the girls answered.

"She's going to be alright," Rachel said finally.

I shifted my head on the pillow to see Mason and Conor standing on either side of the door like tattooed guards, their expressions tight.

I met Conor's eyes. His usual stern, gruff expression softened. Then broke.

Mason wiped at his eyes and said, "Damn straight she's going to be alright."

The crack in his voice made me want to cry all over again.

I glanced around the hospital room for a bassinet, for a light blue or pink blanket, for any sign of... I felt the pain of those stomach cramps and the heat of the blood on my thighs all over again. I was almost too afraid to ask.

But I had to know.

"My baby?"

I looked between Aurnia and Rachel, who were staring at each other.

"Please," I croaked.

Eithne took my hand. "Still in ICU."

She looked to the other two girls as if to check if it had

been the right thing to tell me. It was clear from their silence that neither of them knew any more than she did.

I wanted to scream. At them. At the fucking world.

But it wasn't their fault.

I felt myself drowning. I held onto Eithne's hand like it was a lifeline. Her hand was small and cool and while comforting, I longed to hold the hand that dwarfed mine, scraped my delicate skin with calluses, and burned with a deep, dark heat.

"Where's Liam?" I asked.

The silence in the room became stiff and hot. Mason and Conor glanced at each other, something unspoken passing between them.

Mason turned to me, rubbing the back of his neck. "Liam had to…sort something out."

Conor just nodded and let out a grunt.

"He went after Balor," I guessed, panic making my voice jump several octaves.

What if Balor managed to get the upper hand? What if he had an army of reinforcements coming to get him? What if they hurt him? What if they—

"Ry," Aurnia said as the beeping on my heart rate monitor jumped. "Ry, please, stay calm."

What if Liam did something stupid and got caught by the police? What if our baby survived only for Liam to never be there to watch it grow up? What if our baby didn't and I was all alone and—

"Should we call a nurse?" Eithne asked, her palm growing sweaty in mine.

Conor's voice cut through the noise of the mounting chaos in the room.

"Rian is with him."

The gentle giant spoke so little, but I was reminded that when he did, it was for a reason.

Rian was with Liam.

If Rian was with Liam, he would be alright. I believed this. I trusted this.

Conor and I held each other's gaze for a moment. I hoped he saw "Thank you" in my eyes even though I wasn't yet capable of speaking it aloud. I thought his curt nod meant that he had.

"He asked us to look after you until he gets back," Eithne said, resuming the gentle circles of her thumb over my hand.

"We'll be here by your side until he comes back," Rachel added.

A silence fell over the dimly lit room as the girls laid their hands over me and the boys continued to stand diligently at the door.

I let my eyes close, my breathing slowly returning to a steady, even pace. None of us felt the need to say anything more. We'd already said all there was to say without speaking a word of it.

That's what family did.

~

Whether I wanted sleep or not, it came for me. I don't know if I fought it and it won. Or if I begged for it and it withheld its hand till it had me on my knees. All I knew was that I was dragged under.

It was only Liam's hand in mine that brought me back to the surface.

I drew in a breath and it was filled with his scent. There it was, air. Life. My love.

"Liam," I whispered.

The tears escaped between my eyelashes as his head came to rest against my chest, his cheek warm, his stubble scratchy through the thin cotton of my hospital nightgown.

"Ryleigh," he whispered back, his voice trembling. "I thought I'd lost you."

The tubes tangled as I reached for him. He wrapped his arms carefully around me, lifting my back from the thin mattress and drawing me close to him. Eyes still closed I clung to him, breathed in his scent, shuddering in relief.

I thought I'd lost you, too.

"I woke up earlier and you weren't here," I said, pulling back to see his eyes. "Where were you?"

A darkness shadowed his brow. His gaze shifted at something that I knew was far off and away from this dim hospital room. I could look over there. But I wouldn't see what he was seeing. And I feared it would divide us forever.

"Liam," I whispered.

"I don't want to lie to you," he said, his voice haunted. "So don't ask me again."

I knew. Of course I knew. I could see it, written as if in black ink in the deepened lines around his eyes. I could feel it in the weight of his body against mine, heavier than when he left me.

I cupped Liam's face and he flinched. When I tried to tug his face in the direction of mine, he resisted. "Liam..."

"*Don't* ask."

"I *know* where you were."

"No," Liam said, anguish seeming to rip apart his vocal cords.

"You were—"

"Don't say it." Liam's gaze met mine with such ferocity.

But I didn't flinch.

"You were giving me my home back," I whispered, running my thumb along his cheekbone, his skin dry from too much recent scrubbing. "You were stealing Ireland back for me. You were returning these emerald hills to my heart."

I brushed aside a fleck of dried blood on his ear. "You were giving our baby a safe place to grow up in. You were giving our baby a wide, big, open world. You were making a home…for our *daughter*."

His eyes widened as my words sank into him. "We…we have a daughter?"

I nodded, tears running down my cheeks. She was still in ICU and not out of the woods yet, but…

"We have a daughter."

RY

Six months later...

I climbed out of the bath, avoiding the mirror over the pedestal sink. It was probably fogged up anyway from the steam. But I didn't want to take that risk.

Out in the bedroom, I leaned over the basket of fresh laundry and grabbed a pair of long baggy pants and a sweatshirt. I threw out all my old miniskirts and tiny tops. I didn't see a way back to that old version of me.

My bathrobe had slipped slightly from my shoulder and when I looked up and caught my reflection in the full-length mirror, I saw what I'd been trying so hard to avoid seeing. My stomach twisted at the sight.

The knife wounds had healed over the months. They no longer hurt. But they sometimes itched, which was almost worst.

With pain, the last thing you want to do is touch it. When I scratched the itch, I was forced to feel the raised skin inch by inch, forced to relive the memory of him cutting me.

The scars were healing. But like me, not fast enough.

My fingertips trembled at my sides as I stared at the jagged line which followed the angle of my shoulder. I knew what I should do: turn around, pull on the pyjamas still warm from the dryer, and snuggle up beneath the covers till Liam came in and kissed the back of my neck. But…

It's still not too late. The pyjamas are right there in your hand. Don't do this to yourself.

I shuddered as the bathrobe pooled around my feet.

Tears pricked my eyes as I stared into the mirror. I lifted a heavy hand to trace the C-section scar on my belly. I didn't mind this scar. It reminded me of our beautiful baby girl. Of our family.

In fact, I tried to hold onto this scar. To only see it in the reflection of the mirror. But my fingertip always seemed to reach the end of it too soon, as it was doing now.

We'd named our daughter Cahira which meant *warrior* in Irish. And boy, was she a fighter. Even born prematurely, she refused to give up.

It seemed the world would relent to her and soon both mother and daughter were released from hospital.

But the shadows of the night that changed everything remained.

Our daughter's birthday would always come on the day of my capture and torture.

My eyes stumbled from scar to scar, all over my body, all over me. Cutting across all the art on my body that I'd loved so much, making me feel and look like a broken doll.

Something no one would ever want to play with. Something rejected and worthy only of being thrown away.

My chin trembled as the urge to cry grew stronger. I hated that when I looked at those scars I thought of Balor. I didn't want to give the bastard even the dignity of space in my mind. But it was impossible to see anything else.

I was a ruined painting. Slashed. Irreparable. A Frankenstein stitched back together. I was horrific. Monstrous.

The door opened quietly and it was far too late to cover myself back up. To hide from Liam what I had been doing.

My cheeks grew pink from embarrassment as the door clicked carefully shut behind him.

Liam came to stand behind me, his warm hands on my hips. Warm hands which had just been holding our daughter. I wished all I saw was her and Liam. I wished I wasn't covered in the evil of a monster.

A tear slipped from my squeezed eyelashes.

"You're beautiful," Liam said softly, his chin on my shoulder.

I shook my head.

Gently Liam turned me around in his arms so that I was facing him. I felt his fingertips at my lips.

"You. are. *beautiful*."

I opened my eyes. His eyes were so earnest, so loving as they searched mine. He wanted me to believe him.

I *wanted* to believe him. For his sake. So he didn't have to see me cry.

But I couldn't.

I remained silent, fighting back a fresh wave of tears.

Liam drew my trembling chin up and kissed me.

I loved the way he smelled, stubborn engine grease beneath his cedarwood soap. I loved the way he exhaled softly as he drew me closer to him, like my body was a relief to him, the way he intensified the kiss when I moaned softly, knowing what I needed even before I did.

I wanted him. Fuck, I wanted him. To have Liam back inside of me, to have him claiming me as *his*. The desire burned deep in my belly.

I knew Liam wanted the same. He was hard against my thigh through his charcoal-grey sweatpants.

Liam's hand slipped lower down my spine. My heart rate jumped with a flare of sudden panic, but I kissed him all the more passionately.

I wanted this, I *needed* this.

Liam brushed his hand along the side of my naked breast.

I flinched.

He stopped kissing me and instead just rested his forehead against mine.

I sucked in lungsful of breath, trying not to hyperventilate. I hated myself. This wasn't the first time this had happened. He'd always been so understanding when I pulled away. But we still hadn't had sex since...

I wasn't sure how much longer it could go on. How much longer he could take only having half a woman.

A tear fell straight from my eye onto the carpet between our bare feet. "I'm sorry. It's not you. It's—"

"Shh, baby, shh. I know."

His gentleness with me almost made it worse. At least if he got frustrated, I would know what he was really feeling. He couldn't possibly be this understanding, could he? There was no way *I* could have ended up with someone like that.

"I know it's been a long time since...and I know I should be better by now—"

"Ry."

"No, but Liam. I—"

Liam pulled me into a hug, cutting off my protests. My arms were caught up against his chest over my breasts and I hated how much I wanted to curl into my myself instead of curling around him.

Even having my nipples against Liam's skin felt like too much, no matter how desperately I didn't want it to be like that.

Burying my face against Liam's shoulder, I shook hard as I cried.

"It's okay," Liam said as he smoothed down my hair. "We can take all the time in the world."

He rested his cheek against the top of my head and held me even tighter.

"We have it, baby," he said. "All the time in the world."

But I couldn't believe him. What if I never got better? What if I could never stand for him to touch me? What if I could never have sex with him again?

He would leave.

Balor would win. From the grave, he will have finished what he started.

He would have destroyed me.

~

"Can you see anything?" Liam asked behind me, clearly an accusation, even though his hands covered my eyes. "No peeking."

I laughed. "Baby, your hands are the size of billboards. I can't see a thing."

He wouldn't tell me where he was taking me for date night.

Liam wore a nice cologne and I'd taken the time to curl my hair while the baby napped before Auntie Aurnia and Grumpy Uncle arrived.

The evening summer air was balmy and fragrant. Only when a cooling breeze swept over us did my spirits drop slightly as I longed to feel it on my skin instead of my jeans and long t-shirt.

"I just don't want to ruin the surprise," Liam said and then a moment later, "We're going in here."

Liam was worried about me seeing, but he should have been worried about me *hearing*. The little ring of the bell told me immediately where we were. Though I had no idea in the world why we'd be at Dublin Ink.

"Ta-da!" Liam announced, pulling his hands away.

Rian, standing beside his tattoo bed, added a more self-conscious, "Ta-da...?" of his own as he smiled at me from across the empty parlour.

I looked up at Liam. Dublin Ink certainly was stocked with liquor and there was probably half a box of Lucky Charms in the kitchen, but it wasn't exactly the kind of dinner and drinks I was imagining for date night.

"What's going on?" I asked, trying to hide my apprehension.

Liam beamed down at me. "I got you a present."

"A present?" I asked.

I resisted dragging my feet as Liam guided me by the small of my back toward Rian.

"What kind of present?"

Sheepishly, Rian lifted his tattoo gun and waved it back and forth.

"A *tattoo*?" I asked, consciously tugging down the long sleeves of my shirt, dread filling my stomach. "What tattoo?

Where?"

Liam took my fidgeting hand as my heart thudded in my chest. He kissed the back of it.

"Trust us?"

The whole time Rian was tattooing I didn't dare open my eyes.

Over the years of tattooing, I'd had plenty of clients who did the same. Kept their eyes sealed shut the whole time, too afraid to look.

But they all knew from the start what would be there on their skin when they opened their eyes at the end. I didn't have a clue what Rian was putting on my skin.

I was in a bathing suit that Liam had secretly packed (and apparently saved along with my old clothes). My nerves were so heightened, my skin so buzzing with electricity that I could hardly feel where Rian was tattooing me.

But Liam had asked me to trust them.

That was all. And that was enough.

Even if the stress of it made me want to cry. Even if I clung to Liam's hand the whole time like it was a lifeline. Even if I felt myself drenched in sweat.

I would trust Rian. I would trust Liam. I *could* trust them.

I was exhausted by the time the gun finally turned off. The muscles around my eyes ached, the leather of the chair beneath my body was slick with my sweat.

I didn't open my eyes when Liam and Rian took my arm on either side and helped me up. My legs felt shaky as they walked me to the corner of the parlour where I knew was the full-length mirror.

When we came to a stop I was quivering like a leaf, my hand in both of theirs. Rian squeezed my fingers reassuringly.

"Ry, baby," Liam said softly, somewhere near my ear. "You can open your eyes now."

For a moment I wasn't able to. I wasn't quite sure what I was feeling: nervous, hopeful, afraid.

I recognised Liam's rough calluses as he brushed some hair from my forehead. I always marvelled at how delicately he could tuck it back behind my ear.

He asked me to trust him.

I trust him.

With one last steadying inhale, I opened my eyes.

And saw my reflection in the mirror.

A wave of emotion swept over me with such force that I nearly stumbled back. My fingers tightened instinctively on Rian and Liam's hands. It took everything inside of me not to curl in on myself, away from the intensity of all that I was feeling.

Rian had tattooed along every jagged scar with gold.

The effect was staggering. I no longer looked marred. I looked whole. The gold lines seemed to weave in between all my tattoos like a thread. Past, present, and future all connected. It looked purposeful. It looked beautiful.

I looked beautiful.

"Kintsugi," Rian replied.

"What?" I fought against the tears gathering in my eyes as I looked from my best friend to my partner in the mirror.

"In Japan they mend broken pots with gold," Liam explained with a smile.

I nodded, jarring a tear loose. It rolled down my cheek, hot and fast. It proved to be the cracking of the dam. There was no stopping the wave of tears that came from my eyes after that.

"They are not beautiful despite their brokenness...but *because* of it."

I grabbed Liam with a speed and strength I hadn't felt in my body in a long time and drew his face down to mine. I kissed him with a renewed fire, welcoming back that heat that stirred my soul.

As I tasted his tongue, savouring him with deeper breaths, I heard the door click shut.

We pulled away from each other, each blushing a little sheepishly: Rian had left.

We were the only ones here.

Liam glanced over his shoulder at the door, which was now locked, the "Open" sign switched to "Closed". "I think he thought we were going to...you know, need some alone time."

Liam looked back at me, hope in his eyes. "But we don't have to...you know."

"...tattoo you?" I arched an eyebrow. I hadn't felt like this since before Balor's attack. Playful.

Liam laughed. "That's not quite what I was thinking."

My lips curled into a mischievous smile as I tapped my chin.

"Oh, then maybe you wanted to...walk me home? To make sure I get there safely?"

Liam drew me back into his arms.

"I'll take you home," he said as he kissed along my neck, sending shivers down my spine, "but *not* to make sure you get there safely."

I lunged for his mouth, our tongues meeting as our kiss deepened instantly.

The lines of tattoo stung as he crushed me to him but it added to the pleasure already coursing through my body from his kiss.

He tugged the strings on my bikini and suddenly I was naked. I kept waiting for the flood of panic to hit me but as Liam slipped his hand between my legs, we both discovered how wet I was.

I pushed at his clothes, needing to feel him, needing him to claim me. To make me wholly *his* again.

He stripped down quickly, throwing clothes across the studio until we were both naked. I let out a groan of pain and pleasure as he pulled me against him, backing me up to the tattoo chair until I bumped it with the backs of my thighs.

He picked me up and sat me on the edge, and I wrapped my legs around his waist.

He broke off the kiss and his fingers brushed across my body softly. He kissed my neck but his lips were gentle, cautious. Like I was breakable.

Did he see me differently now? Did he just see Balor's marks on me? Was I no longer his to claim?

My jaw ached as I tried not to cry.

"Shit. Baby, I'm sorry. Does it hurt?" he asked, his voice hesitant, his fingers coming up to wipe a tear away.

I grabbed his face in my hands and forced him to look at me so he could *see* me.

"I *want* it to hurt."

Liam's eyes widened. "But—"

"Choke me," I demanded. "Fuck me. Make me yours. *Claim* me."

For a long moment Liam just stared at me. Dread collected in my stomach. Oh God. He was disgusted by me. He would never be able to fuck me the way we used to fuck.

Balor had ruined us.

Then he moved so fast I didn't see it coming. His hand closed around my throat, stealing my breath.

At once my world stilled. Everything except him and me fell away. *Yes.*

"You are mine in every way," he growled as he pushed me back onto the leather.

"This body—this beautiful fucking body—is *mine*."

I let out a whimper as he slid his hand down my body, firmly, like he was taking back every inch of my skin for me. It stung as he brushed over the new tattoos but I didn't care, the pain added to the pleasure his callused hands gave me.

"Your breath—your fucking *life*—is *mine*."

His hand squeezed around my neck as if to make a point.

I let out a groan as need gripped my body, as I rocked my hips forward on the leather, begging for him to touch me.

"Look at this fucking perfect pussy, weeping for me."

He parted my folds and dove down with his tongue, licking up the wetness dripping from me, using both of his hands now to hold my legs open wide for him. I felt so exposed but it made me ache for more.

"So fucking sweet. And every drop is *mine*.

Tingles spread all over my body and my back arched off the leather as he lapped at me.

"Touch your beautiful body while I eat this sweet cunt," he said, his voice rumbling against my folds. "Good girl. Play with those perfect tits."

I did as he commanded, running my hands over sensitive skin, over my aching nipples, claiming my body back as Liam reclaimed my pussy for me.

The pleasure began to build and I tugged at his hair, as I rocked my hips onto his face.

His hand came down flat on my clit and the burst of pain radiated through me before pleasure swept after it.

"So impatient," he reprimanded.

I let out a moan.

"Please," I begged. "Fuck me."

He chuckled. "Some other time, I'm going to tie you down and tease you for so long that you'll be crying for me to put you out of your misery."

My heart skittered at his words. My clit throbbed at his promise.

Yes, piece by piece he'd reclaim all of it back for me.

"But not today," he said, standing and positioning his hard cock at my entrance. "Today, I can't fucking wait to be back inside you."

His palm encircled my throat. He used that grip to hold me in place as he pushed his cock inside of me.

Pleasure welled up from the depths of me at the way he stretched me. Our twin groans echoed through the empty studio. His hand tightened around my throat, as he fucked me, hard, my breasts bounced with each thrust.

"Your pussy takes me so well, baby," he groaned, his eyes hooded. "Your sweet tight cunt never forgot who it belongs to."

"Oh God," I choked out, "I'm close."

His eyes flashed. "I'm going to fill you until you're overflowing with my cum so there's no mistake about who you belong to."

He tightened his hand around my throat and spots danced in front of my eyes. My orgasm exploded through me in waves, racking my body in shudders.

"Yours. Yours. Yours," I muttered as I rode the orgasm.

As he grunted and came inside me.

As he half collapsed on top of me, his face falling between my breasts to rest upon my heart.

"*Mine*," he said simply. "And I am *yours*.

EPILOGUE

RY

"Let me just tidy up my workstation and I'll be ready to go," I said as Liam walked through the door of Dublin Ink.

It was date night and we had a babysitter looking after Cahira at home.

"No rush."

He kissed me long and deep, only pulling away when the catcalls of the rest of the Dublin Ink gang got too loud. Someone threw a scrunched-up ball of paper at us—probably Mason.

"Jaysus Mary Joseph, get a room," called Rian, but there was humour in his tone.

I batted Liam away and turned to my station.

"I was thinking," Liam said, sliding his hands, callused and still grease-stained from work, around my stomach. "Maybe I'd like another tattoo."

"You think?" I said, tracing a scar along the back of his hand.

He turned me to face him and there was a strange seriousness in his eyes. "I want another tattoo."

"Oh…okay then."

There was a sudden stirring in the room. Aurnia, Mason, and Conor all found excuses, mumbled over one another to leave the parlour.

"Tea kettle's whistling," said Aurnia. It wasn't.

"I think Rachel is calling me," Mason said. She wasn't.

"Left my bike with the keys still in, I think," Conor grumbled. Over his dead fucking body would he ever do such a thing.

I looked over at Rian, who was critiquing one of Eithne's most recent drawings. I raised an eyebrow as if he would find it all just as strange.

But he stood, arms stretched overhead and said, "Eithne and I need to go…buy art supplies."

Eithne followed after without a word, without anything but a poorly concealed grin. She followed Rian right up the stairs.

"Um, I don't think the store is up there," I shouted after them.

After all of them actually, the whole lot of them, liar after liar, disappearing up the narrow old stairs without even glancing back in my direction as I shouted at them.

"We're not going to have sex!" I called.

With an arched eyebrow, I said to Liam in a low whisper, "We aren't having sex, are we?"

Liam just laughed and shrugged his red flannel shirt from his muscular shoulders.

I narrowed my eyes and glanced back over my shoulder at the now empty stairs. "You know, that doesn't really answer my question."

I looked up at the high ceiling as if I could see through it. Were six pairs of ears pressed to the vintage rug in Mason and Rachel's bedroom? Were they giggling together, all crammed into the bathroom with the clawfoot tub?

"*Are* we having sex?" I asked once more, this time with desire taking the place of confusion, my voice sinking into the depths of lust.

Bare chested, Liam arranged himself on my tattoo chair. He picked up the gun, which was lying on the silver tray atop my workstation and opened my fingers to place it against my palm.

"Tattoo," he said, grinning at me.

"So tattoo isn't code for a crazy new sex position."

Liam chuckled. "Not today."

I huffed in pretend (or mostly pretend) disappointment.

"Fine," I grumbled, drawing out the word like a petulant teenager.

Liam smirked and slipped his hand under the neckline of my shirt to pinch my nipple.

"Now you're just being mean," I said, pointing the tattoo gun at his throat, much the same way I had the first night we'd met.

Liam took my wrist in both hands and tugged the tip of the needle down to his heart. It was the only space on his chest left without a tattoo.

For a moment or two, I stared at the place where the needle pressed lightly, my artwork surrounding the empty place like water rushing into a sinkhole.

Liam's chest rose and fell steadily. There was no hitch in his breathing. No racing of his pulse.

At night I traced the lines of the tattoos I'd given him. My life across his body. But it had always been there. That untouched expanse. That unacknowledged absence. That missing piece.

When I looked up at Liam, he was waiting for me, the response to a question I hadn't even yet asked right there on his tongue.

"I'm sure."

I drew in a long inhale. I didn't have the strength inside of me to keep my breath from shaking.

"I—" I shook my head. "I don't know what to put there."

Liam's smile was reassuring.

"That's alright," he said softly, tucking a strand of dark hair back behind my ear. "I do."

He wanted my name in a gentle curve and Cahira's name to complete the infinity sign. I kissed him when he was finished describing the design. When our lips touched, heat against heat, I saw how I wanted it to look perfectly behind my closed eyelids.

I didn't even need to sketch it out first. I would go right in with ink. We would go right into it no matter what, for better or worse, permanence, eternity.

I laughed to hide the prickle of tears as I pulled back to begin my work.

Neither of us needed to say much as I tattooed him. Everything between us was communicated by the needle: pain and beauty, blood and ink, forever and forever.

"It's perfect," Liam said into the mirror I held out for him afterwards. He steadied my shaking hand with his and whispered to me, "You're perfect."

Liam cleared his throat. "Well, I guess it's time to pay up then."

I laughed and dismissed him with a wave of my hand. "Right, right. Very funny."

It was our little game. One last time.

"Come on, Ry," Liam insisted, nodding toward the cash register, "ring me up."

I relented and Liam followed me to the counter. Looking at him with an *"Are you happy?"* look, I punched randomly at buttons.

The machine dinged as the cash drawer popped open.

"How much?" Liam asked, reaching for his back pocket.

Playing my part, I said, hands on his hips, "At least let me offer you a discount if you insist on paying."

Liam drew up one of his eyebrows. "A discount for what?" he asked, his voice low.

I circled my finger in the air, thinking.

"Oh, I don't know," I said, grinning up at him.

The last rays of sunlight illuminated his eyes.

I smirked. "For finding me. For stalking me."

He'd admitted everything he'd done in pursuit of me. How he'd watched me and followed me.

But I couldn't be angry at him for long. His shadowy presence had stopped Balor from snatching me.

Nor could I stay angry that he'd installed a secret tracker in the bracelet he'd given me. We wouldn't be here if he hadn't.

"...for saving me," I added.

Liam paused with his hand still stretched toward his back pocket.

I continued, "For stealing my breath away, in more ways than one. For loving me, for trusting me. For healing me. For giving me the greatest gift in the world."

I placed a kiss at Liam's jaw.

"For loving me."

I lowered myself back down from my tiptoes. I smiled up at him, half of my world.

"Is this the part where you ask me to go on a first date with you as payment?" I asked, grinning like a schoolgirl with a crush.

Liam finally pulled his wallet from his back pocket. He had a wry smile as he said, "I think we're past first dates."

I held out my hand for whatever bills he was going to give me. The heaviness of what he dropped into my palm surprised me.

"I was hoping you'd take this instead," he said.

I stared down at the diamond ring. Ink from my palm already stained the vintage ivy curling around the gold band and the sharp corners of the rock.

I looked up at Liam as he dropped to one knee.

"Ryleigh Carroll," he said, cupping my open hand in both of his. "Mother of my daughter. The love of my life. Will you also be my wife?"

I blabbered a *yes, yes, hell fucking yes* and Liam swept me into his arms, his lips crashing onto mine.

Everyone coming down the stairs at once sounded like a stampede of animals.

"I told you they weren't fucking!" Mason shouted over the calls of congratulations.

I laughed through the tears as Liam set me back down on the ground.

Amongst the chaos of the celebration I felt a hand at my elbow.

I turned with pink cheeks, nearly breathless to find Rian beside me. My best friend. Frowning.

His fingers squeezed my forearm as he looked between Liam and me.

I sucked in a breath. Liam's smile faltered for a second.

But then Rian's face broke out into a genuine smile.

"Congratulations, guys," he said, his voice quiet amongst all the noise and yet still crystal clear in my ear. "It couldn't happen to two people I love more."

Rian flung his arms around both our necks and pulled us into a hug. The tears I'd been holding back broke from the dam as I clung to the two men I loved most, my heart healed in every way possible.

If you loved the Dublin Ink Series and want more enemies to lovers, age gaps, forbidden love and hot tattooed Irish men, check out the Irish Kiss Series.

BOOKS BY SIENNA BLAKE

DUBLIN INK

Dublin Ink

Dirty Ink

Dark Ink

Devilish Ink

IRISH KISS

Irish Kiss

Professor's Kiss

Fighter's Kiss

The Irish Lottery

My Brother's Girl

Player's Kiss

My Secret Irish Baby

IRISH BILLIONAIRES

The Bet

The Fiancé

The Promise

BILLIONAIRES DOWN UNDER

(with Sarah Willows)

To Have & To Hoax

The Paw-fect Mix-up

Riding His Longboard

Maid For You

I Do (Hate You)

Man Toy (Newsletter Exclusive)

ALL HER MEN

Three Irish Brothers

My Irish Kings

Royally Screwed

Cassidy Brothers

DARK ROMEO UNIVERSE

Dark Romeo (standalone)

Bound by Lies (#1)

Bound Forever (#2)

A GOOD WIFE

Beautiful Revenge

Mr. Blackwell's Bride

Paper Dolls

ABOUT SIENNA

Sienna Blake is a dirty girl, a wordspinner of smexy love stories, an Amazon Top 20 & USA Today Bestselling Author.

She lives in Dublin, Ireland, where she enjoys reading, keeping fit and adding to her personal harem of Irish hotties ;)

Printed in Great Britain
by Amazon

42524884R00219